The Guardians: **Night of the Phoenix**

Richard Austin is the pseudonym of a popular
science fiction adventure writer.

Also by Richard Austin in Pan Books

THE GUARDIANS
THE GUARDIANS: *Trial by Fire*
THE GUARDIANS: *Thunder of Hell*

Richard Austin

THE GUARDIANS
NIGHT OF THE PHOENIX

PAN BOOKS
London, Sydney and Auckland

First published 1985 by Jove Books, a division of
the Berkeley Publishing Group, New York
This edition published 1990 by Pan Books Ltd,
Cavaye Place, London SW10 9PG
9 8 7 6 5 4 3 2 1
© Richard Austin 1985
ISBN 0 330 31572 2

Printed in England by Clays Ltd, St Ives plc

*For Patricia "Copperhead" Jackson
and John "Dangerous" Donigan*

PART ONE
——————— **DARK DAWN**

PROLOGUE ——————

The long winter is nearly over. It hasn't been the last winter of the world, so long predicted as the consequence of nuclear war. But for many, it's been close enough.

Now, though, it seems a new day is about to dawn. Those who made it through the months of ice and darkness have settled into a round of life that by now seems normal. They're beginning to rebuild—with the help of fragments of the top-secret Blueprint for Renewal, gathered over the past months by the elite team known as the Guardians.

Caches of food and matériel, assembled under the Blueprint, have begun to be discovered and utilized; miracle gene-tailored seeds and instructions on how to use them to achieve unprecedented crop yields in a fantastically short time are being disseminated from Dr. Georges Mahalaby's living lab, New Eden, in California's Sierra Nevada; specially picked experts are beginning to fit the pieces of a shattered nation back together. Not all the Blueprint has been recovered, not by a long shot. But enough has been recovered to give a lot more people a lot more of a chance than they would otherwise ever have had.

3

A new day is dawning. It won't be easy—far from it—but it might be a bright day indeed.

Across the ocean, however, black storm clouds have been gathering over the harsh months of winter. And now the storm is about to break.

CHAPTER
ONE ————————————————

"Still nothing, Billy." Fighter ace Casey Wilson, formerly of the United States Air Force, had to pitch his voice to carry, even though Billy McKay sat not three meters away with his back pressed against the honeycomb-cored rear tire of Mobile One. The icy, driving wind had still plucked the words to tatters by the time they reached the bull-necked ex-Marine's ears.

"Shit." McKay scuffed at the frozen ground with the heel of his combat boot. "What the hell you think's the matter?"

Casey shrugged. He had a fur-lined cap crammed down on his head, and blinked rapidly as the wind whipped strands of lank blond hair into his eyes. He hugged himself, trying not to shiver in the open hatch. "Who knows, man? Could be sunspots. Or maybe funky atmospherics. Even radiation; the real high-energy junk left over from the One-Day War should have decayed long ago, but we still get anomalous interference all the time."

A voice spilled from the depths of the V-450 Super Commando armored car: "If you have to talk to that nut McKay,

for Chrissake go out and freeze with him and *shut the door*."
Even in this wind, there was no mistaking the downhome
Missouri twang of Commander Sam Sloan, the ex-Navy line
officer who was inside trying to coax some response out of the
vehicle's awesome array of high-tech communications equipment.

"Yeah, Billy, like, why don't you come inside?" Casey's
lean cheeks glowed pink, making him look even younger than
he normally did.

"Go on and shut the fucking hatch," McKay growled. "I'll
be in in a minute. It just drives me fucking crazy, being cooped
up twenty-four hours a day with you yoohoos." Looking
hurt, Casey shut the door. Grimacing, McKay kicked at a
clump of gray grama grass. Still dry and friable despite the
slushy snow clodded around it, a few strands crumbled and
whipped off in the wind amid a brief plume of snow.

Out here in the Great Plains, away east of where Amarillo
used to be—its Air Force base having made it a primary target
under Soviet counterforce doctrine—the wind blew wild and
free, unfettered for thousands of klicks by any terrain feature
much more significant than an aggressive anthill. For a March
night, it was a lot like January. Sleek gray clouds stampeded
overhead, trampling the bulbous face of the moon. Snow
came intermittently like teasing flicks from a quirt, maybe
presaging a full-dress blizzard, maybe not. The plains wind
bored right to the core of you, set your bones resonating inside
you with cold like a giant tuning fork. *So I'm crazy to sit out
here with my nuts freezing together when I could be inside
in the warm*, McKay thought sourly. *I just can't hack that
damned tin can. I'm getting claustrophobic.*

Deep down inside, where the cold rang like hammer blows,
McKay knew that wasn't the whole story. He was just plain
restless. He stood. His high-tech superinsulated parka made
him look like the Michelin tire man, though it left him a sur-
prising degree of mobility. What it didn't seem to do was take
much of the edge off the cold. He stretched, turned, yanked
open the hatch, and boosted himself into the vehicle.

Inside the warm air was like dragon's breath on his face.
The only illumination was the soft amber glow of instruments
up front, where Sloan sat hunched over his console, murmur-

ing into a microphone. Next to him Casey Wilson sat sideways on the driver's seat, the bombardier's jacket he insisted on wearing instead of Guardians winter issue hanging open, his cap gone and replaced by the lightweight headset of a Sony Walkman, his fingers beating out rhythm on the leg of steel-gray fatigue trousers. McKay dogged the door, his hand brushing the buttstock of an evil-looking Maremont lightweight M-60 machine gun held against the hull by padded brackets.

Chagrin twinged through him. He'd gone outside without his primary weapon, and his combat-modified .45 was none too accessible beneath bulky winter gear. *Shit. I'm getting slack.*

"Good evening, Lieutenant McKay."

McKay glanced left. In the dimness aft of the turret root he could make out the matronly form of Dr. Andrea Dobrovic sitting in a fold-down chair beside the engine compartment, plying a notebook computer by the shine of its built-in work light. "Evenin', Doctor."

It was getting so he could barely keep track of their names, much less their specialties. Hell, he could only picture this one by working at it: a plump, pleasant woman with Brillo hair, round pink weathered cheeks, and Coke-bottle glasses, dressed in red Pendleton shirt, faded green Army jacket, threadbare green cords, and work boots. High fashion, after-the-holocaust style. They'd found her at an agricultural research station in western Oklahoma, where she was some kind of animal geneticist. According to plan, they'd pulled back here into the Texas Panhandle to rendezvous with the pickup plane from Heartland; Oklahoma had gone back to being Indian territory, in a manner of speaking. It was the home of the Church of the New Dispensation, founded by the late prophet Josiah Coffin and currently under the management of ex–boy wonder television evangelist Nathan Bedford Forrest Smith. Having been instrumental in the collapse of the church's first great crusade—to say nothing of having in person scragged its looney-tune founder—the Guardians enjoyed considerable pride of place on the New Dispensation's shitlist. Nor was the church particularly sympathetic either to the Blueprint for Renewal, the top-secret plan for rebuilding

America under which the Guardians operated; or to President Jeffrey MacGregor, who presided over the Guardians and, nominally, what was left of the United States, from the vast underground complex of Heartland in north-central Iowa.

McKay knew full well that Smith and his bloodthirsty church were a thorn that sooner than later would have to be pulled from the side of an America undergoing reconstruction, and he more than halfway hoped to bump into one of their patrols, maybe with luck even a detachment of fanatical Brethren of Mercy, so that there'd be that many fewer nut cases to deal with later. No such luck; they cruised in, collected Dr. Dobrovic, then cruised back here to what Heartland judged to be a safe rendezvous spot, without the slightest hitch.

That was the whole damn problem with life these days. Too few hitches.

Shaking himself, ostensibly to rid his broad shoulders of a dandruff of windblown snow melting on them, McKay moved forward to the front of the compartment and leaned over the electronics console.

"Either that's a grizzly bear breathing down my neck or our illustrious leader's decided to give up on communing with nature," Sloan remarked, not looking up from his computer screen.

"Everybody's a comedian," McKay growled. "What have you got?"

"Nothing. Not a damn thing." Sloan rapped the back of his knuckles against the screen over the idiotically blinking cursor. "If I didn't know better, I'd say Heartland isn't even broadcasting. We're getting zip on their frequencies. Not even carrier hum—and that means the computer can't find any signal, either."

McKay frowned. He rubbed his massive chin with fingers still stiff and unwieldy from the cold. "Maybe you ain't crazy. Heartland's got enough power they could come in over the fillings on our teeth if they wanted to, even at this range."

"But there should be something," Casey Wilson said. "They're supposed to get in touch with us at twenty hundred to confirm the rendezvous for tomorrow."

McKay sneered. "No shit? I don't know what the fuck we'd do if they hadn't sent a boy genius along with us to tell us which way was up."

Sloan turned quickly in his chair. "Now, hold on a minute! You've got no call to go jumping down Casey's throat."

"And when I want your opinion," McKay said, stabbing a finger at Sloan's chest, "I'll send a request through channels, Navy boy."

Sloan's square homely-handsome face darkened. "Just who do you think you're—"

"Billy." The soft voice of ex–Green Beret Tom Rogers, the fourth member of the team, drawled into McKay's ear from the tiny speaker taped behind it. He was on watch up in the turret. "I think I see something moving."

McKay swung away from Sloan, reaching out for his M-60, ready to bale out if trouble broke. He'd fought in the Marine Force Recon and on innumerable shadow missions for Studies and Observations Group, Southwest Asia Command, and his viewpoint remained that of a seasoned "leg" infantryman: an AFV was fine for the shelter it provided, transport, and its knack for keeping off small-arms fire. But when things got serious, it was a big fat juicy target, and just filled to the gunwales with high-explosive high-octane fuel. In spite of the protection the armored hull gave, if it came to the crunch, McKay wanted to be *outside*.

"Never mind, Billy," Rogers said. "It was just a trick of the light. Sorry, Billy."

McKay frowned, opened his mouth. Then he shut it and shook his crewcut blond head. Pulling down a seat from the hull beside the machine gun, he plopped heavily down into it and crossed his arms over his chest. Tom Rogers was the other man with ground-combat experience in the elite team called the Guardians. He was at least as seasoned as McKay, possibly more so—most of the missions he'd been on during his career with Special Forces had been so classified that not even McKay, who knew a few things about how to dig details of covert ops out of the camouflage of official records, was able to get any background info on them back during Guardians training. And Rogers himself was about as talkative as a stone statue; he was the last man in the world to cloud up and start spilling war stories any time he got two beers in his gut at one time. But McKay knew a hard-core, seasoned trooper when he saw one, and Rogers definitely fit the bill. And Tom Rogers *never* started at shadows.

The truth is, I was being an asshole, McKay thought. He dropped his chin to his chest. In his own low-key way, Rogers had pulled the fuse out of the potentially ugly—and utterly pointless—shouting match between McKay and the other two. But, shit, it wasn't his fault alone. They were all jumping on each other these days; even Tom Rogers was getting a little testy now and then. McKay closed his eyes.

It all started with World War III. From the four main branches of the Armed Forces they had been assembled: Billy McKay, the maximum Marine; Tom Rogers, perfect master of the arts of shadow war; K.C. "Casey" Wilson, the top-scoring American fighter ace since Korea; and Samuel Sloan, the hero of Sidra Gulf. Disparate men from differing backgrounds, with but one thing in common: they had proved themselves in battle. Not that they had simply displayed bravery; in the troubled years leading up to the Third World War, tens of thousands of men—women too—had had ample opportunity to display that quality. The men picked to be Guardians required more. They had to possess superior savvy, superior cunning, and, above all, the ability to keep it absolutely together under fire.

Like four rare and exotic metals, they were carefully chosen, forged together into a new and remarkable alloy, then honed and tempered into perhaps the finest implement in man's long military history. They were drilled intensively in all the skills of the modern warrior, from the arcana of urban combat and antiterrorist techniques to survival under the most primitive conditions in jungle, mountain, desert. They learned the intricacies of communications, of mechanics and field medicine and electronics; small-boat handling; ambush, escape, and evasion; how to wage guerrilla war, diagnose disease, balance books. Scarcely an area of human endeavor escaped the compass of their grueling regimen—and the mind-busting classroom work was accompanied by a schedule of physical training of the type normally reserved for Olympic athletes.

The mission: In the event of nuclear war, to convey the President of the United States out of Washington, D.C., to a designated safe haven. Or so they were told. Each Guardian was closemouthed as only a hardened professional could be during the period of training. But McKay felt sure that, like him, the others wondered why so straightforward a mission required such intricate and varied training. Still, it was a job . . . and a challenge. And that perhaps, at core, was truly what drew the four Guardians together: none of them could resist a challenge.

When the balloon went up—the collapse of the Soviet/Warsaw Pact land offensive in Europe driving the Politburo to the ultimate recourse of a modern superpower—the Guardians ran headlong into their first surprise. The man they were supposed to protect, rugged, hard-talking archconservative President William Lowell, had flown off in his National Emergency Airborne Command Post, ordering the four of them to remain on the ground. They would stay at the White House with Vice President Jeffrey MacGregor and the Chief Justice, in case anything happened to the President. If it didn't, the giant EA-4B Flying White House would simply land the President near one of his bolt-holes; there was no need for the Guardians to accompany him.

McKay had come within an ace of rebelling. Dammit, their brief was to protect the *President*. That the change in orders stranding them on the ground was also, in effect, stranding them on ground zero—with chances of survival none too high—never even occurred to McKay and his comrades. What mattered was that each man had lived through eighteen months of hell in order to protect the President's life at just this crux. They had *earned* the privilege, and here they were being left behind.

But orders were orders. The Guardians and the Vice President sat out the thermonuclear exchange safely in the War Room deep beneath the White House while President William Lowell flew off into history—communications with his aircraft broken during the attack, airplane and President presumed lost.

The Guardians found themselves carrying out their original mission after all. They escorted President MacGregor, newly sworn in by Chief Justice Shaneyfelt, through the streets of a shattered Washington and then in the desperate cross-country dash to the shelter of Heartland. On the way they fought blood-maddened mobs, looters, and hunter-killer teams dispatched by a traitorous faction that had taken over control of the Central Intelligence Agency. Of three vehicles that set out for Heartland, two were lost, as well as the entire complement of Secret Service men who had insisted on accompanying the President on the run from the White House. Despite fearful odds, the Guardians delivered Jeff MacGregor—young, handsome, liberal, chosen as the crusty Lowell's running mate in an attempt to forge a broad-based coalition—to Heartland safe and sound.

Which is where they learned their *real* mission. In the years before the war, a number of concerned government officials had begun to assemble something called the Blueprint for Renewal. This was a treasure trove of high-tech knowledge and equipment: a network of the nation's top minds in science, business, and administration, together with substantial caches of equipment scattered across the country. Locations of participants and matériel were kept secret; for security reasons, the master key to Project Blueprint was kept in the possession of President Lowell. Using that list, once the dust of World War III had settled, the Guardians would start putting together the pieces of the blueprint for the renewal of a shattered America. There was only one catch. The master list had been lost with Lowell.

Working frantically, the technicians of Heartland, President MacGregor, and the enigmatic, scar-faced former Green Beret major known only as Crenna, whose brainchild the Guardians were, had managed to scrape together a few pitiful clues as to who *might* have been participants in Project Blueprint. The Guardians had gone hunting for them—and for more clues. They battled road gypsies in mohawks, spikes, and black leather, the fundamentalist fanatics of Josiah Coffin's New Dispensation, a radical terrorist network headed up by former California Lieutenant Governor Geoffrey van Damm. Worse, they found they weren't the only ones after the Blueprint: Yevgeny Maximov, international financier and man of mystery who had made himself master of post-war Europe, knew of the Blueprint—and would stop at nothing to get it. Progress had been slow, but progress was made—until, in California, they located one Dr. Jacob Morgenstern.

Morgenstern was one of the original architects of the Blueprint for Renewal. He held a substantial chunk of the Blueprint in his head. Once he was safely delivered to Heartland, the pieces began to fall into place at a fabulous rate.

That was the trouble.

The mystery and excitement were gone. The Heartland techs were cranking names of Blueprint personnel through their computers as rapidly as Morgenstern could reel them off. If they were judged likely to have pulled through the war, the Guardians were dispatched to collect them. It wasn't always as much of a piece of cake as this most recent pickup had been, not by any means. But aside from an occasional shooting scrape with scavengers, road gypsies, or the goons of various organized and armed power blocs scattered across the continent, the Guardians had become little more than glorified taxi drivers. There was danger, all right. But there wasn't any *challenge* anymore.

McKay started, lifted his chin, and opened his eyes. "Huh?" Instantly he wondered if someone had actually spoken to him, or if he hadn't just imagined it in his sleep. He got ready to rip a new asshole for anybody who wanted to give him a hard time about it. He glared around the amber-lit gloom with bellicose eyes.

But Casey and Sam Sloan were staring back at him with faces drawn taut as towlines, heads tilted as if listening to something unbelievable. "Billy," Sam Sloan said. "You'd better listen to this."

"Whatever is the matter?" came Dr. Dobrovic's pleasant soprano voice from the rear of the vehicle.

McKay waved her to silence. "Get it the hell onto my earphone."

The voice rode a powerful signal, punching through atmospheric interference like a bullet through cotton cloth. It was a familiar voice, deep, gravelly, self-assured. The voice of a man accustomed to power. The voice of a dead man.

"I have returned to take up the reins of power," William Lowell was saying. "I have occupied the secret complex that is the current seat of government in this country with the aid of our allies, the Federated States of Europe. Vice President MacGregor, who attempted to usurp the office of President, and whose pusillanimous conduct of that office has endangered the welfare of all Americans, has been placed under arrest, pending trial for treason.

"The FSE has extended the hand of friendship to us in this, our hour of need. Their forces aided me in thwarting this heinous scheme to usurp the power of the Presidency, and will continue to help me in restoring order to this great land of ours. Most of them are good American boys who were fighting the Communists when the war broke out, and were stranded over there when things fell apart. I must ask each and every one of you to cooperate to the fullest with them, American or foreign friend.

"Our nation faces grave danger; the forces of anarchy stalk the land. But with the help from our friends across the water, and with the help of God and the American people, we will soon straighten things out and turn this country around again. America is still a great nation. It's time we pulled her back from the brink of the abyss. We can do it. I promise you this as the duly elected President of the United States of America."

A pause that seemed to crackle with more than interference, then a familiar chuckle, dry as a back-country road. "It's good to be back."

CHAPTER
TWO —————————————————

"It's crazy!" Sam Sloan exclaimed, doing his best to pace with his lanky frame bent halfway over in the cramped compartment. "Jeff MacGregor under arrest—I can't believe it!"

"It's what President Lowell says," said McKay, sitting on the fold-down seat with arms crossed, "so you'd better believe it."

"But why, Billy?" Casey asked. "He was doing his duty. Just the same as we are."

"President Lowell must have his reasons," Tom Rogers said.

"If that's even Lowell," Sloan said, hacking the air with his hand for emphasis. "How do we know he's not an impostor? Where's he *been* all these months?"

"Reckon he'll tell us in his own sweet time," Tom Rogers said laconically.

"No way of knowing whether that's the real Lowell or not," McKay said. "But it sure as hell sounded like old Wild Bill. And we're sworn to serve the President. So I'm damned well going to go along with whatever he tells us until it's proved it ain't him.''

"But who *is* the President, Billy?" Casey Wilson asked. "MacGregor was sworn in, man. He's served eight months already.''

"William Lowell is the man I voted for," came the apprehensive voice of Dr. Dobrovic from the shadows in the rear of the vehicle. "He should be the President, shouldn't he?''

"I never voted in my life, myself," McKay grunted. "But it looks to me like Lowell's the man with the better claim. MacGregor—'' He shrugged massively.

Sam Sloan struck himself on the forehead with the heel of his hand. "I don't believe it! I've known you and Tom Rogers for over two years now, McKay. In that time you've impressed on me again and again the importance of loyalty to your teammates—to your buddies. We've *fought* with MacGregor. And you know how hard he's worked these last eight months, trying to pull the country together."

McKay stared at the corrugated deck beneath his boots. He couldn't meet the gaze of Sloan, who stood over him with fists clenched at his sides. "You're right about buddies, Sam," Tom said quietly. "But that's the bitch about being a soldier. You help them when you can. But if your mission requires it, you got to let 'em go.''

"But it isn't fair!" Mercurial as always, Casey was showing yet another side of his personality. There was the laid-back *californio* with the tan and the yellow Zeiss shooting glasses, and there was the fighter jock, tense but in control. This was just a bewildered kid who looked ten years younger than he was. "MacGregor hasn't done anything *wrong*. We can't just sit by and let him be treated like a traitor."

McKay shook his head. "MacGregor's getting a bum deal. But, shit, I don't make policy. And neither do you. We're grunts, Casey. They tell us saddle up and go, and we saddle up and go. That's all there is to it.''

Casey's eyes shone. "That's not American, man. That's not the America I grew up with.''

At the brink of speaking, Sam Sloan was drawn up short by a sudden beeping from his console, accompanied by a blinking red light. "Heartland," he said, frowning.

"Now we know why they were off the air, anyway," McKay said.

Turning, Sam Sloan slid into his seat with a fluid grace that belied Billy McKay's usual image of naval officers. Sloan had been exceptional in more ways than one; he'd never given in to the sedentary way of life, but had become a fitness nut, working out relentlessly in the weight room of the cruiser *Winston-Salem*, pounding out miles each day around the decks. He was an Olympic-class marathon runner. He could practically run McKay into the ground, and it was a constant source of mortification to a man who was not only a Marine but an ex-Parris Island drill instructor to be reduced to chasing after a damned candy-assed Navy man.

Sloan punched buttons on the console. "Guardians acknowledging. This is Sloan. Over."

"This is Heartland." Though the Guardians had no way of knowing all the technicians working in the vast subterranean complex, the voice somehow sounded *wrong*. Harsh, unfamiliar. "We're confirming rendezvous oh-eight hundred tomorrow morning. Repeat, confirming rendezvous." The voice rattled off a set of coordinates.

Sloan looked at McKay. His brown eyes were bleak. McKay nodded his blocky chin once.

"Roger, Heartland. We'll be there."

"You worry too much, McKay," Sam Sloan said from the electrical systems operator's seat next to the driver. "What are you so nervous about, anyway?"

Hunched at the back of the vehicle in his bulky winter parka, ignoring the slow rocking as Mobile One lurched down the abandoned strip of highway, Billy McKay was checking the backpacks to make sure their emergency kits were in order. "You can't be too careful," he mumbled. "Never know when something might go wrong."

"What makes you say that?" Sam Sloan demanded. "You're the one who insisted we play ball with the . . . new regime."

McKay glared up at him, blue eyes icy beneath almost invisibly pale brows. "What do you mean, new? Bill Lowell was elected President—Jeff MacGregor never was. Or have you forgotten that?"

Sloan exchanged looks with Casey, who was back behind the wheel. The young ex–fighter pilot bit his lip.

"Oh dear," said Dr. Dobrovic. "Please don't fight, gentlemen."

"What's it to you?" McKay snarled. "You're flyin' right out of this godforsaken wasteland. What do you care about us grunts?"

The doctor's round face fell. "Billy." It was Rogers's voice, falling softly but firmly in McKay's ear. The mild intimation of reproof was Rogers's equivalent of outraged indignation. The ex–Special Forces officer had old-fashioned notions about the proper way to speak to women.

McKay nodded his heavy features into a grimace. "Yeah, okay, I'm sorry, Doctor." He resealed his pack, set it aside, boosted himself off the fold-down seat, and lumbered forward to peer out of Sam Sloan's forward view slit.

The Panhandle extended endlessly under a sky the color of spoiled milk. The land wasn't perfectly flat here. It more resembled a collection of large flat slabs skewed slightly in all directions, dotted with sorry clumps of vegetation and dusted with snow. To Billy McKay's eyes, accustomed to the brownstone, brick, and asphalt canyons of the Pittsburgh of his childhood, and the rolling green hills of the East, this country looked no less unnatural and uninviting than the deserts of California.

Outside the wind rushed by Mobile One and thumped its hull with open-handed blows as it passed. The highway thrust straight as a knife blade before them, black beneath scurrying drifts of snow. Visibility wasn't great; nothing seemed to be coming out of the pallid sky, but the snow was powdery-dry, and the wind sucked it into billowing white plumes. Ahead, McKay could make out a big broad billboard sticking up to the right of the road six or seven hundred meters away, faded by sun and wind and weather, advertising Salem Lights in the ghosts of letters. Sloan glanced irritably up at him. "What are you so twitchy about, anyway? The rendezvous is all set. Nothing can go wrong."

"Yeah, Billy," Casey put in. "Things're going better than usual, man. Pickup plane is already on the ground, even." There was an unmistakable touch of condescension in the Southern California voice when it said the word *plane*. To ex-fighter jock Casey Wilson, an airplane was a high-tech fighter aircraft, a superb refined creation; quick and supple as a greyhound, sensitive as a Stradivarius violin; precise as a surgical laser, like the new F-29 with its forward-raked wings, or the older, but exquisite, F-16 in which he'd scored his own seven kills in the Near East. The DeHavilland Canada Twin Otter parked expectantly on the asphalt one thousand meters away, its twin props lazily rotating on its high-mounted wing, was just barely an aircraft at all. More of a bus with wings.

McKay winced. "The last time somebody told me nothing could go wrong," he snarled around the stub of his cigar—unlit, to save the atmosphere inside the vehicle—"I got my ass blown out of a helicopter by an RPG."

He felt a touch on his arm and half turned, biting back a snarl. It was Dr. Dobrovic, pudgy face congealed in concerned contours, who had braved the uncertain motion of the armored car to come forward. "Please don't say that, Lieutenant McKay. Everything will be all right, won't it? I—I've been through so much."

McKay glowered down at her for a moment. *Gotta be polite to the bigwigs*, he thought. *What the fuck? She's a nice enough old bat.* "Don't worry, ma'am," he said, taking the cigar out of his mouth. "Just having a little joke. Everything's gonna be okay."

"McKay." Sloan stared down at the electronic wonderland of his console, where a few megabucks' worth of state-of-the-art sensors and software monitored everything from the surrounding radar picture through background radiation to wind velocity. Sloan had been exchanging recognition phrases with the crew of the Otter. Now he was frowning back at the insistent red wink of an LED indicator. "RF monitor's picking up carrier hum from a fairly strong transmitter nearby."

"So?"

"Our RDF—that's Radio Direction Finder—"

"I know what it goddamn means."

"—says it's coming from—" He lifted his head to peer

skeptically through the laminated glass-and-plastic-armor view slit. "—from behind that billboard up there."

Bringing the well-chewed cigar stub to his mouth, McKay's right hand halted in mid-arc. "Jesus fucking *Christ*!" he yelled. "Casey, *get us the fuck* outta *here*!"

There was no visible sign of danger. But the Guardians were nothing if not a well-oiled machine. Instantly the tanned blond California kid, who alternated between twitchy nervousness and being so laid-back as to seem barely conscious, went away to be replaced by the ice-cold combat pilot. McKay's bellowed warning was still bouncing around the inside of the V-450's hull when he had the brake pedal hammered down and was cranking the wheel to the right, letting momentum and the road's slick surface torque the car's ten tons around in a high-speed bootlegger turn. The big car teetered far over, groaning on its suspension. At this speed and under these conditions, it was a knife-edge maneuver, *pushing the envelope* with the cool daring of a pilot with plenty of the right stuff. McKay had to grab on to the back of Sloan's chair to keep from being flung down; with his left hand he snatched frantically for Dr. Dobrovic. Screaming, she was hurled against the left side hatch of the APC.

The billboard exploded. It bulged outwards and popped like an overinflated balloon, shredded into burning wisps by the supersonic passage of a 105-millimeter projectile and a volcanic rush of hot gases from the barrel of the cannon mounted on the M-1 Abrams tank hunkered like a giant toad behind it. The shell struck the left-hand door. Its shaped-charge HEAT warhead went off, squirting a jet of incandescent copper through the foamed-alloy armor like a blowtorch through butter. The discharge vaporized Dr. Dobrovic's body between pelvis and clavicle, plated the turret root with gleaming copper, and filled the compartment with flame and smoke and noise and a hideous compound stench.

Mobile One reeled under the impact. Its broadside-skimming motion halted; for a moment the tires squealed impatiently on snow-slick asphalt, and then the big car shot perpendicularly off the road and went bounding off across country.

Somehow McKay kept his feet. He was coughing uncontrollably, flapping his left arm without knowing why he did so. He stopped, then realized that the left sleeve of his coveralls was on fire. Feeling like the Scarecrow in *The Wizard of Oz*, he beat the burning sleeve out against his leg and fumbled with a small fire extinguisher clamped above Sloan's console. "Casey, Tom, Sam," he choked. "Is everyone all right?"

His voice rang hollowly inside his head; the blast had temporarily deafened him. Through Sloan's seat back and the deck plating beneath his boots he felt a trip-hammer vibration that told him Tom Rogers had opened fire with the heavy ordnance in the turret. McKay practically lifted Sloan out of his seat and propelled him toward the rear of the vehicle. *"Get the gear! We're going to have to bail out!"* he bellowed, hoping the bone-conduction speaker taped behind Sloan's right ear would enable him to hear the words. He looked around.

The back of Casey Wilson's seat was on fire. Pale blue flames flickered in the hair at the back of his head, and the plastic spacer at the rear of his Scorpions concert tour baseball cap was melting. Ignoring the pain, Casey steered the wildly bucking car across the snowy landscape, slewing it wildly this way and that to complicate the tank-gunner's targeting solution. He shut his right eye when McKay hosed him down with the stinging-cold CO_2 from the fire extinguisher, but otherwise didn't move a muscle. *Christ, the kid's hard-core*, McKay thought in admiration. He turned away to join Sloan, frantically pulling equipment out of lockers, and just missed being splattered by the shot that tore off the front of the vehicle and set it spinning in a frenzy like a Tonka truck kicked by an unruly child. He pitched against the hull, the receiver of his own LWMG smashing into his forehead, and then he was falling *upward* as Mobile One began a slow, gut-wrenching roll, over and over and *over*....

McKay had the reflexes of a panther, but for all the agonizing slow-motion deliberation of the roll he couldn't stop himself being tossed around the smoke and flame and metallic hardness of Mobile One's interior like a rock in a tumbler. At last the irresistible seismic motion stopped with a great jarring crash, and he slid down the turret root to slam against the buckled deck plates. Flames gushed a Niagara roar. He lay

there for a moment, feeling as if his body had been turned to
glass and then smashed, sticky wetness filling his eyes, conflagration stinging his face and the backs of his hands. Sharp
loud corn-popping cracks reverberated through the hull,
followed by a ringing demon clatter—small-arms ammunition
cooking off in the heat of a fire.

McKay stirred feebly. *Time to get the fuck* outta *here*.
Strong hands gripped him, helped him to his feet. He blinked
through flame-shot smoke, saw Sloan's square face, grim but
collected beneath a layer of grime, soot, and blood.

By some miracle Mobile One had landed on its tires. Still
numb from the battering he'd received, McKay wiped blood
from his eyes and staggered with Sloan through a sheet of
flame to where Casey Wilson slumped in the driver's seat.
Most of the car's bow was gone. The two men tugged at the
unconscious driver, but his seat belt held him fast. There were
belts on both front seats. They had always seemed a silly touch
to McKay. Now they'd saved the already wounded Casey from
a savage smashing bout. He looked pretty bad as it was; he'd
obviously sucked frags and flash damage from the second hit,
plus an unguessable amount of blast injury.

The seat belt's release mechanism was jammed, pinned by a
steel fragment like a bug on a board. McKay pulled out his Ka-
bar combat knife and hacked through the webbing. He helped
Sloan wrestle the unconscious man out through the opening
that gaped where Sloan's own combat station had been, then
turned back to the Dante-esque interior of the car. He threw
open the intact port-side hatch and began pitching out all the
gear—rations, packs, weapons—that he could get his hands
on. A rhythmic shudder in the warped metal beneath his melting bootsoles told him that somehow Tom Rogers was still
making the two turret guns go.

Through a whirl of smoke and wind-blown snow Sam Sloan
materialized, grabbed McKay's wrist. McKay tried to pull
away. Sloan made frantic gestures. He mouthed the words
she's gonna blow. McKay grabbed the M-60 out of its clips,
jumped out of the burning vehicle, ran thirty meters on rubber
legs, and flopped to the prairie. Sam Sloan followed, holding
his Galil/M-203 combination in one hand and dragging a pack

and a couple of disposable antitank rockets by their slings with the other.

The earth lurched beneath McKay, and flame and smoke geysered forty meters to his left. Sloan flopped down as the chunks of frozen earth rained down all around. The M-1 had fired again, somehow managing to miss the stationary V-450. McKay scoured blood from his eyes again, squinted through the blowing snow. He could see the pale firefly sparkles of muzzle flashes against the prairie. There were men out there shooting at them. Small surprise.

The cool professional in him marked Sam Sloan's performance. Since the formation of the Guardians, McKay had been concerned about how well an ex–fighter jock and a naval officer would respond to combat on the ground. That concern had never been entirely laid to rest, even though both Sloan and Casey Wilson were by now seasoned ground-combat veterans many times over. At this moment, though, Sam Sloan was perhaps calmer than McKay himself. Iron behemoths whaling away at each other with big guns was the combat environment he'd been *trained* for. The main difference was that the guided-missile cruiser *Winston-Salem* in which Sloan had seen action in the Gulf of Sidra could have swatted both Mobile One and her larger, more powerful opponent like flies with a fraction of its secondary armament. He was almost certainly a lot less impressed with the big squat Abrams than McKay was.

And Rogers—McKay twisted, craning his neck to look back at the stricken Mobile One. Flames bellowed out the split-open bow and the open hatch. Ghostly orange flames flashed ryhthmically from the M-19 and .50-cal through the smoke wreathing the turret. McKay understood now why the tank hadn't wiped them out yet: Tom Rogers had managed to lay down a line of white phosphorus grenades, drawing a curtain of thick white smoke between them and the tank. He'd done more than that; McKay belatedly registered that he had seen the Otter twisted and burning from 40-mm hits almost a kilometer away, sparing them the dangers of observation or attack from the air. Rogers had obviously hit the aircraft while Mobile One was still moving—or, incredibly, *after* it had finished its roll. Tom Rogers was one hell of a troop.

He still wasn't fireproof. "Tom," McKay said, hoping the mike taped to his larynx and the pocket-sized communicator attached to it were still functional. *"Tom."*

"I read you, Billy." As calmly as if he were announcing it was time for dinner.

"Get the hell out of there. She's gonna go up any second."

"There's about a platoon out there shooting at us, Billy. They're five, six hundred meters away, and I want to keep them from closing to effective range—"

"Tom, you're sitting on a goddamn time bomb, and the wind is whipping your smoke to shit, and in about ten seconds that tank's going to get a good look at you and blow your ass to Wisconsin. *Get the fuck out of there!*"

"Negative, Billy. You-all get clear. I'll cover you."

Mechanically, McKay had been flinging down the bipod of the LWMG and checking the fifty-round belt in its Australian half-moon ammo box for twisting, alternating with brushing a loose flap of skin out of his eyes. *Shit*, he thought. He knew goddamn well that a little thing like burning to death wouldn't *even* stop Tom Rogers from sticking by his post to cover his buddies' escape. "Fuck that. Casey's hit bad. It's going-to take all three of us alive and well to get him out of here."

"But Billy—"

"Rogers, de-ass that can *now!* That's an order."

"Roger, Billy." McKay glanced back over his shoulder. Mobile One's turret hatch popped open. Tom Rogers emerged, carrying his own Galil Short Assault Rifle and his pack, his face a mask of blood beneath his tanker's helmet. He flowed down the side of the burning vehicle like a snake and seemed to vanish in the snow shimmer that clung to the ground.

A dazzling column of yellow flame spurted ten meters out through the open hatch, and Mobile One exploded. McKay pressed his face to the ground. Food, extra weapons, medical supplies, umpteen millions of dollars of the finest silicon-lattice electronics—and home for more than half a year. Gone, just like that.

Also their wheels. And they were a long, long way from anything resembling home.

Another shot from the tank smashed the wreck like a giant's fist. Concussion drubbed McKay. When the fury passed, he croaked, "Tom, Sam? Do you read me?" After a heart-stopping eternity, two ragged affirmatives crackled in his ear. "Fan out and try to keep them busy. I'm gonna do something about that tank."

Turning, he crawled back to the scatter of equipment hurriedly thrown out of the stricken vehicle by Sloan and himself. Mobile One lay on its back, a dead beetle wrapped in fire. Groping with fingers raw from burns and numb with biting cold, he quickly found what he sought: the stubby plastic tube of a throwaway AT-4 antitank rocket. Slinging it over his broad back by its webbing strap, he scuttled off across the snow-swept prairie on a tangent to the line between the distant tank and its stricken prey.

Though inventoried as smoke rounds, white phosphorus rounds were in fact meant to serve as incendiaries as well. They were better as the latter. They tended to send up dense spires of white smoke, drifting upward like tentacles with gaps between, instead of comforting curtains; the protective screen laid down by Tom Rogers's M-19 by now looked like a picket fence with most of the pickets gone. It didn't do much to overcome the tremendous feeling of nakedness McKay had as he scuttled forward in his gray-mottled white winter camouflage. Left and behind he heard the hard rap of a hand-held grenade launcher. Though his combat-honed reflexes instantly registered it as outgoing, he hit the dirt anyway, plowing up powdered snow and hardpan behind a hummock of dead grass. White smoke spouted from the prairie; another WP round. The ambushing infantry was probably out of range of Sam Sloan's little M-203, but it didn't hurt to have the bad guys know it was there. The Guardians' worst problem right now was the possibility of a hard concerted push. Anything that might keep the bastards' heads down helped.

He jumped up and ran, darting in short random rushes before diving down again, trying to come around on the attackers' left flank. His rocket had no more effective range than Sloan's grenade launcher—about four hundred meters—and if at all possible he didn't want to have to shoot at the Abrams's massive front armor. He also wanted to be able to enfilade the ambushing platoon if they moved forward to mop up their victims. He hoped like hell he wouldn't have to. He was focused on that damn tank like a laser beam.

He threw himself forward, hit the ground, rolled, heard the small furtive finger-snaps of rounds passing overhead. From behind he heard another thump from Sloan's grenade launcher, and the crackle of Tom Rogers's Short Assault Rifle, playing pitiful counterpoint to the big band across from them. The sound of the ambushers' M-16s was like a curtain, stitched angrily across by a Minimi 5.56-mm machine gun. The tank's main gun boomed. Its shell tore chunks out of the frozen prairie with high explosives. McKay picked himself up and ran, wind-driven snow stinging his cheeks like needles.

For all the apparent invincibility of the M-1, sitting there smug in its white-paint-dappled armor, it was no longer the overwhelming factor in the fight. By blasting the area around the wreck of Mobile One with high explosives the iron monster might incidentally swat Tom, Sam, or Casey—if the boyish ex-pilot was still alive. Peering out into the windblown snow through the glass-and-plastic laminate of narrow vision blocks, the tank's crew didn't actually stand much chance of spotting any of them. Heading down a round-bottomed draw that cut his path transversely, McKay felt a transient flicker of glee, like a spike on a power line. *Think they're hot goddamn stuff in that steel box of theirs*, he thought. *If they ain't got a vehicle or a prepared position to shoot at, they ain't shit*.

The gully got deep enough that he could drive on without anybody being able to see him for the moment. He straightened, quickening his pace. He had to get to the tank, and fast. It may have been comparatively useless at the moment, but he reckoned its loss would take the starch out of the ambushers. Whoever their attackers were—and he didn't want to think about that too much right now—they weren't any too strak. They had already underestimated their opponents once, leaving a radio fired up in the concealed tank, apparently ignorant that its emanations would shine like a beacon to the ultra-sophisticated electronics of the Guardians' armored car. If they lost their ally machine, their morale just might unravel. He hoped.

"Billy." Rogers's voice, vibrating through his mastoid process from the tiny speaker behind his left ear.

"I read you, Tom."

"They're moving forward. Look out."

"Roger." He dropped onto the gentle slope of a gully wall and peered over the lip. "Shit," he said aloud.

Dark forms moved forward across the mottled landscape. Casey Wilson's evasive maneuvering had triggered the ambush at a range inconvenient to both sides—about six hundred meters, out of range not only of McKay's antitank rocket and the M-203 grenade launcher fastened under the barrel of Sloan's Galil SAR, but beyond effective range of the ambushers' small arms as well.

According to modern doctrine, infantry wasn't so much meant to *fight*, as it was to poke around until it blundered into an enemy, and keep him occupied until artillery or air strikes ranged in. Soldiers these days weren't taught to shoot so much as fire off lots of bullets, and the weapons reflected it: lightweight, often throwaway rifles firing lightweight ammunition that, while high-velocity, lacked range, accuracy, and killing power, but was splendid for throwing out and sustaining a high volume of fire. Billy McKay's family had been USMC since there was a USMC, and until very recently the Marine Corps had cherished a tradition of marksmanship. That legacy made something inside McKay rebel at the idea of trying to fight with a glorified .22.

His main weapon packed more punch. He poked the barrel of the Maremont over the edge of the draw, threw down the bipod, snugged the butt against his shoulder, and locked it there with his left hand. There were fifty rounds of 7.62-millimeter ammunition on a belt coiled inside the half-moon-shaped Australian ammo box clipped to the side of the machine gun; three similar boxes rode in the compartments of the Rhodesian-style ammunition pouch on McKay's broad chest. Not only did the big 7.62 slugs have considerably more range than the enemy's 5.56, but the Maremont was a true machine gun, a streamlined M-60; and unlike an assault rifle, it suffered no deterioration of performance when fired on full automatic. He sighted on a hunched-over figure among those closest to him, about two hundred meters away, and squeezed the trigger briefly.

The figure dropped in the boneless, limb-sprawling marionette way of a man struck instantly dead. Other figures dropped to the ground and began casting about in nervous confusion. As intended, McKay had put himself off to the left of the attacking units, who now found themselves in the uncomfortable position of being caught in a crossfire. As if to underline their predicament, a white phosphorus grenade from Sloan's 40-millimeter launcher exploded fifty or so meters past the man McKay had dropped. Another man leapt out of the core of the smoke anemone, slapping at himself like a man who had blundered into a swarm of angry wasps. In a moment, coils of smoke streaming from his bulky winter gear enveloped him completely. He fell thrashing. If he'd just had sense to tear off his parka before the ravenous little phosphorus flakes had eaten through it, he might have saved himself. He didn't. McKay aimed his machine gun at the hapless soldier, waited. A couple of his buddies popped up from concealment and converged on him, bent low. McKay bowled them both over with a single burst. He began to work the gun back and forth, laddering off bursts, three-four-five-six, and down again. If they took enough grief from their flank, maybe they would bolt—

A giant boot caught McKay in the side and flung him ten meters down the draw. Only when he rolled to a stop in a cloud of powdery snow was he aware, after the fact, of the flash of light and heat that had briefly enveloped him. Dazed, he blinked at drifting afterimage suns. The smoke and dust of an HE shellburst were settling out not forty meters away from him. *Underestimated the pukes,* he thought blearily. The enemy infantry had reacted more professionally than he'd anticipated, spotting the plume of powdered snow thrown up by the M-60's ferocious muzzle blast, and radioing his position to their buddies in the tank. With that realization singing along his nerves like a charge of electricity, he jumped to his feet and ran.

A shell passed over in God's own thunder. He flung himself down. Noise and chunks of frozen earth cascaded down on him. Dropping the machine gun, miraculously still held in burned and bruised hands, he fumbled the tube off his back.

It was an AT-4, a shoulder-fired rocket jointly developed by the Americans and the Swedes. It was intended to punch hard and raise extreme hell once it got through armor. But its 84-mm warhead didn't seem like much to pit against the awesome frontal glacis of a main battle tank.

The big Abrams was on the move, seeming to float in the ground haze of snow. The beast was three hundred meters away, inside his rocket's range. Behind him he heard the popping-corn sound of a firefight in progress. The Minimi was still at it, and it sounded as if the bad guys had a 40-mm grenade launcher thumping back in answer to Sloan's. McKay was confident his two unwounded teammates could hold their own. This apparently flat land offered a good deal of cover, and the blowing snow made visibility lousy. With their intensive Guardians training, Tom and Sloan could play hide-and-seek with the bastards until they got in close. It was McKay's job to make sure they didn't.

The tank creaked and moaned and rumbled like an iron giant wakening from deep sleep. McKay tried to make his six feet, three inches very small. To fire the goddamn rocket, he was going to have to sit up and prop it on his shoulder—and when he did, there was just no way somebody in the tank wasn't going to see him, ground haze or no. In the meantime, there was no point in inviting unwanted attention from the 7.62 coaxial MG mounted next to the cannon.

The Abrams rolled in like a steel tide. McKay popped the protective covers off the fore-end venturi of the missile, took a deep breath. *Now or never*, he thought. He slipped the safety lever forward and over the Kevlar-lined plastic launch tube and sat up, bringing the weapon to his right shoulder with a single fluid motion.

He centered the open triangle of the front sight inside the rear sight's circle. The big tank, seeming to flow over the ground like mist, spilled out to all sides of the sights; the bastard was *close*. McKay aimed for the juncture of turret and deck beneath the ledgelike overhang of the turret's armor, and fired.

The missile whooshed from the tube, commencing an angry crackling buzz as its drive motor kicked in. The AT-4 had a speed of over a thousand feet per second. With a HEAT warhead speed was unnecessary for penetration. The advantage lay in better accuracy, giving its target less time to move—and less time for the firer to sit exposed to the tank's angry attention before the missile struck.

The tankers were alert. The rocket launcher's backblast had just kicked a vast plume of smoke, snow, and dry grass off the prairie when the co-ax machine gun cut loose. During a very long time in which McKay's heart beat once, ponderously, like the tolling of Big Ben, the enemy gunner probed for McKay with angry copper-jacketed fingers. Then came a sunbright flash, right on target, followed by the distinctive *crack!* of a HEAT round going off.

The Abrams's Chobham armor was meant to be proof against much heavier charges than that carried by the AT-4. But the nasty little rocket didn't pack a conventional punch.

For just a slice of a second, McKay thought he saw hell-red light flare up through the vision block of the driver's periscope. He was already in motion, casting aside the discarded launcher and rolling across the hard-frozen land like a man on fire trying to put himself out. Crenna and his gremlins, back in Heartland, had done everything to assure their fair-haired boys got only the best equipment. But he also knew all too well how often high-tech stuff failed to live up to the advertising brochures—and the M-1 Abrams was one tough son of a bitch. It seemed presumptuous as hell to think about knocking it out with a single dinky missile.

McKay hugged the planet as if he hoped to melt into it molecule by molecule. *One thing is for sure*, he thought grimly. *The beast won't be bothering Tom, Sam, and Casey.* Tankers hated few things more than infantrymen armed with antitank rockets. The Abrams's crew wouldn't rest until they had rolled McKay out into a red-brown smear on the prairie.

The M-240 machine gun in the turret stopped. A moment later, the sixty-ton monster veered abruptly right and stopped. A feeble red furnace glow began to bake off the sloped front plate, visible even in the wan daylight. A moment later,

McKay heard a rumble of muffled explosions. The air slid out of him in a long shaky breath as hatches opened and tankers started tumbling out like kids for recess.

"Billy," Tom Rogers said in his ear. "They're pulling back."

And that was that.

CHAPTER
THREE _____

Impassive as Lenin in his tomb, Yevgeny Maximov sat smoking his *makhorka* cigarette while makeup people swarmed over him like wasps, daubing him up for the cameras. In a matter of moments he would be addressing the Federated States of Europe, which he had ruled as his personal demesne since the radioactive dust of the Third World War had first begun to settle out of the stratosphere, on the great adventure upon which the peoples of United Europe were now embarked.

A sporadically religious man, Maximov regarded what had happened as little less than a miracle. Entropy had begun to claim the jerry-rigged Federation for its own, even as the protem heads of the stricken European nations were being coerced or cajoled into swearing their fealty to Maximov and the Internationalist Council of which he was then chairman. The economies of the social-democratic West had been declining for years before the war; its safety cushion of surplus was woefully thin, the means of production suffering from indifferent maintenance, from development governed by political expediency rather than regard for the marketplace. The one thing that could be said was that the Western Europeans were better off than the Soviets, who had been suffering food shortages in increasing severity for over a decade before the Soviet leadership, seeing their conventional offensive into Western Europe beginning to dissolve like sugar poured in a running stream, had pressed the big button.

The post-war situation would have daunted a lesser man than Maximov. He had, however, certain advantages. For one thing, the physical plant of Europe proved rather more durable than its human population—less vulnerable to the heat, blast, and radiation of the thermonuclear exchange, and not susceptible at all to the plagues that frolicked in its wake. Economic devolution notwithstanding, the holocaust survivors found themselves heir to stockpiles more than sufficient to keep them alive—for a while. Second, there was the marvelous passivity of the European population, traditionally happy to entrust their fates first to the aristocracy and subsequently to the cradle-to-grave Socialist reformers who succeeded it. Confronted by catastrophe greater than even the Black Death, they were ready to follow a man on horseback. Yevgeny Maximov was such a man.

For years before the war, he had been the mystery man of Europe. He was widely known to be a Russian emigré, a man who moved constantly in the highest circles of money and power, like a Russian-born Bernard Baruch. Insofar as the public might have heard of him at all, they would likely associate his name with the Internationalist Council, the coalition of government officials, businessmen, intellectuals, media personalities—the molders and shapers of public opinion throughout the Western World—assembled to work toward the common goal of establishing what they termed a "rational world order." Which meant a *centralized* world order. For all the humanitarian rhetoric in which the council cloaked itself, those members who worked their way into the elite, onto the council itself, realized that when the abstract terms were stripped away, *centralization of power* meant power was centralized into the hands of a chosen few *individuals*. As, invariably, was privilege. With noble self-sacrifice, the members of the Internationalist Council were only too willing to provide those hands.

They had a hidden agenda as well. While they worked openly to establish their new world order, they worked covertly to undermine what order existed. Secretly they subsidized protests and repression, terrorism and brutal response alike. Disruption of trade and economy, though, to the despair of their analysts, disruption generally required little encouragement in those areas that most readily adopted the council's program. Eventually, they intended to create such overwhelming chaos that the world would embrace them in weary relief when they stepped forward to offer the benison of their leadership. The crowning touch, the final leap in chaos, was to be the Third World War.

But something went wrong. The protracted struggle that would exhaust the superpowers and complete the slide into world disorder never materialized. For years the Western defense establishment, from which the council drew no few of its numbers, had been glorifying the Soviet military in terms that would have gladdened the heart of a Hollywood flack of the 1930s. In the crunch, Soviet competence and durability failed drastically to meet expectations. It was the Soviets, not NATO, who, their backs to the wall, first employed nukes—and what ensued was no token exchange that would frighten the participants into malleability, but hell with the hinges off.

Still, such was the legitimacy the council had built up, in European politics at least, and so strong was the European desire for unification—as gentlemen of the ilk of Napoleon and Adolf Hitler had found—that it was perfectly natural for Western Europe to submit to the council's benevolent dictatorship. That accomplished, Maximov had taken the centralization-of-power principle to its logical conclusion. He called a meeting of surviving council members in his fortresslike villa in the Bernese uplands of Switzerland and had them all massacred, in such a way that the deed could be portrayed to media as a terrorist attack against the FSE, justifying his declaration of emergency and assumption of plenary powers—i.e., a police state, with bells and whistles.

To support his own version of the New Order, Maximov didn't only enjoy a substantial secret police establishment built on an elite coterie the council had assembled before the war of co-opted KGB operatives and members of the Western services alike. With America smashed and out of touch, the Soviet Union shattered by thermonuclear onslaught, its survivors facing the violence of sectional separatists and several hundred million angry Muslims to the south, the commanders of both the Warsaw Pact and the NATO forces that had been locked in the struggle in Europe likewise tendered their submissions to Chairman Maximov. Nothing, it seemed, could go wrong.

But, of course, it did. Surplus generated by the cataclysmic drop in the population dwindled rapidly. Shortages became the order of the day. Barbarians howled at the frontiers, and within the Federation Maximov's military might and secret police could not protect the survivors against those who chose to prey on their fellow men—particularly since among the most avid predators were Maximov's satraps themselves. Docile the Europeans may have been, exhausted they may also have been, but there was still a limit to human endurance. Like the thatched roof of a hut with the sparks of a nearby inferno falling on it, Europe began to take light with a thousand insurrections.

The key to restoring order, Maximov knew, was production. If the population had enough to eat, decent clothes to wear, decent shelter above their heads, electric power to run the ridiculous conveniences that would let them pretend they were leading a modern, civilized life, they would be less willing to incur the savage consequences of disobedience. Yet despite the armies of planners and analysts the Internationalist Council had gathered under its aegis, production within the FSE remained at a virtual standstill. But a solution existed—a miraculous talisman, possession of which would solve his empire's woes overnight: the Blueprint for Renewal.

Alarmed by escalating international tensions and the increasing vulnerability of technology-based society, certain parties in the United States government had initiated a top-secret program to provide for the reconstruction of America in the event of thermonuclear war. They assembled a master plan, based on a network of experts and caches scattered in secret locations across the country, to be activated after the war to insure the quickest possible recovery. The master key to the plan was contained in a set of electronic storage media, which accompanied the President of the United States wherever he went. In the event of war, the key would be transferred with him to whatever secret emergency command post he chose for refuge—Heartland in Iowa, for example, or Mount Weather or Raven Rock not far from Washington, D.C.—and the Blueprint would be put into action.

Since he had first learned of the Blueprint's existence through various informants highly placed in the United States government itself, Maximov had been trying to get his hands on it. He'd had no luck. Under the direction of the shadowy Major Crenna and former Israeli paratrooper and economist Dr. Jacob Morgenstern, Project Blueprint itself had resembled an elite military unit; its members were deeply committed, fired by enthusiasm for the project, and totally beyond any blandishments Maximov might dangle before them. His alternative, then, was to wait for war, then steal the Blueprint.

Came the One-Day War. President William Lowell took off in his National Emergency Airborne Command Post, and vanished. With him vanished the master listing for the Blueprint itself. At a time when both America and the man who would be her master most desperately needed the Blueprint, it was lost.

Maximov initiated an all-out effort to get hold of it. As he should have surmised, the Americans did also. They fielded the Guardians, an elite team supposedly formed to escort the President of the United States to safety in the event of thermonuclear war. Lowell's last-minute decision to entrust himself to his converted 747 had proved fortuitous for the Guardians, since it left them not just alive but guarding the person of his successor, Vice President Jeffrey MacGregor. In that capacity, they had once thwarted Maximov already.

In a bid to seize control over the stricken nation, one of Maximov's minions, a man code-named Trajan who headed a faction that took control of the Central Intelligence Agency during the One-Day War, attempted to grab MacGregor before he could reach safety in the massively fortified secret complex of Heartland. The Guardians eluded them, winning through to the Iowa facility. There they had learned their true mission: to reassemble the Blueprint for Renewal.

What ensued was a mad scramble for the scattered fragments of the Blueprint. Working on fragmented clues and computer projections, the Guardians and Maximov's men raced to find and secure components of the lost Blueprint. So far, honors went to the Guardians.

The man called Trajan—known to millions of Americans as conservative novelist and gadfly W. Soames Summerill—had attempted to build a power base out of a charismatic religious cult that swept the Midwest immediately after the war under the leadership of mad, radiation-resistant prophet Josiah Coffin. That initiative had fallen apart when the Guardians succeeded in killing the First Prophet Coffin himself before a crusading army of his Church of New Dispensation in Colorado's San Luis Valley, a conflagration in which Trajan himself disappeared.

Next Maximov had dispatched his right-hand man, the dapper KGB-colonel-turned-traitor Ivan Vesensky, a trained spy and killer with the grace of an Olympic skier and a jet-setter's demeanor. By stages Vesensky flew to California to take command of a network of wild-eyed would-be revolutionaries he had seeded in that state years before. Under the direction of former Lieutenant Governor Geoffrey van Damm, it had already resurfaced, and with Vesensky for a gray eminence seemed likely to accomplish by terrorism in California what Josiah Coffin had come within an ace of doing in the Midwest through revivalism. Unfortunately van Damm was as thoroughgoing a madman as the Midwestern preacher. His craziness, combined with the amazing factionalism endemic to revolutionary movements anywhere, had greatly aided the Guardians in kicking that scam to pieces too. Not only did they bring van Damm's People's Republic of California tumbling down, but they'd gotten away with no less a personage than Dr. Jacob Morgenstern, one of the Blueprint's founders, who carried a substantial chunk of the master plan in his grizzled, sunburned head. Arch-operative Vesensky, who had barely escaped with his life from van Damm's raging paranoia, had been forced underground with no resources left but his native wit and cunning. Those were formidable resources indeed, but for one man alone, even one as supremely able as Vesensky, to mount a serious threat to the Blueprint would require effort and a long, long time.

In the meantime, the Blueprint was rebuilding rapidly, dangling out of Vesensky's—and Maximov's—reach like a lush ripe fruit.

Then Maximov got a call from a dead man.

"Your Excellency," shrilled the wispy creature in the neon green smock. "You'll have to extinguish that nasty cigarette now. We have to powder you now so your makeup doesn't smear." Maximov blinked, scowled, his bushy black eyebrows looking like caterpillars bumping heads. He had just been working up a nice rosy glow of satisfaction, and this confounded fairy had doused it. Still, if one intended to be master of the world, one must make certain sacrifices.

He took a last, deep draw at the cigarette, pulling the smoke with malice aforethought into his lungs. Only a true Russian could find pleasure—or profess to—in smoking those infernal *makhorka* cigarettes with their long cardboard tubes; harsh beasts, tasting of burning leaves and, of course, cardboard. Most Russians valued few symbols of upward mobility so much as the smoking of Western cigarettes, mild as baby's hair in comparison to the dreaded *makhorka*. Ukrainian by birth, Maximov took perverse pleasure in continuing to smoke the things.

He sighed smoke and stubbed out the cigarette in the ashtray instantly proffered by another besmocked attendant. The makeup crew adjusted the cloth protecting his black suit and began spraying him with a fine mist of aerosol powder to fix the makeup on his blunt heavy features.

The adjective *bearlike* has been much overused in description of Russians; nevertheless, Yevgeny Maximov bore a striking resemblance to just that animal. When he stood, the bald spot on top of his head was almost two meters above whatever surface lay pressed beneath the soles of his immaculately polished shoes. He had a powerlifter's body, broad of shoulder, massive of chest, with a grandly imposing paunch that was mostly muscle the consistency of firebrick. The hands protruding from his sparkling white cuffs were hirsute and powerful as a bear's paws; the broad, bearded face, the heavy brows and deep-set eyes, all suggested the ursine. Power—personal, political, physical—radiated from him like heat from a stove.

Squinting his eyes shut against the spray, he thought, *Ah, Trajan, my very good friend. I underestimated you. I did indeed.* When the Church of the New Dispensation was defeated in Colorado, Maximov had naturally assumed the Guardians had done Trajan the great favor of killing him—a favor in view of what Maximov would have done to him after a failure of such magnitude. Then came the call, relayed across the Atlantic via a satellite that had sailed serenely above last summer's thermonuclear tumult from a secret Company base in North America. A familiar stick-dry voice whispering of French-Canadian separatists and the great treasure they had to offer. At a single stroke, the man named Trajan—who had somehow, miraculously, escaped from the debacle in the San Luis Valley—had placed the means for achieving Maximov's goals in this hands.

It hadn't been an overnight solution. It had taken time, a commodity of which the Chairman had little, and cunning, with which he was far more plentifully supplied. It had required months of top-secret preparation, concentration of much of the FSE's dwindling resources. And yet it would all be worthwhile; yes indeed.

In a matter of minutes Chairman Maximov would mount a podium in the special broadcast studio in his newly occupied headquarters in the seventeenth-century *Schloss Ehrenbreitstein* in Germany, set high on a cliff overlooking the town of Koblenz at the confluence of the Rhine and Moselle rivers forty kilometers south of the ruins of Bonn, to announce that the Federated States of Europe had embarked on a glorious new crusade. American troops, supported by their friends the FSE, had crossed the Atlantic in order to restore order to the stricken power—under the leadership of the last elected President of the United States, William Lowell, who supposely had died in the One-Day War.

While emphasizing the "hands across the water" aspect of the exhibition, the carefully crafted speech would allude to alleged stockpiles of American wealth that had survived the war, in which the hungry, huddled masses of Europe might expect to share as a reward for their aid to their good friend. Nor would the fact—never stated in so many words—that the adventure would mean substantial reduction in the number of

Americans in Europe escape the listeners. That would be another public-relations plus, and not simply because of resentment of having to feed tens of thousands of foreign mouths; whenever possible Maximov had chosen to use interlopers, American General Mark Shaw's soldiers or the Russians of Marshal Beriev, as blunt instruments against dissidents too tenacious for secret and conventional police forces to subdue. The Chairman's propaganda had subtly encouraged the public to think of the two armies as occupying forces, thus shifting resentment away from the government that was their actual master.

Finally, Chairman Maximov would enlist his subject's humanitarian feelings in this great crusade to restore order to the once great power across the water. It would be a truly stirring peroration.

Such a splendid gift you bestowed on me, my friend. More than sufficient to buy and pay for the two things Trajan demanded: his life, and vice-royalty over America. The consummate businessman, Maximov was only too willing to set aside his earlier determination to kill Trajan by millimeters for his earlier failure. As for his "rule" over America, behind the looming figurehead of Bill Lowell . . . Trajan was quite mad, of course. Yet it was a useful sort of madness. Nor, in this age of diminished expectation, could Yevgeny Maximov readily discard tools, however cracked, that might still prove serviceable. Let Trajan savor his triumph. Plenty of time, later, when the situation in North America had stabilized, to eliminate him and replace him with a more stable subordinate.

Scowling at his reflection in the mirror, Maximov lit a cigarette and filled his lungs with harsh smoke. "I cannot decide," he rasped to the makeup artists hovering over him, "if I resemble more exactly a cheap whore or a freshly embalmed corpse." He flung his fresh cigarette to the scuffed linoleum floor. "Now get this confounded rag off of me. I have a speech to make."

CHAPTER
FOUR ─────────────────────

Sheltered from the fierce blast of a blizzard in a corrugated metal culvert that passed beneath a long-ungraded farm road, the Guardians took stock of their situation. McKay and Sloan had patched each other up and smeared white zinc oxide ointment on burns, and now sat at either end of the meter-and-a-half-high tunnel watching the snow blow by while Tom Rogers hunkered over Casey in the light of a solar-battery handlamp.

After the Abrams brewed up, the survivors of the ambushing platoon had retreated as a brand-new storm settled in to stay. Pleased to find that being blown ass over teakettle by the tank's shells hadn't bent the barrel of his Maremont, McKay hooked one of the two Aussie ammo boxes still left in his chest pouch onto the weapon's receiver and fired a few precious rounds after them, not for effect, but to ensure they kept going in the right direction. That was one of the weaknesses of soldiers trained for the modern combat environment: they came to depend too much on big brothers, on armor, artillery, called airstrikes. When their apparently invincible tank blew, the ambushers' morale went up with it. As McKay pulled back through snow, he thought he heard the mumble of truck engines firing up a klick or so away.

When he got back to where Mobile One was burning itself out, he found Tom Rogers working on Casey. He had the ex-pilot's coveralls open and some kind of drip in his arm, and was prying his body armor off his chest with his Gerber Mark II Commando knife. Fifty or sixty meters away Sam Sloan lay in cover, keeping a watch for trouble as if he'd been doing this all his life. McKay knelt next to the team medic. "How is he?"

In truth he didn't look too good. A few strands of hair blew limply across a mask of blood, dirt, and soot. Much of his steel-gray uniform coveralls had been burned or blown away, and the chest area looked like raw hamburger. "Hard to say," Rogers said, taciturn as always. "He was concussed, but he's coming out of it some. Has burns on his hands and the left side of his chest, and he had shrapnel tear into his rib cage. Internal damage I can't tell about yet. I do know he has lost a lot of blood." He nodded at the drip, a bottle suspended from a small folding tripod beside Casey's arm. "I'm putting a Ringer's in him to keep up fluid volume."

"Can we move him?"

Rogers' brow wrinkled slightly. "Rather not."

"Not my goddamn question. Can we move him, or is he going to die if we try?"

Rogers raised his eye to McKay's. They were strange eyes, a dull, dead gray, like shark's eyes. Much as he liked the ex–Green Beret, McKay never liked looking him in the eye too long. After a moment, Rogers said, "Yeah, we can move him."

McKay bobbed his heavy chin. "Then get him wrapped back up. Come on in and give me a hand, Sam. We got miles to make."

They gathered up what supplies they could. McKay had considered traveling light, but decided instead to haul off everything they could carry. They had to put what distance they could between themselves and their dead armored car, but the storm would hamper anybody looking for them and cover their tracks as well. Since they were reduced to beating their feet anyway, the enemy—whoever the hell that was—automatically had the mobility edge on them. Better, McKay judged, to hang on to as much as possible. They needed any kind of advantage they could screw out of the situation, now. Besides, they could always ditch the stuff.

For all that he looked like some kind of adolescent California surf bum, Casey Wilson was all whipcord and steel, like any good fighter pilot. He revived enough to stumble along with his arm around somebody's neck. There was no way he could hump his own pack, so the other three rotated, one scouting a little ahead, one supporting Casey, one hauling a double load.

Having been put through the best survival-training courses available, none of the Guardians had illusions about it being necessary to stumble on through a driving snowstorm at any cost—thereby burning calories on exertion and exposing the maximum surface area to radiate away precious body heat—any more than they had any ridiculous notions of needing to fight off sleep at all costs. If they were caught in a snowstorm, the best thing to do would be to find a hole or other shelter, get as cozy as they could, and cork right off, preserving as much metabolic energy as possible. Without shelter they had to do as best they could, even if that was only huddling with their backs to the storm. But now, storm or no, the odds were pretty good that *somebody* would be coming back to take a look at the wrecks. They couldn't afford to be nearby when that happened. So they pushed on.

Take the most intensive, man-killing training and conditioning courses in the world: American Ranger and Force Recon, British SAS, French Foreign Legion, old-line Rhodesian SAS and Selous Scouts. Add them all together and multiply them by about two. That'll give a fair approximation of what Guardians training was all about. Each man had been driven to the absolute pinnacle of physical and mental conditioning—and each Guardian was an exceptional specimen to begin with. But what they had was barely enough. Forging along a tangent to their original line of travel, keeping their noses pointed in what they hoped was the right direction by regular compass checks, they didn't dare to stop to rest. When, after hours of white frigid hell, Casey's legs finally gave way beneath him, he almost pulled a weary Sam Sloan to the frozen ground with him.

Eyes closed, Casey shook his head. "Go on," he mumbled through stiff lips. "Go on. Can't . . . go anymore—"

McKay unslung his lightweight M-60 from around his bull neck and handed the weapon to Sloan. "Fuck that," he said. He stooped, hauled Casey up over his shoulders in a fireman's carry, and stood.

They marched on. By 1500 they'd reached the end of their tether, and what light there was was beginning to fail. They were trying to avoid roads, since any pursuit braving the elements would almost certainly follow them, so it was pure dumb luck that they had fetched up against this farm road just at the point it crossed a small shallow draw.

Now, out of the main force of the storm and sight as well, Rogers was giving Casey Wilson a more thorough examination. What he found wasn't encouraging. "He's got a finger-sized chunk of shrapnel stuck in his chest. Pointing like a dagger at his heart. It's a miracle it didn't shift and kill him on the march." The little W-shaped furrow appeared between his eyebrows. Rogers was fretting over permitting his patient to be moved against his better judgment. "Also, he's lost too much blood. I only got one more Ringer's lactate salvaged from the wreck. That's barely going to be enough to keep him going for twelve hours more."

Sam Sloan turned a long, weary face from the far end of the culvert. "What about transfusions?"

"He's O-negative. Any of us could take a transfusion from *him*. But he can't take one from any of *us*."

"What about trying to hunt up some citizen with the right blood type to transfuse him?" McKay asked.

Rogers looked at him a moment. "Don't have no way to type the blood, Billy." They *had* had the database of the fabulous fourth-generation computer built into Mobile One, interfaced with a nifty little set of medical peripherals that could run an astonishing variety of tests on a patient. It was all twisted junk now.

"We're being hunted, McKay," Sam Sloan said. "Is it safe to go around knocking on doors?"

McKay shook his head. "Okay, it was a shitty idea." He longed ferociously for a cigar. He had a couple in the breast pocket of his coveralls, but after that explosion had pitched his ass down the draw, they weren't much use to him, unless he wanted to scrape some of the remnants together and poke them into his face like a pinch of snuff.

Casey stirred beneath the bedrolls that covered him, muttering something. "What'd he say?" McKay asked.

Rogers shrugged. "He ain't lucid. He's asking after that cap again." During the trek from the wreckage, Casey had drifted in and out of consciousness. During his most lucid moments he demanded to be left behind. Most of the time, though, he just rambled, mostly about his most prized possession, a Bruce Springsteen *Born to Run* tour cap. It was a collector's item whose value was beyond reckoning. McKay himself couldn't see making all that fuss over a twenty-year-old baseball cap, but it meant the world to Casey. In fact, the young ex-pilot had a whole collection of caps with rock and roll groups' names on them; none of the others could remember if they had seen him wearing his Springsteen cap this time out. Rogers spoke low to the boy, soothing him.

McKay turned his head and looked out into the weather. There was a good ten centimeters of fresh snow on the ground, but what was coming down wasn't so hagridden by the driving east wind as before. "There's a cache not a hundred klicks from here," he said. "It'll have some containers of fluorocarbon replacement blood in it. Also a medkit with a chem-tab blood typing set in it, in case he needs more and we can hunt up a few friendlies."

"Long way to walk, Billy," Rogers said.

McKay shrugged. "Maybe we won't have to. There're still some farmers hanging on out here. Maybe we can promote some transport."

"This is New Dispensation territory, McKay," Sam Sloan pointed out. "We might not get too friendly a reception from those religious fanatics. Also, whoever ambushed us is liable to be looking for us."

McKay swung his legs out of the culvert, stood up, stretched, feeling the wind hitting his face like a blast from a firehose. "So who said we had to ask?"

An hour and a half later they were hunkered down behind a piece of fading yellow farm equipment McKay couldn't iden-

tify, and was damned if he would ask Sloan about, for fear
he'd get one of those goddamn superior "you're a pore li'l city
boy, ain't you?" looks. They were watching a swaybacked
little frame farmhouse with a pitched roof that was peeling
like a sunburned back. An old-time barn with a hipped roof
stood off a ways from the main house. Parked in front of the
house were a blue Chevy pickup with a rear window that
looked as if it had been starred by a bullet, and a Fast Attack
Vehicle with two MG-3 machine guns and what looked amazingly like a man in *Bundeswehr* winter cammies sitting in the
driver's seat, tapping gloved hands on the steering wheel.

"What the fuck, over?" Billy McKay whispered. Sloan said
nothing. He simply jacked forward the action of the M-203
grenade launcher slung under the barrel of his Galil, removed
the blunt-nosed WP round that was chambered, slipped that
back into one of the twenty-four pockets of his special gren-
adier's vest, took out a multiple projectile round half the
length of a normal 40-mm grenade, stuffed that up the spout
and pulled the weapon closed. The M-203 was now a very
large, very powerful shotgun.

Eyeing his companions sidelong, McKay almost nodded.
He'd been fretting about the necessity of bringing the ex-Navy
man along ever since they had left the cramped culvert. Sam
Sloan had proved himself again and again in the days since
the One-Day War, but McKay still couldn't overlook the fact
that he lacked the years of experience at this kind of warfare
McKay and Rogers had under their belts. He'd been worrying
about it even more since they spotted the farmhouse with the
funny-looking little car out in front of it. But they snooped
and pooped forward, keeping a good forty-meter interval between them, rendezvousing behind this big combine or harrow
or whatever the fuck it was with the enclosed cab parked not
twenty-five meters from the FAV. And Sloan had performed
as if he had been doing this all his life. Short rushes, hit the
dirt, watch the driver scratch his neck and fidget, watch the
house for signs that anyone was looking out past the drawn
chintz curtains or emerging, then up and run forward again,
bent low, ready to drop flat again in less time than it took an
eye to blink.

McKay didn't recognize the make of car, but he knew

perfectly well what it was. In recent years the trend in the West had been away from vast land-going battlewagons in favor of small, highly maneuverable, fast—and best of all—cheap, wheeled vehicles. By the end of the mid-1980s the U.S. Army had adopted the Highly Maneuverable Military Vehicle concept, lightly armored vehicles about the size of a big jeep. Far smaller and harder to spot than any tracked FAV—a very desirable trait in an epoch in which a major axiom of warfare was "if you can see it, you can kill it"—the HMMV (pronounced "hum-vee") made a lot of sense as a scout, but it also proved itself over and over as a casualty-recovery vehicle, fast-deploying personnel carriers, and, packing a launcher for a beefy TOW-II wire-guided missile, more than a match for a Main Battle Tank.

So if the HMMV was a good idea, why not go a step farther? some military thinkers reasoned. The result was the Fast Attack Vehicle.

What the FAV most resembled was a road gypsy's dune buggy, sort of like the corpse of a Volkswagen Rabbit that had been picked away by vultures until only a skeleton was left. This one was completely open to the elements except for low armored gunwales and a sharply sloped sheet of armor out front. Otherwise, it consisted of four independently suspended tires, balloon-wide for low ground pressure, a rollbar cage over the top with a spare tire lashed overhead, and an engine in back. It carried three men: a driver, a front gunner, and a "stinger" gunner manning a rear-firing pintle gun. McKay himself was skeptical of the concept—he just wondered if somebody weren't a little too fond of playing "Rat Patrol." Still, he had to admit that the little fuckers could run rings around any HMMV made, and could be devilishly hard to hit if the driver had any conception of evasive tactics. Something of a reactionary, McKay was a confirmed "leg" man—and that didn't just mean his taste in women.

Sloan, meanwhile, was frowning at the thing as if he had just seen it drive out of the space-chandelier mother ship in *Close Encounters*. "Somebody would have to be pretty crazy to actually fight in that thing," he opined. "I'd rather ride a jughead mule into battle myself."

McKay grinned at him. "Or the battleship *Missouri*." He

peered at the car. "What's that insignia?"

Sloan squinted. The snow had quit falling from the sky, but was now being blown along the ground in billows by the unstinting wind. Miserable as the snow, either falling or blowing, had made their trek, both men were grateful for it. If whoever had them on his shit list was really looking for them, they might well have fancy people-sniffers or infrared sensors mounted on helicopters to track them down with. This weather made it very unlikely anyone was going to try taking choppers after them.

"Nothing I'm familiar with. It looks like a blue circle with a white map of Europe inside, and a blue five-pointed star superimposed on it." He glanced to McKay. "You think it might be FSE's symbol?"

"You think of anything else it might be?"

Sloan shook his head. "What do we do now?"

"There's our wheels, just sitting there waiting for us." He unslung the M-60 and lowered it to the ground. "If we can take out that driver, we might be able to just drive the fucker off, and nobody'd be the wiser."

He crept down to the opposite end of the machine, unslinging the other weapon he toted all this way from around his neck. As a footslogger from way back, he instinctively rebelled against toting along anything he didn't have to, but the cool, appraising side of him told him it might be handy to have just such a tool along. It was an MP-5 SDX, a submachine gun with integral silencer, part of a lot specially made for select antiterrorist forces in .45 caliber by Heckler and Koch. It was a superb weapon for quick and nasty infighting, especially when quiet was important. As an infantry weapon, however, it was pretty piss-poor. It had only slightly better range than a pistol, and that only in semiauto modes; it was also too damn susceptible to the dust and shit that were liable to get into the works and would be until somebody got the idea of vacuuming battlefields ahead of time. On the other hand, McKay's Maremont made a noise like the trumpet of doom.

He crouched, slid out the telescoping buttstock and snugged it to the shoulder, then sighted along the fat suppressor. He still had his big Ka-bar combat knife, and he'd used that for sentry removal on occasion in the past. But for him, unlike

Tom Rogers, a knife definitely wasn't the weapon of choice. The popular press and movies aside, it was damned hard to kill anybody with a knife, and taking out a sentry with a blade was a desperate, bloody business. You had to be prepared to hang on to the son of a bitch and choke off a cry of warning or just plain pain until he died—and even if you slashed his throat, that could take an eternity a clock might measure as only a couple of minutes. McKay lined up the sight on a brief interval of neck between the helmet and the fake-fur-lined collar of his target's camouflage suit and hesitated.

He was an Expert-rated marksman, and the MP-5 was very accurate for a submachine gun. At this range, with time to aim and the buttstock extended, he could put a whole thirty-round box into a hole in a target not much bigger around than a single slug. If he cut the guy's spinal cord up at the neck, that would be about it. If all he did was punch through a bunch of muscle in the throat, the wound would still probably be lethal, but the recipient might raise something of a fuss before he died. A head shot would be better—but McKay liked taking a chance of whanging a bullet off the coal-scuttle-shaped helmet even less. "Sam," he subvocalized.

"Here."

"Can you chuck something over on the ground beside that son of a bitch? So he looks down?"

"Sure. I was the champion pebble skipper of Langford, Missouri, when I was a kid." Sloan felt in his pockets. He came up with the small tarnished disk of a pre-1965 dime, a genuine silver coin favored as a medium of exchange among survivors of the holocaust. *We could be needing all of these we've got*, he thought wryly, then took aim and pitched the coin underhand in a long arc.

It pinged off the vehicle's frame by the driver's left ankle and dropped into the snow. The driver looked down. McKay shot him through the base of the skull. He jerked once as a final random signal blasted out of his medulla, then slumped forward across the wheel.

McKay slipped off the boltlock, cycling the action once by hand. There was no such thing as a fully silenced firearm, but a .45 slug fired through an integral silencer, moving below the speed of sound so there was no accompanying crack, from a weapon locked to keep the bolt from clacking back and chambering the next round in the magazine, came pretty close. The sound produced might have come from a sharp rap of knuckles on a table. Nonetheless, McKay waited a tense few dozen heartbeats to see if anybody'd heard the shot.

Sloan grinned at him. "Nobody heard you."

"How the fuck do you know?"

"You can tell you ain't a farmboy. With this wind howling and rattling things inside that farmhouse, you could hammer on the door a whole half minute before anyone took notice."

"Shit," McKay said eloquently. "Cover me." With the MP-5 held across his chest and ready to fire full auto, he got up and ran hunched over to the FAV.

When he was halfway there the door to the farmhouse opened. Two men in winter camouflage stepped out onto the porch, talking back over their shoulders. McKay was already in motion, a running dive for the rear of the FAV. The man with the black beret clawed for a sidearm. Sloan's rifle cracked. The little SS-109 slug punched through his body armor and tumbled, slicing like a tiny buzz saw through his heart and right lung. He dropped like a bundle of wet laundry.

The man behind him brought up an AUG, one of those funny-looking little bullpup Austrian rifles. From behind the vehicle's right rear tire, McKay gave him a short burst in the center of the body. Triple impacts tossed him against the door-frame and cracked most of his ribs, but failed to penetrate. He was hard-core. He jerked off a burst one-handed, restricted to three rounds by the rifle's regulator. He was also either lucky or good. McKay barely had time to wince back behind the tire before one shot cracked past his right ear, another thunked the tire and the third spanged off the FAV's armor and went screaming off like a horny banshee. From the combine or whatever the hell it was Sam Sloan squeezed off three rounds full auto. Two of them struck the soldier's much-abused chest, and this time didn't stop.

"I owe you one," McKay called back to Sloan. He picked himself up and went into the house.

Inside they found a typical middle-aged farm couple, jerky-dry and visibly nervous. The three soldiers had shown up about an hour before, they said. In heavily accented but understandable English the officer in the beret had asked them if they had seen any armed men lately. The descriptions of the men they were looking for came mighty close to the two interlopers. Informed that the couple hadn't seen anyone, they invited themselves for coffee, the standard Panhandle hospitality of the reluctant hosts having been short-circuited by the suspicion that they might be Russians. Apparently sensing this, the officer assured them that they were German. He'd sat down with his buddy at the dining room table and explained that they were looking for traitors, armed and dangerous ones, who were known to be on the loose in the area.

At this McKay's face turned magenta and a big vein throbbed in his forehead. "Traitors, my—" He bit off the word just in time. "We ain't traitors."

"We're the Guardians," Sam Sloan put in smoothly. "Maybe you've heard of us."

The woman gasped. "You're the men Reverend Forrie says such turble things about onna radio!"

Her husband nodded and stroked his chin with mesquite fingers. "That's who they told us you was. Said you was mixed up in some kind of revolution."

Laying a hand on McKay's arm to forestall another outburst, Sloan said, "They were lying to you."

"Yeah. Well, I tell ya. Don't cotton much to foreigners coming in here with guns an' all." His eyes flicked from side to side in his leathery face. McKay was still glowering at him with his shoulders hunched and nostrils flared.

"Now, you folks won't tell anybody we've been here, will you?" Sam Sloan asked.

The thin wife clutched her husband's arm. "They'll kill us if they find they been here and we din't tell 'em." The man looked at her, aghast. She had just given these two heavily armed strangers the best reason in the world to shoot them both where they stood.

"If they find out their men died here, they'll probably take reprisal against you," Sam Sloan said. "We'll take the bodies with us—and what they don't know won't hurt anybody, right?"

Out in the yard, they gathered up the three bodies, relieved them of their gear, and stacked them in the back of the FAV, wedged in between the seat and the machine gun mount. Sam Sloan's stomach did rolls like a destroyer in heavy swell. *Wonder if I'll ever get used to this kind of thing,* he thought as he gingerly tucked a dangling arm back into the open car.

He slid into the driver's seat and started the engine. McKay glowered behind the forward machine gun, arms folded across his chest. He was still fuming over the insinuation of treason. "I'm sorry we had to kill the three of them," Sloan said, casting a quick glance over his shoulder as he let in the clutch.

"Yeah," McKay grunted. "Coulda used a prisoner."

They drove a few klicks north toward the Oklahoma border. When they judged they'd gone far enough, they veered off the blacktopped county road they'd been following and moved out cross country to dump the bodies out of sight of the road. Then they came back to the pavement, which had cracked badly since the last repair, and jostled on northward again. They had maps of the area in their packs, and McKay and Sloan had both memorized the locations of the caches nearby.

As they rode they listened in on the vehicle's radio. There was sporadic traffic in English, as well as German, French, a guttural language that might have been Dutch, and, curiously, Russian. It indicated there were a couple of hundred men in the area searching for them. Reassuring; that wasn't nearly enough to cover the area they might be hiding out in. Apparently, the interlopers had no sooner seized Heartland than they'd sent a company or two down here to the Guardians' would-be rendezvous site. Why there hadn't been more on hand than a platoon backed up by the Abrams to greet them, neither man could guess. Probably just snafu. This thing had all the earmarks of a fucked-up operation—fortunately for the Guardians. Nobody even seemed unduly disturbed that the stolen vehicle's crew hadn't reported in. Communications foul-ups were standard for any operation, and this one had more than its share, to judge by the irate radio traffic.

They rolled across the Texas-Oklahoma border somewhere between Hitchland and Perryton. Even before the Third World War, people had been thin on the ground in this part of the world. Now they saw no lights through the drifting snow, no sign at all that anybody lived here anymore. Once or twice they passed the dark huddles of small towns that seemed to have withered up and died. But nothing moved but the wind and the snow. And them.

They drove north a ways on U.S. 83, dodging the occasional oblong snow-mound of a derelict car. Just before the highway crossed the Beaver River they turned right. A wire fence blocked their way. A brief argument ensued, McKay wanting either simply to cut it or just drive on through, country boy Sloan outraged at the very prospect. In the end Sloan won, and they drove several hundred meters back the way they had come before they found a gate. After all, *somebody* might still be using this land, and they were almost certain to be having a hard enough time that they didn't need strangers busting down the fences to let their cattle wander off. McKay hated delay like poison, but he got Sloan's point. They drove several klicks on compass bearings. The FAV showed a slight tendency to skate, but mostly just glided all but effortlessly across the snow with a thin crunching.

Two klicks away from where the cache should have been, McKay ordered a halt. "We don't want to run this sucker without lights. I'll go scout the place out, let you know if it's safe."

Sam Sloan hung on to the steering wheel. His fingers seemed to be freezing in place, locked around it, despite the thick gloves. It was a tense moment. Heartland was taken, their mission compromised; had the intruders managed to crack open the complex's database? If they had, the two Guardians could expect a reception committee to be awaiting them at the cache.

"Be careful." It was all he could think of to say.

McKay nodded briskly. "Don't sweat it. I don't think nobody's here. We didn't pick up any traffic to indicate they got anybody here—and these geeks never even *heard* of radio security." He grinned briefly. "Hang loose." Then he simply faded from Sloan's sight as if dematerializing.

For all his fatigue and his own minor wounds McKay traveled quickly, purposefully. He moved through an eerie anechoic desolation. There was no starlight, no moonlight, yet enough illumination filtered down through the low-hanging ceiling of clouds to make the snow-covered prairie seem to glow with a soft translucent light. The drifting snow cut down visibility to not much more than a hundred meters, and McKay's snowbird camouflage of white with horizontal streaks of dark gray and tan blended well with the prairie. He was traveling light. He'd left his pack and the beefy machine gun back at the vehicle, and was carrying the silenced MP-5. He wasn't going to be engaging in any blazing firefights, not if he could help it. Even though his desperately low supply of ammo for his M-60 had been augmented by the treasure trove of the FAV's ammunition load—400 rounds of 7.62 ammo on disintegrating links that his Maremount could digest just as pretty as you please—he had no illusions of slugging it out alone with a whole platoon. He was a hero, but that didn't mean he was stupid.

When he judged he was halfway to his objective he began to veer to his right, following a southeasterly course. Any ambushers would expect them to drive straight in from 83. He intended to slip in from the other direction. It was a pretty shaggy-assed assignment, to pick your way across this featureless white void by compass readings and sheer dead reckoning. But McKay moved with a confidence that bordered on arrogance. This was his sort of job, the kind of close-to-the-edge work he did best.

Closing in from the east, paralleling the course of the Beaver, he spotted the windmill ahead of him like a frozen metal dandelion. He went down on his belly in the snow and watched.

Nothing. Just the windmill, sighing and creaking and banging in the wind, the stark flatness of a frozen-over stock tank next to it. No sign of movement, no alien shapes or signs of disturbance, not even enough to give him that old subliminal tickle of *wrongness* that he knew so well from his days in Force Recon and SOG. Just the wind, and the snow, and the cold.

He rose, crept forward. The muscles of his belly shrank toward his spine in anticipation of a withering blast of gunfire, but they didn't really mean it. In his gut McKay knew there was no ambush here; the Guardians' cache system hadn't been compromised. Feeling the beginnings of elation within him, he checked over the area carefully. Again nothing, no sign anyone had been there since the snow, since the war, even. "It's okay, Sam," he said aloud. "Come on in." Two kilometers' separation stretched the little communicators to the edge of their performance; that was something else they'd miss about the loss of Mobile One: the ability of the big radio set in the Super Commando to boost their signals over a much greater range. He was half afraid that his own signal wouldn't carry, but in a moment he heard Sloan's relieved acknowledgment.

He knelt. Cold-numbed fingers fumbled open an access panel at the base of the windmill next to where the drive link of the wind-powered pump entered the earth. Off to one side of the assembly of gears and rods was a small slot, unnoticeable unless you were looking for it. McKay drew his Guardians identity card from a buttoned pocket of the coveralls beneath his winter gear and slipped it into the slot. With a slight *pop* a meter-and-a-half-square section of ground next to the windmill suddenly tilted a few degrees like the world's smallest tectonic plate, opening a handspan gap through which warm air from underground breathed a soft exhalation of condensation and spilling miniature landslides of snow to the side. McKay swung open the concealed hatch and descended into the bowels of the earth.

Sam Sloan frowned. "Jesus, McKay. Why do you want me to stop? We're almost there."

Sitting to his side with one hand idly clutching the pistol grip of an MG-3, McKay said, "Don't get any answer."

Sloan braked the FAV to a halt. Ahead of them the county road they were following intersected the little farm road under which Rogers and Casey were concealed. He peeled his hands off the wheel and started rubbing them together, flexing them to limber them up. He hated to stop driving; it had been taking his mind off the cold.

"Tom, this is Billy. We got the stuff. Do you read? Tom?"

"Probably a malfunction," Sam Sloan said. He was the group's communication officer. "You should know how easy it is for communications to get messed up. One little thing goes wrong with our sets, and we're out of touch."

"They've worked all right before."

"So maybe they're due for a breakdown."

McKay shook his head. "Uh-uh. We ain't just waltzing in there." He started climbing out of the car. "I'm gonna go check it out."

Sloan stared at him in disbelief. "We don't have *time*. Tom didn't know how long he could keep Casey going in this cold."

Not listening, McKay was checking the magazine of the MP-5. ":Don't like it," he grunted. "We—"

"*Billy. Sam.*" Both men jerked as if they'd been zapped with cattle prods. Impossibly, it was Casey's voice, a feeble croak, attenuated and bristling with static. "*Stay away. They —they got us!*"

CHAPTER
FIVE ——————————————————

"Shit," Sam Sloan said.

"Casey! What the hell's goin' on?" McKay almost shouted. *"Got us—can't—hey, get your hands off me, man—"* There was a faint pop, then silence.

Sloan looked at McKay with old man's eyes. "What are we going to do?"

McKay slammed the magazine home with the butt of his hand. "Let me go scope it out," he said. "Think you can drive and fire the machine gun one-handed?"

"Lieutenant McKay." McKay glanced around, suddenly tense, before he realized the sound had come from behind his right ear. "Lieutenant Commander Sloan. Are you there?"

"That's *Commander* Sloan," McKay snarled. That he held command over a man who ranked him by as many pay grades as Sloan did had been an unspoken friction point between the two since the inception of the Guardians. But even if Sam Sloan was a fancy-ass Annapolis black-shoe Navy son of a bitch, no fucking Eurogoon was going to scant his rank. "Who the fuck is this?"

"This is Sergeant Eklund, U.S. Army. Ah command the

59

platoon that's taken your Lieutenant Wilson and Lieutenant Rogers prisoner.'' It was a Texan voice, on the high-pitched side. *What, are they drafting goddamn Boy Scouts now?* McKay thought. "Ah'm willin' to discuss the terms of your surrender.''

"Yeah, we gotta do that sometime—over a campfire in hell.'' He half expected Sam, who believed in making nice, to protest, but Sloan just looked at him out of a skull's face.

"Maybe you wanna reconsider that, Lieutenant.''

"No way. I don't know what the fuck you think you're doing, but you're detaining legally constituted emissaries of the United States government. If you don't let 'em go, the shit's gonna come down on you good and hard.''

"If y'all don't surrender pretty quick, it's gonna come down pretty hard on Lieutenant Wilson.''

"You think you're gonna pull us in with hostages?'' He balled his free left hand into a fist, clenching it so tight the tough fabric around his forearm strained and started to give at the seams. Twice when he was with covert ops with SOG, he'd killed a man with a single blow of his fist. He looked forward to making Sergeant Eklund number three—unless he decided that would be too quick. "If you do anything to Casey—''

"Ain't a question of us *doin'* anything to him, Lieutenant. It's more a question of what we cain't do. Lieutenant Rogers say he needs that replacement blood right away.''

"Maybe if you let us talk to Lieutenant Rogers,'' Sam Sloan said.

"Oh. Yeah, Ah reckon Ah can do that. Just a minute. I'm talkin over his communicator. Your friend Wilson's so messed up, we never even thought to check if he had one too. He put one over on us.''

A few moments of fumbling, then, "Billy? Rogers. They're telling the truth. Casey is having a lucid spell, but he's fading fast.''

McKay closed his eyes. That cornball old phrase, *loneliness of command*, beat against his temples like the clapper of a big brass bell. He flicked off his communicator, gesturing for Sloan to do the same. "I'm goin' in. I'll take the stuff. I won't order you to surrender.''

Sloan stared at him. In a moment he looked away. The big ex-Marine wasn't used to showing his feelings, and now Sloan couldn't stand to look at the pain on his face. "This isn't my line of country, McKay. Where can I do the most good? Inside or out?"

If it had been Rogers, McKay might have suggested that he hang back and let McKay try to sell this Sergeant Eklund some sort of song and dance that the fourth Guardian had fallen down and busted his neck. Rogers' entire military career had been devoted to operating in hostile territory alone, or nearly so. But Sam—for all his Guardian training, McKay didn't feel he could lay that burden on him. "My gut feeling is we maybe should stick together. Besides, you're our diplomat, and we just might need one of those. Maybe you could talk some sense into these assholes." He unclenched his fist finger by finger and dropped his hand onto the roll bar. "Besides, if it gets too hairy, I'm sure we can work it so one of us gets away."

He turned his communicator back on. "All right, Eklund," he gritted. "What are your terms?"

According to the sergeant's instructions they kept the light day packs they'd taken with them, and their personal weapons as well. McKay shouldered the fifty-kilo medical kit. The weapons and effects they'd taken from the dead Germans they left piled in the FAV.

Leaving the little attack car sitting where it was, they trudged fifty meters down the road, then stopped. Sam Sloan took careful aim and put a 40-millimeter HEDP grenade with a shaped-charge warhead into the gas tank of the little vehicle. It blew up with a yellow-white flare, a scream of brightness against the dark. He added a Willy Peter grenade for good measure.

"Hey! What was that explosion? What's going on?" Eklund's voice shrilled instantly in their ears. *His voice is really cracking,* Sloan thought numbly. *Do they think that we're so easy that they send adolescents to hunt us down?*

"Just building a little bonfire to warm our hands at before we come in," McKay said. He stood a moment, looking directly at the burning wreck, and the fuck with his night vision. *Leave nothing to the enemy* was the law he lived by, in Force Recon and SOG.

Maybe shoulda threw our personal weapons in too, he thought. Eklund had specifically permitted them to carry them, hung around their necks with long Israeli slings, and McKay had said okay. The weapons had become talismans, little slivers of hope. Maybe it was all delusion, twenty-four-carat bullshit. But their weapons and sidearms seemed to represent whatever tiny chance they had.

"I thought you'd leave him, Billy. I really did," Sam Sloan said.

"If I thought the mission required it, I woulda," McKay said. "But I kinda got a feelin' America can't spare any Guardians right now."

In the wreck, ammunition began to cook off, reaching into the night with tentacles of fire. "Fuck it," he said, stating the creed he'd lived by as a Marine, "and drive on."

They started walking.

There were twenty of them, either a long squad or a short platoon. They'd brushed off the snow by one end of the culvert, scraped together a bunch of dead grass, sprinkled some gas on it, and set it alight for a campfire. They'd brought up a truck, an ancient canvas-back deuce and a half that looked like something from a World War II movie, and parked it to one side to form a windbreak of sorts. They all clustered around, the twisting fire throwing a wan glow on haggard half-shaven faces. Several of them stood with leveled weapons as the two Guardians came marching up, weapons still slung and hands held high as per instructions. The rest just sat, looking at them or into the fire.

McKay's professional eye noted that they did indeed seem to be dressed in the rags and remnants of Army uniform. It was too dark, the light too skittish, to make out unit insignia, but it looked as if they were wearing different types of shoulder patches. He didn't think any were the Europe-and-star emblem of the FSE. The weapons, slung or leveled, were mostly M-16 A-2s, the standard U.S. Army–issue rifle; McKay also noted a couple of older A-1s, several civilian

longarms, the blunderbuss shape of an M-49, a single-shot
grenade launcher that fired the same round as Sloan's M-203.
Not a very strak outfit, it appeared. But there was a certain
wild-eyed wariness to them, to the way they watched the
Guardians, the way they held themselves, the way their eyes
seemed to burn from well back in the sockets: a hair-trigger
readiness. He'd seen that look before, in guerrilla bands
who'd been out in the *maquis* for a while, in the faces of SOG
teams who had spent too long under the gun. You couldn't
take such men for granted. They were like a steel tow cable,
under tension and starting to fray. They might break at any
moment, and if they did, and you weren't looking out pretty
sharp, you might just wind up cut in half.

A hulking figure stood up from the fire. In the shifting glare
McKay saw a shoulder patch, three black chevrons above one
black arc: Staff Sergeant. The figure stepped forward, hand
on a sidearm holstered at one hip. *Big son of a bitch,* McKay
thought. He caught pale highlights in the crewcut hair on the
man's bare head. Automatically he wondered, *Can I take
him?* You couldn't really see what he was made of, with his
bulky winter gear on and in this light, but McKay didn't have
three inches on him, and he moved with the same big-cat
grace, the aura of power under careful control, as McKay did
himself.

"That's far enough," the figure said. That adolescent voice
sounded incongruous coming from such a hulk, though it had
a gruff peremptory buzz to it now. "Y'all put your hands
behind your necks and unsling your weapons real careful-like,
drop them on the ground. Then do the same with your gun-
belts. Also your knives, and any sneaky little high hideouts
you might have." The Guardians complied. The sergeant ges-
tured. "Mason, Ballou—search them. Do it careful, now—
you remember what we found on that other one." *That other
one* would be Rogers. He customarily carried enough concealed cutlery and ordnance to outfit a small insurrection, or
at least a healthy putsch. Unless these dudes were a lot sharper
than they looked, in fact, the odds were good he still had a few
surprises in store for them. For what that was worth.

Two men came forward, a tall black dude and a white guy
with lank, dirty-blond hair. They patted the two Guardians

down, thoroughly if not expertly. "Okay, Sarge," the black said. "They's clean."

"Can I take this goddamn pack off now without anybody shooting me?" McKay asked. "My corns are killing me."

The crewcut head turned toward him. "You McKay?"

"You got that right. And this dude that looks like Jim Garner's younger brother is Commander Sloan."

A nod. "Staff Sergeant Marla Eklund. Wish Ah could say Ah was pleased to meet you."

The heavy medkit was halfway to the frozen turf when McKay heard Sloan say, "Wish we could say the same—ma'am."

McKay tried to stop in mid-motion, almost throwing his back out trying to arrest the downward progress of 110 pounds of medical supplies. "What the fuck?" he rasped.

"That's no way to talk to a lady," Sloan said, showing teeth. McKay let the pack down easy.

"So what are *you* starin' at?" the sergeant demanded. "Ain't you never seen a woman before?"

McKay straightened. "I've seen woman sergeants before, and any was too damn many. You run this show?"

"Ah do."

Bent over, Tom Rogers emerged from the culvert. A couple of troopies hovered nearby with rifles at the ready. He ignored them. "Could you bring the ruck in here, Billy? We ain't got much time."

Chivvied out of the culvert by Tom Rogers, who took distinctly after a mother hen in discharging his duties as medic, McKay and Sloan went out to sit by the fire with Sergeant Eklund's troops. The squaddies treated the two Guardians with a sort of watchful awe that under other circumstances McKay might have found gratifying. They had a smaller cook-fire going in what appeared to be an old Sherwin-Williams paint can, and the two Guardians were given plates of canned beans boiled with canned Vienna sausages.

"Look, would you just tell us what the hell is going on?" McKay said around a mouthful of congealing beans.

"Don't talk to the sergeant that way," a voice said sharply. McKay glowered at its owner. The man was around medium height, slightly shorter than Sam Sloan, heavyset, with full cheeks and a large-pored nose. He wore a boonie hat over straight black hair tied into a queue that hung well down his back. He'd been introduced as James Tall Bear, and McKay recalled the exotic hairstyle had been a concession offered by the Army to Indians a few years back, when Native Americans started to become a popular minority group.

"My friend doesn't intend to be offensive, ma'am," Sloan said, smiling at the sergeant in a way that, inexplicably, irritated McKay. "It's just that we've had kind of a hard day."

"All right. At ease, now, Jim." The sergeant took another bite of beans. In her thick, tattered combat gear, she looked to have the figure of an old Irish washerwoman. Her face was broad, high-cheekboned, with a strong jaw and snub nose. It seemed to have had grime and soot and weariness trodden into it like the floors of one of the Pittsburgh public schools McKay had gone to before his parents dropped him in parochial school.

He was still glaring at her. "I still want to know what's going on."

A shrug. "We've got orders to bring you all in. Don't know as I should tell you more'n that."

"Shucks," Sam Sloan said, his voice taking on a twang like a hillbilly banjo, "seeing as how we're going to be spending some time together, we might as well be friendly." And he grinned. McKay knew that grin. It was well calculated to warm the heart of any red-blooded American girl. Sloan was a handsome bastard, in his own way.

He was a sly one too. The country in his voice was pure contrivance. Now, nothing would turn off any real Texan quicker than somebody faking country, and the ones McKay had met could spot a phony way out past handgun range. But Sloan came by his honestly. He really was an old Missouri farm boy. Even as he could dredge up his shitkicker accent of times past, he could tip his nose back and lower the room temperature with the Ivy League best, thanks to his training at Annapolis. McKay, who'd never lacked for success with the ladies, still found himself envying Sloan the versatility of his approach.

But it wasn't any aw-shucks folksiness or masculine charm that made the sergeant peer into her beans for a full minute as if she saw something swimming in them, shrug, nod, and look up again. It was plain rack-hanging *boredom*, something McKay knew well. You spend your time out in the boonies with the same bunch, month after month. If an outfit comes together it's *us* and the rest of the world is *them*. You'll fight for any one of your buddies, die for them. It's what really holds armies together. But, Jesus, sometimes you just got sick of looking at the same old faces all the goddamn time. Listening to the same old jokes till they seemed to hang in the air like farts and old cigarette smoke.

"No harm in it, I guess. India Three's been up at Fort Sill—that's what they call us, India Three; we're just an ol' scratch platoon." A slight grin. "I scratched them up and whupped 'em into shape myself.

"Anyhow, Major Dugan—he's been our commanding officer, like—well, three, four days ago, he got some kind of message. Made him awful thoughtful. He called up some of his officers and had a big confab with 'em. Nobody told us nothin', though." The snub nose wrinkled. "Shoot, the world blows up, and it all stays the same. Nobody tells the squaddies diddly. So, anyway, next day he orders a bunch of us to move out to Amarillo, where they had that new B-1 bomber base." She grimaced. "That's where I was stationed, back before the war. Me and Ski and Rosie and New and Gillet. We got plastered during the war. How we made it out, I'll never know. Anyhow, since it'd mostly cooled off, they'd had details down there trying to salvage what they could. Took a turn or two down there, ourselves."

"It's a drag, man," said a tall skinny black squatting on his haunches. He had an olive drab rag tied around his head and looked exactly like Jimi Hendrix. "Spooky. Amarillo looked like somebody pick it up a mile or two, then drop it. Real ghost town and shit."

Eklund shrugged. "Not much spookier 'n anyplace else. We been some places, seen some things. . . . Anyhow, they'd gotten one of them runways patched up good enough to use. We got there, secured the area, and damned if these three big old C-141 cargo planes didn't come droppin' out of the sky. Must have been a couple of battalions on board, plus a lot of light equipment like them cute little fast-attack vehicles. Not just

Americans, neither. I mean, mostly, but also there were like English and German and Frenchmen with 'em too. That was yesterday—heck, maybe day before now. So today—yesterday—the officer in charge of them, this Colonel King, he's a long skinny hombre who looks like a telephone pole that decided to get up and walk away. Anyhow, he tells us they're setting a trap to catch some terrorists, we was supposed to come out here and help make sure they didn't slip away."

Alarmed, Sloan glanced at his comrade. McKay's face glowed like the coals at the bed of the fire, and a vein on his forehead bulged as if it was about to burst and spray scarlet steam. If possible, terrorists occupied an even lower rung on McKay's cosmic ladder than traitors did. "They didn't tell you any more than that?" he asked. His own voice rattled a little more than he'd anticipated.

Eklund bit her lip. "Didn't tell us anything about who we were after, at first. Then the rumors started goin' 'round —y'all know how that works."

"Couldn't believe it, that you Guardians was traitors 'n' shit," the Jimi Hendrix clone said. "Still can't, man."

Sloan turned narrowed eyes toward him. *A possible ally?* "C'mon, Chi," another soldier said, rhyming the name with *rye*. "You knows orders is orders."

"Shit," Chi said.

With the greatest effort McKay had controlled his impulse to bounce to his feet and start swinging. By now he just about trusted himself to speak, so he started to. "Billy," said Tom Rogers from the culvert's mouth, and he stopped, and looked.

The former Green Beret was wiping blood from his hands with filthy rags. "Got the splinter out of Casey's chest, and got a few liters of the fluorocarbon blood into him." A breath McKay didn't realize he'd been holding gusted out of him. "Looks like he's going to be okay. But we'd better not move him for a spell."

"You're to be picked up in the morning," Eklund said, looking at McKay.

"My patient is in very serious condition, Sergeant. Unless your superiors are plannin' to provide first-rate modern care for him, I'd rather he stayed where he was. Least till he gets some strength back."

"No way, Lieutenant."

"Shit," Chi said, unfolding himself. "Man's sick. Hell, these dudes is national heroes, like."

"They're terrorists," a young woman's voice said from the darkness.

Chi slapped the contention away with one hand. "You believe everything you hear, Sandy? Great, 'cause I got this twelve-inch dick—"

"Cool it," Tall Bear said.

"Yessir, Corporal sir, I'se coolin' it, yessir."

The stocky Kiowa scowled. "That's improper usage, soldier—"

"All right," drawled Eklund, "that's more'n enough." She stood up, looked from Rogers to Sloan and finally to Billy McKay. "You-all're soldiers. And there ain't been nothin' proved against you. New, fire up the radio. Let's see what we can do for our patient."

CHAPTER
SIX ―――――――――――――――――

Just like Wild Bill, Jeffrey MacGregor thought, *to have cells built into his secret hideout.* From everywhere the ventilation system hummed its endless idiot ditty, without tune, without life. Without hope.

Not that the room was uncomfortable. All of Heartland's personal quarters had the same lack of character, the Holiday Inn interchangeability. His own Presidential suite was a little better, having been designed to President William Lowell's specifications when the vast subterranean complex was being constructed as his personal redoubt. He found some of the details startling—the lush four-poster waterbed with massage controls, the mirrored ceiling—but at least it gave the feel of having been designed with a specific person in mind, rather than some faceless Everyman. The holding cell contained a living room–bedroom combo, with a bed that folded down out of the wall, a kitchenette in one direction, small bathroom with shower stall in the other. The walls were cream, the furniture muted oranges and earth tones; it might have come out of an organic fast-food restaurant. The room contained no clock, an omission the subtlety of which MacGregor was just beginning to comprehend.

How long has it been? The question was growing in him like a tumor. He was sure it was more than a day, less than a week. With no day-or-night cycles to mark time by, he couldn't tell more than that. He dimmed the lights and slept when he felt sleepy, dialed food from the pneumatic-delivery system in the kitchenette when hungry. He was starting to feel like the character trapped in the crypt in Poe's "Premature Burial."

MacGregor leaned back on the couch, laced his fingers behind his neck. He missed the outdoors. He had since they'd first come to Heartland, months ago. He'd always loved to go hiking, backpacking, or even just for a walk in the park. Since last summer he'd been immured in the climate-controlled caverns of the secret complex, unable to so much as see the surface world because of security precautions. But always he'd been able to tell himself he could go outside if he really wanted to. Now he lacked even the comfort of that pleasant fiction.

Feeling a little self-pity, are we? He smiled wryly. Maybe he should do some calisthenics, submerge his brooding in exertion. *After all, how often do deposed heads of state get treated so well?*

How they'd gotten in he didn't know. He was in his bed—in Lowell's bed, with the satin sheets and the little motors to soothe you with standing-wave fingers—and suddenly the door had opened, the room had filled with men. Men in uniforms—American uniforms. Pointing guns at him.

They were very polite. They permitted him to shave—*Were they showing contempt for me, not sending anyone into the bathroom with me, knowing I wouldn't have the guts to slit my throat with toenail clippers or something equally melodramatic?* Dazed, he'd dressed in a white Adidas jogging suit, the first clothes that came to hand. He'd demanded to see their commanding officer. The man in charge of his captors, a tall light colonel with prominent ears and a weary face, had told him General Harkness was too busy to see him now. His other questions had been turned away with a tired headshake; no, Lieutenant Colonel Hughes could answer no more questions.

In the eternal synthetic noon of the corridor outside he'd heard faint sounds that reminded him of summer nights when fireworks displays announced the end of each baseball game in the stadium a few miles from his home: firefight sounds, muted by soundproofing. His escorts' eyes were wary under the rims of their coal-scuttle helmets. For the first time he noticed their shoulder patches. With a small shock he recognized the insignia of the post-war Federated States of Europe. "What's going on?" he asked. He got no answer. With polite insistence they'd led him to the nearest elevator bank, and down and down into captivity.

Maybe if I'd bolted—they wouldn't have shot at me. Would they? Probably they would; no way to tell now. *If only the Guardians were here.* But no. He'd served his military time; he knew this had been a very slick, tightly run operation. The nation's best security minds had worked overtime to make Heartland impregnable—and yet he'd never had an instant's warning. The fortress was garrisoned with a battalion of hand-picked troops, but somehow the intruders had gotten in unnoticed and blitzed them. It had been an inside job, he knew; someone, some traitor in their midst, had let in the attackers. Just as well McKay and his men *hadn't* been here; they'd simply have been captured, or, more likely, thrown their lives away in futile resistance. Better they should be elsewhere. Maybe they could carry on the fight. They were better equipped than *he* was, certainly. They could do something besides meekly follow his captors like a clichéd lamb to a slaughter.

He shook his head. Morbid self-flagellation wasn't going to get him anywhere. He stood up. Time to work out. He stretched, got to his feet.

The door opened. Lieutenant Colonel Hughes stood there. It didn't look as if he'd slept in however long it had been. "Mr. Vice President," he said. "If you'd accompany me."

MacGregor cocked his head, unconsciously repeating a gesture that made him look uncommonly boyish and bright, one of his trademarks. Mr. *Vice President?* "Where are we going?

Hughes's mouth compressed to a line and his eyes fell. "I'm not permitted to tell you, sir."

Outside waited a squad of soldiers. MacGregor nodded and grinned at them as he came out, working hard for non-chalance. They looked at him with the same blankness you see in a shark's eyes. Hughes nodded at them, then walked at MacGregor's side to the elevators.

The elevator halted at Level Sigma. Not particularly surprised, MacGregor walked out. As he expected, he was led on along the corridor toward room 33. Whoever had taken over the complex had no doubt appropriated his former offices.

The door slid open at their approach. MacGregor stepped boldly into it and stopped cold. A man sat across the crescent desk from him in the swivel chair in which he'd spent so much of the past eight months, gazing down at the inset computer console. Despite being seated President William Lowell gave the impression of size; his shoulders were broad inside his brown suit coat. The hair on his head was grizzled, somewhat long.

He raised his head and MacGregor felt his knees start to dissolve. "Bill," he croaked, sagging against the doorjamb. "Thank God you're alive."

Hazel eyes regarded him from deep within dark sockets. "Jeff," he said at length. It was the same old voice, deep as a mineshaft, compelling, flint-edged. But there was something different about it, some unfamiliar current that ran deep, like a subterranean river. "Come in."

MacGregor staggered to a sofa upholstered in amber plastic, sitting down with less than his accustomed grace. The weariness and stress and dread of the past hours rushed upon him like the snowmelt of the postponed spring outside. "Bill," he said, rubbing his eyes, voice quavery with relief. "I thought—I thought you were dead. I thought—" He raised his head, swept lank hair from his eyes. "I can't tell you how glad I am to see you."

Whatever William Lowell had been through had left its marks, he could see that now. The harsh rocky masses of his face were masked by age-spotted skin that seemed to hang on them with no more life than cloth. The neck, once as thick as a fighting bull's, had wasted away to wattles and cords and blue veins; it was clearly willpower alone supporting the weight of that huge proud head.

"I'm disappointed in you, Jeff," the old man said.

MacGregor frowned. For a moment his befuddled mind

couldn't comprehend the words. "What—what do you mean?"

Sagging eyelids descended with such weariness it seemed they'd never open again. But they did. "You tried to supplant me, Jeff. And you weren't man enough to do it. That makes it worse. Much worse."

"I don't know what you're talking about."

For an instant a hint of the old fire flared at the backs of those eye sockets like distant artillery. "Don't play coy! You set yourself in my place, and promptly set about letting the country go to hell."

MacGregor's brain whirled. This was all coming too fast. He wondered if this weren't all some hateful hallucination, if the unceasing pressure of the days since the One-Day War hadn't uncoupled him from reality. "I—Jesus, Bill, we thought you were dead. After we lost communications with your NEACP—"

Lowell's open palm struck the desktop like a club. "Spare me that crap! You saw your opportunity and you took it." His head swung ponderously from side to side. "You don't even have the balls to admit it."

MacGregor blinked at him. His carefully cultivated non-chalance had evaporated the instant he saw a man he was convinced was dead. In his exhaustion he felt an idiotic impulse to burst into tears. *This can't really be happening,* he thought. "The line of succession," he said brokenly. "You vanished. We—assumed—you'd been killed. Chief Justice Shaneyfelt swore me in. We all did . . . what we thought we had to."

Lowell shook his head. "Jeff, Jeff," he said, all fatherly, the vehemence of a moment before gone like the light of a switched-off bulb. "You don't know what this has done to me. I trusted you, Jeff. I elevated you to the second-highest post in the land. And this is how you pay me back."

"We thought you were dead." *I sound like a broken record,* part of MacGregor knew.

For a moment Lowell gazed off at the graceless painting. "You're in a serious situation here, Jeff. Very serious."

"What do you mean?"

"What you've done can't be overlooked. I'm sure you felt you had your reasons; under other circumstances, I'd be inclined to look for a way out. You're an ambitious young man —nothing wrong with that; wouldn't have picked you as a running mate if you hadn't been. And with the world blowing up, you probably felt this was your chance. Probably even felt you were justified in seizing the reins of power."

Jeffrey MacGregor stared at him, feeling as if his own face were a papier-mâché mask that was about to start cracking and peeling away. *What he had done* was sanctioned by all the laws of the United States of America, as well as mandated by his own not inconsiderable devotion to duty, another trait that had recommended him to Bill Lowell as a running mate, along with the need to bring the photogenic young MacGregor's liberal backers into a coalition with Lowell's right wing. Yet talking to the President—inevitably he was thinking of Lowell as that—was like trying to bat away fog.

"But the very circumstances render leniency out of the question. The nation is dying for want of the positive leadership you could never provide. So I have to be firm. Son, I'm going to have to charge you with high treason against the United States of America."

MacGregor sat very still. It was as if a kind of invisible shroud had descended around him, dulling his senses, insulating him from external reality. As though through a wall of a cheap hotel room he became aware of Lowell's basso rumble droning on: ". . . mitigate your position, if you cooperate with us fully. Are you listening to me, Jeff?"

Numbly he nodded.

"We have a problem," Lowell said, speaking with unnatural clarity, "you might be able to help us with. Something's happened to the computers here at Heartland. We can't get any information out of them on the Blueprint for Renewal. We think you could help us out on this one, and we might be able to work things out for you if you cooperate. Jeff? Jeff?"

A quavering scream, dwindling abruptly to silence. "He's fainted, Excellency," a technician in a stained white smock said to Trajan from the interrogation cell.

"Yes. I'm perfectly capable of seeing that for myself." Nostrils dilated in distaste, the man called Trajan frowned through the impact-resistant glass that separated him from the unpleasant reality of the white-walled, glare-filled room.

Next to the technician, a mostly naked Jeff MacGregor slumped in a heavy metal chair that was bolted to the floor, drooling onto the sparse curly brown hair at the base of his throat. Wires ran from between his thighs to a console behind which sat a second technician. The man raised a worried Peter Lorre face to Trajan's window.

"I've tried upping the current, Excellency. He doesn't respond."

Trajan sighed theatrically. He was a tall man, clad in a blue blazer, with a white turtleneck beneath, and gray slacks. His head was narrow, his hair slicked back and oddly colorless, features aquiline, eyes prone to squint. His upper lip had withdrawn peevishly, displaying prominent incisors. The elegance of his ensemble was marred by the creases of his pants, which had long since lost their edge. The inside of his collar was grimy. The two uniformed men in the room with him stood as far away as they could without showing the fact.

He turned to one of them, his gray-blue eyes icy as the wind blowing across the Iowa landscape, hundreds of meters above their heads. "The President and I require results," he said curtly. "I find the clumsiness of your men most disquieting, General Harkness."

"They're experts in their field," the big man with the American uniform and the single star on his shoulders burst out. "They know how to do their jobs."

Trajan swiveled his head and stared at Harkness until the ruddy tint seeped out of the big man's complexion. "If they are, indeed, experts," he said in a menacing voice, "then they should have no difficulty extracting the requisite information from a subject as weak as this." He turned and stalked out of the little room.

In dismal silence Trajan stilted along the corridor to the elevators like a great heron, with a pair of aides scurrying behind. His mood was black. *All these months,* he thought, *the preparation, the effort, the anguish—anticipation.* He shook his head. *Will it truly be for naught?*

Incompetent as they no doubt were, the bone breakers

Harkness had brought over from Europe with him would surely experience little difficulty in breaking MacGregor. The man was a typical liberal, a man of no substance, no bottom. He'd tell them, soon enough, how to lay their hands on the pieced-together Blueprint for Renewal that Heartland's computers had thus far denied them.

But a tiny voice chittered at the back of Trajan's skull: *What if MacGregor doesn't know?*

Ignoring those doubts Trajan turned right at the door of his office, which was nondescript, not much more than a cubicle. As he sat in the leather swivel chair, his communicator buzzed. "Yes?" he snapped.

"Excellency, we've got a communication from Oklahoma."

He leaned forward, at once whippet-taut. "Yes? Yes? Get on with it, man."

"A communication from the commander of the detachment that captured the Guardians last night, Excellency. It requests permission to delay moving the prisoners. It seems one was injured, and needs time to recover."

The Guardians, Trajan thought with a thrill. *At last I've got them, at last.* He himself intended to supervise their debriefing; he very much looked forward to that. And he desired that they all be in the best of condition for the occasion, oh yes. He started to give assent, stopped himself, scowled. "Refresh my memory," he told the disembodied voice. "Was the apprehending unit part of our expeditionary force? Or was it, ah, indigenous?"

"Er, indigenous, Excellency."

The expeditionary force, from Brigadier General Harkness on down, Trajan thought, was a passel of idiots. He was surrounded by idiots; idiots had betrayed him before through their incompetence, made it possible for those bumbling barbarians the Guardians to devastate his brilliant operational plan and reduce him to a hunted fugitive. But the indigenous idiots were worst of all. Worse, they weren't case-hardened by service to Maximov and the FSE, as the handpicked expeditionary force was; they might have naive feelings of kinship for the Guardians, even admiration.

And the Guardians were, in their own brute way, clever. Given time, they might play upon the sympathies of their captors, win freedom. How like Trajan, to be thwarted by idiots again!

"Out of the question," he said. "There can be no delay."

"Their captors say they won't be responsible for the health of the injured one if he's moved," the voice said hesitantly.

"Assure them that they *are* responsible."

"Yes, Excellency. I shall."

He started to turn his attention elsewhere. A thought struck him. "Oh. One minor emendation."

"Excellency?"

"The pickup team. An American unit might fall prey to hero-worship of their prisoners—and any disturbance of the smooth flow of the proceedings would have most regrettable consequences for everyone concerned." A smile tugged back thin lips. "See that the danger is prevented."

"Yes, Your Excellency. It shall be done."

CHAPTER
SEVEN

"Shit," Sergeant Eklund said. She threw down the mike and headset of the big radio mounted in the deuce and a half and stalked back toward the fire.

To the east the sky was turning milky along the flat horizon. The terrible wind had died away, to everyone's relief. A couple of hours before stars had appeared in patches overhead, but they hadn't lasted. Hunkered down in his parka, McKay raised his head and looked at her across the fire. "What's the matter?"

"Finally got word from Amarillo," the sergeant said. "They say we got to move y'all today." She dropped to the ground next to Sam Sloan. "Shoot."

"Casey won't be much good to any damn kangaroo court if he's dead," McKay growled.

Eklund looked hastily away. "This just ain't right, Sarge," Chi said.

"Mebbe we should let 'em go," piped up Torrance, a little wiry white dude who walked with a bad limp.

Tension closed around the fire like a noose. In the hours since their capture, the Guardians—mostly McKay and Sloan,

since Rogers was ministering to Casey pretty much full-time—
had been getting to know their captors. Sloan had mostly
played the diplomat, laughing and joking and putting them at
their ease; McKay mainly tried not to snarl too much. He
knew what game was being played. They needed all the allies
they could get, just now. But he wasn't much of a goddamn
actor.

That was okay; Sloan was. By now the two men reckoned
they had at least half the group on their side. The three women
other than the sergeant—Sandy, who despite her name sported
a long black braid; round-faced black Mary Alice; and Gillet,
a redhead with tired eyes—seemed favorably inclined to them.
So did most of the blacks, who made up better than a third of
the "scratch platoon." On the other hand Eklund's second in
command, the chunky Kiowa corporal, obviously had no use
for the Guardians. A couple of the others were openly hostile:
a tall emaciated white dude with a shock of black hair above
an axblade face who answered to the probably revealing
moniker of Runner—*runners* being the unmounted urban
equivalent of road gypsies—and Ballou, a sandy-haired peckerwood even taller than Runner and just as skinny, except for
furniture-mover's shoulders and fists like mauls.

It was McKay who'd gotten them on Ballou's shitlist—and
at the same time broken ice with a lot of the others. After
Eklund put her call into Amarillo to ask permission not to
move the prisoners until Casey's condition stabilized, her unit
had been too wired by the day's events to sleep—unusual for
seasoned troops, and an indication of just how badly
somebody wanted their captives. They'd settled into the usual
troopie routine of smoking and joking. Ballou'd been at pains
to establish himself as boss raconteur.

"Know any Polack jokes?" he drawled, puffing on a
scavenged Camel. "Won't let me tell no nigger jokes. But ol'
Ski, there, he ain't big enough to take me. So I tells Polack
jokes as I please."

Private Podolski, medium-sized and dark-haired, had
studied the toes of his boots carefully. McKay fixed the big
Southerner with an Arctic gaze. "Yeah," he said. "I know a
good Polack joke: What's black and white and got six busted
arms?"

Ballou drew back his head like a turkey cock and blinked skeptically. "Why, cain't say as I knows that one," he declared, in tones that made it clear that if *he* didn't know it, it plumb weren't worth knowing.

"The last three assholes who tried to tell me a Polack joke," replied William Kosciusko McKay, whose middle name was his mother's maiden name. That got the biggest laugh of the night and made most of India Three start treating the Guardians as part of the gang. It also got Ballou sitting off to one side in a frigid sulk, patting the receiver of his M-16 and eyeing McKay.

But ragged-assed as they were they were still a military unit, and the only voice that mattered was that of Sergeant Marla Eklund. And *she* was determined to obey orders, personal feelings aside. It was a hard-core outlook for a woman. McKay regarded women as emotional creatures incapable of such determination. He would've admired her for it under other circumstances.

"That ain't a bad idea," Rosie said. "We could just kinda turn our heads, tell 'em back at Amarilla they done run off when we weren't looking."

"What the fuck," shot back Private Gutierrez, whose name everyone pronounced Gootuh*rezz*. "I thought they didn't wanna move that Casey dude. How they gonna run away?"

Ballou thumped the buttplate of his rifle on the frozen earth. "You gone plumb soft in the head. These here's traitors. What you wanna let 'em go for?" He slapped the receiver. "Maybe we oughta take care of 'em ourselves, like."

"Watch who you're callin' *traitor*, you wool-hatted son of a bitch," McKay said. "I'll shove that M-16 so far up your ass the flash suppressor'll tickle your fuckin' tonsils."

Flushing, Ballou started to his feet. "At ease," Tall Bear rapped. Ballou subsided, glaring red-eyed at the Indian.

"Really, Sergeant," Sandy said. "Couldn't we let them go? I hate to think what'll happen to them, and you know they're not . . . what they're accused of being."

"I don't know nothin' of the sort, Sandy. I reckon there's some misunderstandin', but it ain't up to us to decide. You boys understand. I got my duty, same's you."

Sloan looked at McKay. "The lady's just as bullheaded as

you, McKay.'' McKay grimaced. She'd used the one argument he could never counter.

Ballou was still looking murder at him. *Fuck him if he can't take a joke.* ''What time's the pickup?'' he asked.

''Man said it ought to be around eleven hundred.''

McKay leaned back and shut his eyes. ''Wake me when it's over,'' he said.

Someone was shaking him. Instantly McKay clawed for his .45, found only the loose flap of his empty Kevlar field holster. He opened his eyes.

Chi had him by the shoulder, standing well to one side to be out of the line of fire—a combat-soldier's reflex. ''Taxi's here,'' he said. ''Sorry, dude.''

He rose, stretched, yawned. A black spot hung against the milk-colored sky to the southeast: the pickup chopper from Amarillo AFB. He briefly bared his teeth, turned, climbed into the culvert.

Inside it was perceptibly warmer than outside in the pale filtered sunlight. Tom Rogers hunkered over Casey Wilson, a position he'd scarcely budged from during the eighteen or so hours since they'd first gone to ground here. The former air-man was asleep beneath a pile of bedrolls, his dirt-smeared face surprisingly peaceful. ''How is he?'' McKay said in a low voice.

''Hangin' in there. Considerin' we got no medicine aside from stuff in the packs, no heat, no sanitation to speak of, he's doin' damn well. He's tough and he's young. That's all he's got goin' for him, but it seems to be enough right now.''

Plump-faced Mary Alice sat across from the recumbent Casey with her knees drawn up. Her glasses reflected the weak sunlight dribbling in from the mouth of the culvert, turning them into blank disks. ''Don't let him give you that, Lieutenant. He's been hovering over the poor boy all night like a guardian angel. If it weren't for Lieutenant Rogers, he'd never have had a chance.''

Rogers shrugged, not meeting McKay's glance in a rare display of embarrassment. ''Lieutenant Wilson spoke several times during the night,'' said the other guard, a Vietnamese named Nguyen, New for short, who was leaning against the corrugated metal wall of the culvert with his M-16 slung. He could almost've stood up straight; they must have bent the height requirements to let him into the Army. "He kept saying something about a Bruce Springsteen cat."

"*Cap*," Rogers corrected softly. "Kept askin' after his cap."

"Jesus," McKay said.

When he backed out of the conduit the hum of the approaching chopper's engines was beginning to differentiate into spokes of sound. His eyes confirmed the identification his ears had made: an old three-engine S-65 Sikorsky Super Stallion heavy chopper, painted in green-and-black camouflage and angling down for a landing. Sloan stood to one side, sipping from a cup of coffee and talking softly to Eklund, who seemed to be ignoring him. The rest of the platoon stood around, most of them looking sullen.

On a ground sheet to one side the Guardians' personal weapons and effects had been laid out. McKay caught Sloan's eye, slid his own to the gear. A corner of Sloan's mouth curved up, and his shoulders quirked in an all-but-imperceptible shrug. He was game, but dubious. The two sentries keeping watch over the stuff, a jittery guy called Steely and an enormous shaven-headed black named Jamake, held their rifles at the ready. Not far away stood Masood with a thirty-round clip in his M-249 Minimi, instead of a belt, so it could be used like an old BAR. He hadn't seemed hostile, but his attitude left no doubt he'd use the Minimi if necessary. Sitting beside the truck with his M-203—like Sloan's, except his grenade launcher was clipped to a standard M-16 A-2 instead of a Galil—over his knees and looking alert was Pfc. Gutierrez. He wasn't all that well disposed to the Guardians. Finally, there was Ballou, grinning all over his face. He saw McKay glance at him and once more stroked the weapon.

"Shit," McKay said. "You musta got your cock shot off, the way you keep jackin' off with that thing."

Ballou's face turned the same color as the sky and he started forward. Tall Bear and Private Gillespie grabbed his arms. He allowed himself to be subdued. McKay laughed silently. The Southerner was an inch taller than he was and probably had reach on him, but McKay had a good thirty pounds' advantage. No wonder Ballou calmed down so quick.

Faces turned as the big Sikorsky began to settle in a cloud of
powdery snow. McKay glanced hopefully toward the weapons, but no luck; the sentries were eyeing him like vultures
perched above a dying man. Eklund walked up to him, arms
crossed over her stomach. "This is it," she said, shouting to
be heard above the roar of engines and seven blades chopping
air. "Ah'm right sorry it turned out this way."

Her arms pulled in the front of her battle dress and parka,
revealing a rack of boobs that McKay normally would've eyed
with considerable appreciation. Now he hardly spared them a
glance. "That's the breaks, Sergeant. You're only following
orders."

The dig went home. She looked away quickly. The Stallion
dropped its wheels onto the dirt road a hundred meters down
from the culvert. The hatch in front of the starboard stub wing
popped open and soldiers began spilling out.

McKay's blood temperature dropped below the surrounding
air's.

"Shit," Rosie called out above the dying turbine whine.
"Never see no camouflage like that before."

McKay had. Never actually worn by anybody, but in plenty
of pictures. And he *had* seen people wearing those kettle-
shaped helmets, and blue berets like the one on the handsome
square-jawed officer who stepped out last. Beneath their
oddly striped winter camouflage the platoon would be wearing
distinctive striped undershirts, McKay knew. Like the berets,
the undershirts were the proud badge of an elite.

Better trained in uniform recognition than the rear-echelon
troopies of India Three, Sloan had recognized them too. His
jaw hung open, and McKay took honest pleasure in seeing him
with, for once, nothing to say.

Eklund's brow furrowed. "Good God A'mighty," she
breathed. "They're *Russians.*"

"Right the first guess. Air-assault troops of the VDV."

Deploying a squad to cover the chopper, the officer stepped
forward with another blue beret trotting obediently behind.
The others followed. The rest of Eklund's people were becom-
ing aware something was very much out of the ordinary. The
unfamiliar uniforms and gear hadn't troubled them initially;

they'd told their captives that the forces sent to Amarillo for
the manhunt included NATO elements, and most of them
couldn't tell one foreign uniform from another. But the
newcomers' stubby rifles had a distinctive broken-nosed pro-
file and banana-shaped orange plastic magazines that were
hard to mistake. The whisper ringed the little laager:
"Wha'fuck's goin' *on?*"

"I'm Taranov," the officer said in perfect English. He and
his men wore the blue and white FSE insignia on his shoulder.
"Captain, *Vozdushno-Desantnyye Voyska*. The Airborne
Forces of the, ah, Federated States of Europe. Who is in
charge here, please?"

Eklund licked her lips. "Ah am, Captain. Staff Sergeant
Marla Eklund, United States Army."

He cocked an eyebrow. "Charmed to meet you, I'm sure,
Ms. Eklund." He looked at McKay and smiled. The ex-
Marine reckoned that if they sold toothpaste in the USSR,
Captain Taranov was just the man to do it. "And this, I
presume, is one of the prisoners."

"Uh, yes, that's right. This here's Lieutenant McKay."

The square chin nodded. "Lieutenant. A pleasure." He
looked around. "I see one more. Where are the others,
please?"

The Soviet troops kept themselves slightly apart from the
startled Americans. "The culvert," Eklund said, voice barely
audible over the idling Stallion's engines.

Taranov nodded, said something in Russian. A burly sergeant started toward the culvert, rifle at the ready. The para-
troops carried 5.45-mm AKRs, carbine versions of the
standard AKS-74 assault rifle. The captain packed a Mini-Uzi
in a hip holster; Western submachine guns were great status
symbols among the Soviet officer classes these days. His aide,
a fresh-faced blond lieutenant, had to make do with a
holstered Makarov pistol.

As the sergeant stepped up to the culvert Tom Rogers
emerged. He stood there staring at the sergeant with a flat
gunmetal gaze. The sergeant hesitated.

Taranov barked something. "No, wait," Marla Eklund
said. "I won't let you take them. I'm not turnin' American
boys over to no Russians!"

The captain shook his sleek head. "I'm sorry, my dear sergeant. It appears you've no choice."

All around the laager weapons snapped to the ready. The members of India Three started, showing a lot of white around the eyes. Numbers were about equal—but Eklund's platoon, while seasoned in a way, was used to running up against looters and bikers. These were jump-trained combat troops. *Soviet* troops.

Drawing the Mini-Uzi from its holster with the slickness of a movie cowboy, Taranov grabbed Eklund by the biceps and swung her in front of him. "This has gone on long enough."

The sergeant by the culvert pivoted his head a few degrees at the movement behind him. As he turned back Tom Rogers' right arm moved in a blur. The scalpel the Guardian had palmed turned over once in the air and socketed itself in the sergeant's right eye. The Russian staggered back with a scream, blood gushing down his face.

Marla Eklund drove her left elbow into Captain Taranov's gut. He doubled up, gagging, and she wheeled and smashed a straight right into his face that knocked him back asprawl into the arms of his dumfounded aide. Eklund was on him like a tiger, clawing for the Uzi.

Sam Sloan launched himself through the air toward the Guardians' stacked weapons. McKay took a strange drifty little step forward to the nearest Russian, who was swinging his assault rifle to bear. Before he could react McKay swung his foot up in a kick that took him in the crotch and lifted him half a meter in the air. As he came down McKay drove his fist like a battering ram into his throat, crushing cartilage like a Dixie cup. He went down choking, face turning black. McKay dived past him, snagging his AKR on the fly.

In accordance with the Leninist pyramid-of-power principle, Soviet soldiers are trained to do *nothing* without orders. Soviet army training is geared to eradicating any tendency toward taking the initiative, particularly in the lower ranks. Tough though they were, the Soviets' reaction was to freeze with indecision. It lasted a millisecond; but that was enough to lose them the initiative, to gain the Guardians and Eklund's platoon the ghost of a chance.

One of the Soviet paras grounded on the road broke the spell, firing a long burst from an RPK-74 machine gun. Just who he was aiming for no one could say, since he couldn't have sprayed the Americans without hitting some of his own team. That may not have mattered to him in an emergency like this, when it had been impressed on all of them that the price of failure to return the Guardians would be summary execution, but more likely he was hoping to panic the Americans by firing over their heads.

It didn't work. Eklund's ragged troopies might not have been trained up to paratroop standards, but they'd spent most of the last year living by the skins of their teeth. It took more than a little automatic-weapons fire to freak them. They were already diving in all directions, looking for cover from which to shoot back.

When the Soviets down by the road came out of it, they were about the only ones standing. Masood tucked the butt of the M-249 under his elbow and cut loose with a hip-high burst. Several Russians went down. Whether any of them were hit or not McKay couldn't tell. He was busy shifting his grip on the AKR and spraying some lead of his own. Accuracy was the furthest thing from his mind; at a time like this, the only thing to do was fill the air with bullets and hope the bad guys flinched first.

Gunfire stitched up snow in front of Sloan. He tucked his head, rolled, came up on his butt. As if they'd rehearsed all week, little Steely jittered forward a couple of steps and kicked Sloan's Galil/M-203 combo spinning through the air toward him. The former Navy officer snatched it by the sling and flopped onto his belly. Steely's throat exploded scarlet and he went down too.

When the machine gun opened up from the road, Pfc. Gutierrez rose, turned, and propped his own M-203 on the hood of the deuce and a half. He dropped an HE round onto the road right on top of a Soviet para's helmet. An instant later the RPK gunner who'd come down with Taranov walked a burst along the flank of the truck and across the small of Gutierrez's back.

Eklund had Taranov's Mini-Uzi. She fired at the lieutenant

hovering a couple of meters away. With the weapon's high cyclic rate it sounded like the cough of a big feral cat. The aide held up his palms as if to ward off the bullets. Red spattered his cammies like rain.

In the blink of an eye, Masood was the only one standing. His action had bought his buddies a little grace, but suddenly he realized it was past time to play John Wayne. The Minimi clicked empty. Before he could go for cover fire converged on him from a half-dozen directions. He dropped onto his butt. His parka hung open, and the front of his threadbare fatigue blouse was soaked in red. He tried to fumble a new magazine into his MG. A burst from the RPK knocked him onto his back. His body arched like a buttress, heels kicking mindlessly at the frozen earth.

Sam Sloan aimed for the biggest cloud of debris thrown up by muzzleblast and triggered his M-203. The multiple projectile round puked a cloud of 000 shot that hummed just above the ground like a swarm of furious wasps. The Soviet machine gunner shrieked shrilly as the swarm tore into him, shredding his face and shoulders.

All three active Guardians had weapons and were firing them—picking their targets, a shot at a time. Behind Tom Rogers, New and Mary Alice were ripping off three-round bursts with a coolness that suggested they'd done this before. An arm whipped up from behind a clump of scrub. A grenade arched to land just in front of the culvert mouth. It went off with an actinic flash and a cloud of dust and black smoke. McKay fired his AKR dry in the direction it had come from as a burst of fire rattled into the pipe. Ricochet whines echoed like banshees' cries. McKay heard screams, thin and sharp as the edge of a shard of broken glass, but someone inside was still shooting back.

Hope to hell Casey's all right, he thought. He jumped half-erect, took off like a sprinter for three rapid-fire steps, glided into the scatter of Guardians' gear right next to Sloan, who was firing his Galil from the prone position. McKay grabbed his M-60 and flattened himself behind it, holding it by front and rear pistol grips, not bothering with the bipod.

And suddenly it was all over. A couple of paras were running back along the road, while two more threw away their

AKRs and stood up with hands held high. The squad on the road fired up the truck and the mostly concealed Americans. Hurriedly Sloan jacked open the M-203's receiver, stuffed in a white phosphorus round, and sent it their way. It landed right in the Russians' midst, and most of them lost interest in shooting at anybody for a while.

Eklund had an M-16. "Push 'em!" she roared. "Keep 'em on the run! Yee-*haa!*" India Three skirmished toward the chopper, blasting away at the remaining Soviets. "Mother" Myles, the fat black A-gunner, darted over, picked up Masood's M-249, stuck in a new magazine, and opened up.

Tom Rogers bounded back into the culvert. New was hunkered over Mary Alice, who was clutching her sides and rolling back and forth, moaning in agony. "She's hit bad," the Vietnamese said. His face streamed tears.

"Casey?"

"He's all right. But Mary Alice—"

"Be back in just a minute," Rogers said, and was gone. Sobbing, New began to tear open the woman's fatigue blouse.

The Soviets pulled back toward the chopper in good order. It wasn't wise. The penetration of 5.56-mm small-arms fire was too chancy a thing to pose much threat to the big Stallion. No so McKay's 7.62. And the Sikorsky was a nice fat target, at point-blank range for the Maremont. As the last VDV para jumped into the open hatch and the wheels kissed the red dirt road good-bye he saw hits sparking its green and black flank just in front of where the U.S. insignia had hastily been painted out.

There was a flash from the engine housing that bulked above the fuselage like a hunchback's hump. "Everybody *down!*" McKay bellowed. The 40-mm HEDP grenade knocked pieces of housing and engines in all directions. Too low for the rotors' freewheeling to do much good, the S-65 dropped like a brick and exploded on the road.

A tidal wave of heat washed over them. "Somebody get to the truck," McKay heard Eklund shouting. He raised his head, opened his eyes. Chunks of burning debris had fallen everywhere, and some were threatening to set the canvas cover alight. He jumped up and ran for the truck, tearing off his coat as he ran, and joined in flailing at the flames.

From behind him came a shot.

He whirled. Marla Eklund stood a few meters away, coolly directing operations. Behind her stood Captain Taranov, his late aide's 9-millimeter Makarov in hand, aimed for the close-cropped back of Eklund's head. He had an expression of surprise on his recruiting-poster face, and his eyes stood halfway from their sockets—more from the catastrophic overpressure of a bullet that had transited his skull from temple to temple than from any emotion. His hand dropped, the pistol discharged into the dirt by his feet, and his legs folded up beneath him.

Every head turned toward the culvert. Casey Wilson stood there, barechested but for bandages, Mary Alice's M-16 slipping from his fingers. Tom leapt like a panther, caught him as he fell.

Marla Eklund shook her head and whistled admiringly. "Owe that boy one," she said. "Hope he makes it."

She turned to McKay. "Better get your traps aboard the truck. Looks like we're all fugitives together now."

CHAPTER
EIGHT ━━━━━━━━━━━━

"So what do we do now?" Eklund asked. "They got choppers and search planes to Amarillo, and the weather ain't bad enough they can't fly. What's gonna stop 'em spottin' us before we gone twenty miles?"

"You wanna try humpin' it outa here?" McKay asked.

"No."

"Then let me think about it."

India Three's casualties were two killed outright, three wounded. Masood died while Tom was working on him. Mary Alice had been hit in the guts by a 5.45 round. It hadn't tumbled as it was designed to do, which was fortunate, since it would have shredded her insides and left her no chance of survival. Or maybe it wasn't a mercy; she was still badly hurt, and had little prospect of getting much decent medical care anytime soon. A skinny little soldier called Cato, who had black hair and a pair of glasses held together at the bridge by what looked like a whole roll of masking tape, had a wound in the thigh from another non-tumbling slug, and other India people had various nicks and scratches. On the whole, they'd been incredibly lucky.

Seven survivors of the VDV platoon turned up, three of them wounded. They were disarmed and herded to the side where the undamaged ones could work on their buddies under the unfriendly gaze of Mother Myles.

In a sort of controlled frenzy India Three gathered up its gear and policed what equipment it could from the Soviet casualties. Spare magazines of red plastic and the little "Krinkov" AKRs were useless without one another; Eklund's people scarfed up both. Their M-16 A-2s were rather more durable than earlier models of the rifle, but they were machines that saw a lot of brutal use, and despite the care Eklund insisted her command lavish on them it was in their nature to wear out or break. The vast unwieldy supply tails of "modern" armies were now outmoded as cavalry—if horse troopers weren't about to make a comeback, that is. What you used was what you could scrounge.

McKay had to admire the way Eklund's ragtag platoon pulled together when the shithammer came down. They'd kept cool during the brief, savage firefight with the Russians, and now they were policing up like professionals, even though they were still very much under the gun. And knew it.

Casey, the fresh bandages wrapped around his chest soaked with blood, was carried to the truck and laid on a pallet of blankets at the front of the covered truckbed, snugged up against a heap of supplies secured by stained tarps. A sheepish New explained that he had been so preoccupied trying to help Mary Alice that he hadn't noticed the Soviet officer struggling to his feet to point his aide's sidearm at Eklund's head. Casey, emerging briefly into consciousness, had glimpsed what was happening, grasped the situation in an instant, and, in that instant, had with his fighter-pilot's reflexes *reacted*. He'd then lapsed back into delirious mutterings, and then to unconsciousness.

Together McKay and Eklund saw Mary Alice settle down next to Casey under the eye of Cato and New. As they emerged into the watery daylight the dour Tall Bear came stumping up and saluted. "We're ready to move out, Sergeant." His belt was festooned with round Soviet flash-bang grenades.

McKay cocked a brow at Eklund. "Since when do you salute a sergeant, Corporal?"

The pockmarked Kiowa looked at McKay as if he were something to scrape off his boot. "The sergeant's our commander," he said flatly.

To McKay's astonishment a flush had soaked up across Eklund's prominent cheekbones. It made her look downright fetching despite her Master Sergeant drag. "Their idea, Lieutenant. Tried to make 'em cut it out, but—"

McKay shrugged. "No skin off my butt." Actually he was impressed, though torture wouldn't make him admit it. India Three looked to Eklund as a real leader. That meant, hard as it was for male-chauvinist McKay to believe, that she was one. Veterans—and these people were definitely that—had zero tolerance for bullshit in the field.

"All right, people," Eklund called out, displaying a good deal of lung power. "Let's saddle 'em up."

"Uh, Sarge," somebody asked sheepishly. "Where we gone go?"

"Y'all let me worry about that. Right now, we just got to go."

India Three began to pile onto the trucks. The VDV captives stood to one side looking impassive. Ballou licked his thin lips. A funny light came into his eyes, and he raised his M-16. Sam Sloan knocked the barrel skyward just as he loosed off a burst. Ballou glared murder at him. Before he had a chance to do more Sloan drove a straight right into his face and knocked him sprawling.

Spitting like a wet cat the lanky Southerner sat up—to find himself staring up the muzzles of Sloan's combo. "What the hell do you think you're doing, you murderous son of a bitch?" the Missourian gritted.

The fire died out of Ballou's pale eyes. "Why, shit, I was jus' policing up the area. We cain't leave these suckers behind."

"We can't murder prisoners. We're not animals."

"Sarge, you gonna listen to this crazy man?"

Eklund opened her mouth, looked sidelong at McKay, locked her lips. Events had forced the Guardians and India

Three to join forces. The question of who would command had just reared its ugly head.

In his time Billy McKay had shot a prisoner or two. But that was when they had no choice, when they couldn't take them along or let them go either one. He was grimly amused at Sloan's bleeding-heart horror at the very notion. On the other hand, he liked the look he'd seen in Ballou's eyes even less than he liked Ballou in general.

"No reason not to let 'em go," he said. "They don't know which way we're heading. Fuck 'em."

Eklund jerked her head at the truck. "Get your rifle and get your butt inside, Ballou." She glanced at McKay again, then said, "Chi, you climb up front and drive."

The India troopers were all aboard. Tom Rogers walked up. "What about our communicators, Billy?" he asked.

McKay frowned. "Uh—right. What about it, Eklund?"

Anger flared in her eyes. "Y'all got secrets you want to talk about without the rest of us hearin'?"

"So what if we do? We're the Guardians, dammit, not a bunch of droopy-tailed legs you found wandering around the ruins."

" 'Droopy-tailed'?" Eklund shrilled in outrage. "Why, you—"

"Now, now," Sam Sloan said, materializing between the two of them. "We're all on the same side. Let's save our anger for the FSE." He turned a few megawatts of charm on the furious sergeant. "You have to understand, Sergeant Eklund, we're still a team. We need our communications to function effectively. And it's in the interests of everybody's survival that we do just that."

"Well . . . all right. Corporal, give 'em their walkie-talkies back."

Tall Bear spoke into the truck. In a moment the calculator-sized instruments were handed out with their earphone and mike cords wrapped around them. "Ol' Mason, he pissed off some," Rosie said from inside. "He want to take 'em apart an' shit, see what they made of."

Slipping his communicator back in its accustomed pocket, Sloan said, "I sure hope the tape still sticks on the mikes and phones."

Rogers was eyeing the clouds apprehensively. "We better get a move on. They're going to miss their pick-up team real soon now."

"Right," Eklund said. "Mother, send them prisoners on their way."

The fat A-gunner, holding his Minimi slung in assault position with one hand on the pistol grip, started waving his other hand at the captives. "Shoo. C'mon now, you honkies, clear out." Sam Sloan said something in Russian. The paratroopers exchanged a look, shrugged, turned, and trotted off over the snowy landscape. One, the youngest, cast an apprehensive look over his shoulder. The others kept stoically on, obviously expecting to be shot in the back at any moment.

"Sorry we don't have time to bury Gutierrez, Masood, and Steely," Sloan said.

Eklund shrugged. "Let the dead bury the dead, the Good Book says." Her tone made it clear they'd had to let their dead lie before.

Sloan and Rogers let Mother Myles clamber into the deuce and a half, then followed him. "I'll ride up front," McKay and Eklund said simultaneously.

For a moment they stood glaring at each other while the wind rose about them like the tide. "You and Chi and Ah are all six-footers," Eklund said, controlling her voice with obvious effort. "Cain't all of us fit up there."

"*I'm* riding up where I can see where we're going. Don't forget we're Guardians, lady. We can commandeer this vehicle if we want."

"Like hell you can!"

"Like hell we can't."

"McKay," Sloan's voice said in his ear. "We have to work with these people, and time's wasting."

"All right, all right. Your driver's real skinny, and I'm the dainty type myself. You can ride in the back if your butt's too broad."

Eklund stared at him a moment, eyes and nostrils wide in anger. She turned and stomped over to the cab, tore open the door, and climbed in. "Hearts and minds, Billy, for Christ's sake, *hearts and minds,*" Sloan said.

"Shit," McKay snorted, and followed Eklund.

She was sitting in the middle of the wide cab with her arms tightly folded. Chi had started the engine and was studiously staring off in various other directions. McKay slid in and shut the door. The cab wasn't narrow, but the rounded firmness of Eklund's hip pressed his. In spite of himself he didn't mind.

"I'd get us the hell outa here," Chi said, "if somebody'd just tell me where to."

"I suppose you got it all figgered out," Eklund said to McKay.

McKay turned to her. "As a matter of fact," he said, showing all kinds of teeth, "I do."

"This is an outrage!" Spittle flew like spindrift from W. Soames Summerill's aristocratically thin lips. "An outrage."

"I—I don't know what happened, Excellency." Brigadier General Alex Harness's broad face was running sweat, though the air conditioner was cranked so high in Trajan's office they both might as well have been outside in the Iowa snow. "Colonel King's men found the wreckage of the helicopter and a number of bodies. Several of them belonged to members of the unit that made the capture. The rest—" His thick shoulders rose and fell in a helpless shrug.

"See? Do you see, man? Yes or no?" Harkness's eyes started from their sockets. He didn't see, but he nodded anyway. "I was right all along. All along! I knew the weaklings would let the Guardians sway them."

"S-sway whom, Excellency?" The general was too agitated to feel his usual resentment at having to call a civilian Excellency. Given that this raging lunatic held power of life and death over Harkness, he'd be more than willing to call him Jesus J. God if he asked. In the few days of their association, Harkness had seen what happened to those who crossed Trajan. It shriveled his nuts to marbles.

"The despicable cowards who took them prisoners! They were Americans, and Americans have no moral fiber, no discipline. But we're going to change that, aren't we, General?"

"Uh, ah—yes, yes, of course we are. Excellency."

"And speaking of discipline," Trajan said, leaning back in his chair, regarding Harness across his desk with eyes like obsidian marbles, "someone has to pay for this fiasco."

Harness's knees began to oscillate. "Yes, Excellency," he managed to get out. *Dear God, let it be quick,* he prayed. *Not the acid bath or the microwave, please.*

Trajan steepled his fingers before his chin. It was a weak chin, not receding, but weak. He'd long since started affecting the gesture to cover that fact. "This Colonel King whom you dispatched to Fort Sill—a good man?"

Harness chewed his lower lip. If he defended the man he might share his fate. But if he said King was no good, the question would inevitably rise as to why he, Harness, had sent him. "Yes, Your Excellency. He was on my staff during the suppression of the Amsterdam riots."

"Ah, yes. That's where a thousand children were taken hostage by security forces and then shot to break the rioters' morale, is it not? A sound move, General. One must deal harshly with rebels. And with incompetence."

"Of course, Excellency," Harness said into the expectant silence.

"Very well. Colonel King deserves another chance. Have the officer he found in command of the remnants there—Dugan, was it not?—have him executed. An example must be made."

Harness moistened his lips with a tongue that felt swollen. Dugan had been at Sill when the pickup team was dispatched from Amarillo AFB; he'd had nothing to do with the mission or its failure. "Yes, Your Excellency."

He stood, trying not to fidget like a recruit on report. He could barely tolerate the smell of the man. "One more thing," Trajan said at last. "This notion of hostages—have King take a hostage from each homestead within, oh, twenty kilometers of the place where the helicopter went down. If the Guardians aren't captured, start executing them. We can't have the populace sheltering criminals.

"And, most of all, General—*find the bastards!*"

CHAPTER
NINE _____

"—proud to recognize the signal contribution to the reconstruction of our great nation made by Dr. Nathan Bedford Forrest Smith over the tragic past few months," the voice of William Lowell grumbled like a cement truck down a gravel road.

"Will you turn that shit *off?*" Rosie demanded, voice rising high in agitation. "How the fuck many times they be playin' that shit, anyway?"

"Least six times a day," Frank Gillespie said, sitting in a swiveling dinette chair covered in cracked red vinyl, cleaning his rifle. "Past five days at least."

"I was hopin' they'd play some music," said Torrance, defensively hovered over the Panasonic ghetto blaster they'd scavenged from a LaBelle's.

Rosie sneered. "They gone be preachin' at us another two hours before they play music. An' who wants to listen to that country shit anyhow, man?"

"Put on Wazoo," Mason said, meaning the big transmitter across the Mexican border in Juarez. "They'll play some decent rock, anyway."

"Shit, Mason, my man. You th' electronics genius. Whyn't

you whip up somethin', get us some good soul music?''

McKay stood up off the crate where he sat, stretched, walked over to the open door of the warehouse, and gazed out across the ruins of Amarillo. He was still a little smug about his brainstorm. The truck gave them mobility without which they'd have no chance to escape. But at the same time it would have been impossible to hide from aerial observation. They could've hidden out during the day and traveled by night. But aside from the difficulty of finding empty buildings big enough to park the vehicle in—not many stands of trees sufficient to hide them from aircraft, out here in the Great Plains—McKay strongly suspected the opposition had night-sensor equipment that could pick them out plain as daylight. Had Casey been fit, the Guardians might have wished India Three the best of luck and tried to slip out on foot; they were all intensively trained in escape and evasion, and tough about Eklund's people. But Casey wasn't. They had to drive, or move off on foot and en masse, or just sit and wait for the FSE.

But where to drive *to?* Where better than in the one direction the pursuit would never, ever, suspect?

They'd seen two aircraft, a one-engine airplane and an old Iroquois chopper, on the drive into Amarillo. Neither paid any attention to the battered truck. They were looking for game making time away from Amarillo, not heading right toward it.

An hour later, as Chi was picking his way into the ruins on the western edge of town, they picked up a transmission that froze their blood. "Target not answering," came suddenly loud and clear from the radio. "Commencing firing run."

"Holy shit!" Chi yelped, and cranked the wheel over while Eklund and McKay frantically searched the sky. The truck jounced into an alley behind a burnt-out Circle K convenience store. McKay had the door open and was ready to bale out when he heard the pilot's triumphant cry: "Got 'im! Lookit that sucker *burn.*" And for the next several hours they listened with unalloyed glee as FSE searchers converged like a school of piranhas on one of their own units whose radio had malfunctioned at an inopportune moment.

Meanwhile they were locating a convenient warehouse to

hole up in. By the time the FSE boys had realized their mistake, after a spirited last stand defense by the victims, the Guardians and India Three were hidden and settled in to ride the storm out.

The bolt-hole lay in a district of warehouses and light industry that hadn't suffered much visible damage from the blasts. This side of the warehouse gave onto a whole acre of self-storage units shaped, for God's sake, like miniature red barns. Rank on rank of the things, hundreds of them. It was enough to depress a brass monkey, but it was better than sitting around inside all the time. Even though India Three had policed it up as best they could, and soaked it with gallons of Lysol, it still smelled of mildew and wet paper and several John and Jane Does who'd died inside on some pretext or another long enough ago that they were skeletons in rags of clothing.

A footstep crunched dirt behind McKay. He turned and frowned. "Casey, for God's sake, you shouldn't be up and around yet. Rogers is gonna pitch a bitch."

"I've got to stretch my legs, Billy. I'm going crazy. It's been a *week*, man." A week after being wounded as badly as he had, most men would've been content to do no more than lie in bed and be attended by beautiful nurses. Here was Casey hobbling up with the aid of a bright yellow cane they'd turned up during one of their forays into the surrounding ruins. His skin was yellowish and shrunk like parchment onto the bones of his face. He may have lost his beloved *Born to Run* cap, but by God his yellow Zeiss shooting glasses had survived somehow, and he had them on.

"Your funeral. You can explain to Tom why you're up wandering around." McKay shrugged and went on out to sit in a scavenged folding yellow lawn chair. He wasn't wearing a coat today. The temperature had climbed clear up into the fifties, though there was still a lot of snow on the ground.

Casey came up painfully and sat in the blue lawn chair next to his. McKay marveled that he didn't tilt to the right as he did. Casey's pet Smith and Wesson M-29 .44 Magnum had vanished in the confusion of eight days ago. A foraging expedition to a nearby shopping center had found an unlooted sporting goods store and come back with a brand-new one, a real Dirty Harry six-shooter with an eight-and-three-eighths-inch barrel just like the old one, and a boy-howdy cowboy hip holster to replace his shoulder rig, which had gotten ripped and burned to shit when Mobile One went. McKay, who never thought twice about hauling his twenty-pound Maremont "pig" around, would've died before weighing himself down with a horse pistol like that. Hell, most footsloggers preferred to carry an extra canteen or two even when a sidearm was allowed; the only reason Eklund wore her 9-mm service Beretta was as a badge of rank.

Though the Maremont was back in the shadows of the warehouse, McKay had his own .45 automatic cocked and locked in its holster, and kept a watchful eye out for dog packs. They had four people spotted up on the roof behind sandbags, with an RPK-74 to keep them company, but you couldn't be too careful. Damn dogs were *smart*.

Casey squinted up through yellow lenses to a gauzy patch of brightness in the center of the sky. "Nice day," he commented. "You can almost see the sun."

"Jesus, you sure know how to look on the bright side of things, don't you?"

In spite of his gruffness McKay wasn't unhappy with the way things were going. The issue radio in the truck kept them up to date on how the search for them was going, which was terribly. They were being reported as far afield as California, New Jersey, and Canada. Apparently the FSE expeditionary force's brass was putting Amarillo AFB through shit changes over their stupidity in letting the quarry slip through their grasp.

Meanwhile the fugitives were safe and sound, not twenty klicks from their pursuers' lair. They were sending out scavenging patrols a couple of times a day, largely to keep busy. Amarillo had taken it hard from the war, what with the grounder at the base spewing fallout all over everything; very little looting had gone down, since there wasn't much of anybody left to loot. They already had enough canned goods to last them past the millenium. The sporting goods store provided an invaluable several hundred rounds' worth of 5.56—the older stuff, meant for weapons with a different twist to their rifling than the M-16 A-2s and the Galils, but still usable. They had medicine, including antibiotics for Mary Alice, who'd been hanging in there, getting neither worse nor better since she'd been hurt. They had drugs of a not-so-medicinal nature too, and booze aplenty. Eklund and Tall Bear let their people do as they pleased about those, as long as they weren't fucked up for duty; those were the rules by which India Three had lived all these months, and those who wouldn't abide by them were long gone.

There were even toys. Sam Sloan had gone out with a patrol three days ago and they'd come back grinning like monkeys, riding in the bed of a commandeered Toyota pickup truck carrying a fucking pool table in the back. McKay had stomped around and hollered about that one. Sloan had just grinned at him. He'd had his revenge, though; he'd whipped everybody's ass at eight-ball, in no uncertain terms.

But the big issue was water. The simplest and most unglamorous of commodities—and one of the toughest problems of supply. Even when you could find it—not always an easy task, say, in the middle of a desert or a dead city—it was a bitch to transport. It was heavy and took up a lot of space, and you had to have something to carry it in. And it took a lot of it to keep a man going.

With all the snowfall of the past months, there was a fair amount of standing water to be found, on flat roofs and whatnot. Little Torrance, the sandy-haired one with the poorly set leg, turned out to be the natural-born scrounger most units seemed to have. He'd come up with a pickup truck with a tank in place of a cargo bed, which some landscaping firm had used to haul water in. They'd taken to sending it out with one party in the morning to bring in the day's water, then sending another patrol out on foot in the afternoon for whatever it could turn up while the stay-behinds boiled and filtered the morning's haul. They were using a bunch of uninstalled bathtubs as holding tanks, and McKay reckoned they had better than a day's reserve.

Hell. They even had *beer*. It shoulda been paradise.

But it wasn't.

As if reading his mind, Casey said, "When are we going to move on, Billy?"

"Soon as we can figure out where the hell to go."

From inside came a burst of laughter, echoing hollowly. McKay frowned. These people could use some better noise discipline. Still, there hadn't seemed to be much need for it. No one was looking for them in these parts. The occasional survivors they glimpsed on their excursions gave them a wide berth. Anybody who spotted them would assume they were either foragers from the base or deserters. McKay guessed there were enough of the latter skulking around the ruins that the FSE boys wouldn't even bother investigating their presence in the unlikely event they were reported.

McKay was itching to be on the road, and he knew his teammates were as well. Eklund's people felt no such sense of urgency; hell, they had nothing on their minds beyond simple survival, when all was said and done. The Guardians were different. They'd been chosen in part for their strong, almost overwhelming, senses of duty. They'd been trained to absolute devotion to *mission*. And right now, none of them was quite sure what that mission *was*.

"Billy," a voice said in his ear. It was Tom Rogers, out with the afternoon patrol. Sloan and Mason had whipped up some modification to the platoon's issue radio that enabled it to boost the sending and receiving power of the little pocket comm units, courtesy of a bucketload of parts liberated from a Radio Shack. "We've had a contact. Podolski's hurt, not bad."

McKay and Casey loked at each other. Sam Sloan materialized in the side door of the warehouse blinking sleep from his eyes, Galil-203 in hand. "FSE?" McKay asked.

"Negative to that, Billy. Locals. We're coming in."

Half an hour later Runner called down from the roof, "They're comin' in."

"Tom?" McKay sent.

"Almost there."

McKay and Sloan went around to the other side of the warehouse, which faced onto a decent-sized street. Across it stood a cinderblock building that housed a computer store and a sandwich shop, with a Shell station next door. The patrol emerged from between the two, Rogers on point, Ballou behind him with the M-203, then Mother Myles with the Minimi, and next Ski with a bandage on his left arm, holding his M-16 in the right. In the rear walked Tall Bear, his black eyes restless beneath the rim of his OD baseball cap.

Eklund came out to join them. She was wearing her fatigues with the sleeves rolled up. Though stained and threadbare, they were more or less clean; she'd insisted that spare water be used to wash uniforms and bodies, another move which won McKay's grudging approval. And that wasn't all. Out of her layers of cold-weather gear, she didn't much resemble an Irish washerwoman after all.

"How bad is it, Ski?" she called out. The stocky trooper grinned at her, showing a gap in his top teeth.

"Just winged me, Sarge. I'll be good as new in a day or two."

"Twenty-two," Tom Rogers said, as they walked around the warehouse. "Went right through his biceps. Clean. Hardly tore the muscle."

"Mother, you're limpin'. You weren't hit, were you?" Eklund asked.

The machine gunner looked sheepish. "Well, I wasn't shot, no."

Ballou brayed laughter. "Fuckin' *brick*. Some scrub hit him in the ass with a brick. Hard target to miss."

"Bull*shit* it was my ass! Got me in the thigh, tha's all."

"Jesus, Tom, what happened?" McKay asked.

They were in the gloom of the warehouse now, with the rest of the platoon gathering round and Casey looking on from his cot, where McKay had banished him after Rogers announced he was coming in. "Had a run-in with a bunch of survivors. Locals. Jumped us near a high school, 'bout four klicks away."

"We didn't hear shooting."

"Wasn't much," Tall Bear said. The Kiowa corporal hadn't warmed much to the Guardians in the last few days, but he wasn't hostile, either.

"They came swarmin' out at us, throwin' rocks and bottles and shit," Ski said. His faced was flushed, his speech slurred. It might have been shock, but McKay just guessed he was excited. He didn't look to have lost much blood. Besides, Tom Rogers didn't seem alarmed, and as far as McKay was concerned that meant there wasn't anything to be alarmed about.

medically. "Real sorry-lookin' bunch. One of 'em popped me with a Ruger 10-22. Then Mother fired off a burst in the air, and that calmed 'em down."

"You'da let me have some of them there multiple projectile gree-nades, I'da got the whole bunch of 'em," Ballou said pointedly to Sloan.

"Glad I didn't," Sloan smiled.

"They must have been pretty uptight, to attack five armed men with rocks and bottles, man," Casey observed.

Rogers shrugged. "Think they were tryin' to drive us off. They were scared, but they were desperate too."

"You-all talked to 'em?" Eklund asked.

"You bet we did, Sarge," Ski gushed. "We went to cover and they went to cover, and we started hollerin' back and forth, and—" Tall Bear nudged him in the ribs, and he subsided.

"He's right," Rogers said.

"What'd they say?" Sloan asked.

"They were part of a group been livin' in an old motel off I-40. Don't know whether they lived through the fallout or just drifted in after things'd cooled down. Anyway, they been scrapin' by, same's we been doing the last week. Then, few days ago, some soldiers from Amarillo AFB hit them. Chased them away from the motel, scooped up their supplies, caught a couple of women and dragged them off. They heard that's been happenin' all over town, especially off on the east side, nearest the base. Been rousting a lot of people into forced-labor gangs too."

"You think they're looking for us?" Gillet asked nervously.

"No way," Sandy said. She laughed mirthlessly. "It looks like they're settling in to stay."

McKay had his cheeks drawn back and was gnawing his underlip. "We're gonna have to move on," he said. "If the FSE people are moving in, it's just a matter of time before they stumble onto us. And somebody's gonna blab to 'em, sure as shit."

"I wanted to grease 'em," Ballou said hotly. "They wouldn't let me."

"Jesus, Eklund, where'd you find this guy? Fuckin' refu-

gees got enough problems already without we start blowin'
'em away.''

"They'd find out sooner or later, anyway," Tom Rogers
put in. "Somebody's noticed we've moved in here, you can
bet on that. There're people all around here. They've just been
keeping out of our way."

"Shit," Rosie said disgustedly. "You mean we gotta move
out of here? Just when we's gettin' *comfortable?*"

McKay sighed like a winded racehorse. "Looks like it." He
wasn't altogther sorry.

Now that the heat was off it was better to move at night.
There was sporadic air traffic from the base at all hours, but
nobody was apt to be paying attention to the low-light televi-
sions or the other after-dark sensors. With any luck they could
slip out of town and be well into New Mexico by daylight.

The truck loaded with provisions and a hundred plastic milk
bottles filled with water, the Guardians and India Three
waited for dark to come down. Eklund came up beside McKay
as he stood in the open door watching the last light bleed out
of the sky behind all those awful mini-barns. "So what's
next?"

His brows came together. "Huh?"

"Ain't much of a conversationalist, are you?"

"I ain't Commander Silvertongue Samuel Sloan."

"That's for darn sure. *He* knows how to talk to a lady."

He turned his head and looked at her. "I didn't think you
were a lady," he said. "I thought you was a sergeant." She
blinked. "You just decide to pass the time insulting me, or was
there something on your mind?"

She glared off at the sunset as if it offended her. The way it
silhouetted the storage barns, maybe it did. "Ah wanted to
know where we're goin' from here—*if* that ain't too much
trouble."

McKay frowned at her. He didn't know why she was so
cranked at him tonight. "Listen," he said, "we don't really
have to go together, your people 'n' mine. We can liberate
some transport of our own and be wavin' good-bye anytime.
If you don't like us, let's split."

She stared down at the toes of her boots. "Lieutenant McKay," she said huskily, "since the war we been gettin' by just fine. We hung together, we *survived,* through all kinda scrapes, all kinda shit. I've led my people, and I've led 'em good. But now we're—aw, hell. We're out of our depth, McKay. We need *help.*" She had to pull the words out like barbed darts from her flesh.

McKay should have felt triumph. All along he'd thought a woman had no damn business bossing a platoon. *So why the fuck can't I gloat?*

The truth was he didn't have it in him. He knew just what kind of miracle Sergeant Eklund had accomplished, keeping her people intact over the past months; hell, he of all people knew what the world after the One-Day War was like. Now she was having to admit there was a situation she wasn't up to facing, and it ate at her. Even McKay could see that.

"Hell," he said, not looking at her. "We owe you one, Sergeant. You put it on the line for us, back there at the culvert." He turned, rubbed his jaw. "We thought of heading into New Mexico, then swinging north to hook up with some people we know in Colorado."

"We've been through that, Lieutenant. What I want to know is what do you-all plan to do next? There's somethin' mighty big comin' down in this country. What're you going to *do?*"

His lips pressed together till they disappeared. "You tell me, Sergeant," he said. "Then we'll both know."

"Billy," Tom Rogers called from where he sat with the others next to the deuce and a half. "Better come here a minute."

The two walked back from the doorway. Sam Sloan came up from checking gear in the truck and Eklund just sort of naturally gravitated to his side. *So what's she see in him?* McKay indignantly wondered. *He ain't even as tall as she is. And why should I give a shit, anyway?*

Most of India Three was clumped in the glow of a kerosene lantern around the Panasonic, from which oozed the syrupy tones of a FSU radio announcer, speaking from Forrie Smith's citadel in the heart of Oklahoma City, the Mecca of the Church of the New Dispensation. "Once again, we have a momentous announcement. The trial of Vice President of the United States Jeffrey MacGregor concluded today at the secret Underground White House. An extraordinary tribunal of civil and military authorities convened by President William Lowell has found MacGregor, thirty-eight, guilty as charged of high treason."

Somebody gasped. Casey was gaping; Tom and Sloan just looked grim and taut in the lamplight. "MacGregor has been stripped of all titles and privileges, and sentenced to death. Execution has been scheduled for the Fourth of July. President Lowell has scheduled a press conference for this evening at seven o'clock, Central Standard Time.

"That's news again: former Vice President MacGregor found guilty of treason—"

Chi reached long black fingers and clicked off the radio. "Shit," he said.

McKay looked at his comrades, "July four, huh? That's just a little over three months from now."

Sitting with elbows on knees, Rogers bobbed his head slowly. "Not much time, but I think we could pull it off."

"You're not thinking—" Sloan began, looking wildly from Rogers to McKay. "You can't mean—"

"I bet they do, man," Casey said.

"But it's a crazy idea!" Sam protested.

A grin slowly illuminated Casey's features. *"Yeah,"* he breathed.

"So don't tell the rest of us what you talkin' about," Chi said. "I mean, shit, why should we care?"

Feeling Eklund's eyes on him, McKay looked at the sergeant. "Don't know about you people, but I think we know what we're gonna do, once we get outa here."

"What's that?" Eklund asked in a carefully neutral voice.

"Only bust Jeff MacGregor's skinny ass out of the most secure facility in the continental United States."

CHAPTER
TEN ──────────────

"Now let me get this straight," the tall and gangly Jimi Hendrix lookalike called Chi said. "You seriously think you gonna break this MacGregor dude out of some top-secret complex that's just crawlin' with all these FSE mother-fuckers?" He shook his head. "You *nuts*, man."

They were gathered around a kerosene-primed fire of dead brushwood in the mountains of the extreme northeastern cor-ner of New Mexico. After bidding farewell to their warehouse hidey-hole—with varying degrees of reluctance—the night before, they'd driven through the hours of darkness. Progress had been slow; it was a long time since the roads had seen any maintenance, which hadn't been that elite in the last few years before the war anyway. There were the usual wrecks and derelicts to contend with, remnants of the panicky futile ex-odus from the stricken city. Also, both McKay and Eklund were reluctant to use the headlights, even taped down to blackout slits. Just because nobody was looking for them in this part of the world didn't mean they were ready to chance attracting attention.

The plan had been to cruise straight west into New Mexico,

then curve up and into Colorado. With a little bit of luck they should have made the San Luis Valley of south-central Colorado by nightfall. The Guardians had in mind joining forces with the retreaters of the community called the Freehold. The Freeholders were a gang of libertarians and anarchists Billy McKay regarded as frankly cracked, but they'd fought bravely against the New Dispensation crusaders last summer alongside the Guardians, and had subsequently linked up with the trade network Project Blueprint founder Dr. Jake Morgenstern had been spinning in California. Also, Angie Connoly, who was as close to being a leader of the community as Freeholders acknowledged, was distinctly sweet on Casey Wilson, a sentiment the former fighter jock reciprocated—though to McKay's knowledge there was at least one lady in California, a long, buxom redhead named Rhoda, who might have had some words of her own about that setup. In any event, the Freeholders would be more than happy to let the Guardians hide out among them for a while. And whatever else you could say about them, McKay suspected they were the last people in these formerly United States who'd ever turn them over to Wild Bill Lowell's FSE goons. In the Freehold they'd be able to lay their plans.

All it would've taken was a little luck—so of course they didn't get it.

Dawn found them crawling along the shoulder of I-40, which was still mostly clogged with abandoned cars, almost to Glenrio on the New Mexico line. A few klicks past, the engine gurgled and died. Eklund chased everybody out and into a creditable defensive perimeter while Chi, who supposedly had trained as a mechanic for his MOS, opened the hood, peered inside, and scratched beneath his 'fro. To Tom's saturnine displeasure Casey insisted on hiking up front to scratch his head too.

Presently the deuce and a half wheezed into life again. Everybody climbed back in, Tom Rogers still clucking at Casey. Having gone through their little dance earlier as to who would sit where and having both made their points, McKay and Eklund crept into the back of the truck and let Tall Bear and Sam Sloan do the honors.

The pattern was set for the whole damn day. Drive along for

a while; choke and die; everybody deass for more head-scratching. McKay grew steadily more twitchy as the day wore on. "We gotta cross Raton Pass in this beast," he said, eyeing a sky covered over with high thin clouds fibrous and hard-bright as glass wool. "Is it gonna make it on one lung like this?"

"Sure, Billy," Casey said cheerfully. McKay'd long ago learned better than to argue mechanical matters with Casey. For one thing he knew a shitload more about it than McKay, and McKay never liked to point things like that up too much. Besides, if you let him, Casey tended to go all metaphysical on the subject. Zen and the Art of Deuce and a Half Mainte-nance.

Raton was a small New Mexican town that looked as if it once had a certain pitched-roof and whitewashed turn-of-the-century look about it. Now it looked like most other small towns, right on down to the Pizza Hut with half the glass in the sign shot loose. It showed signs of life. There was a bypass on I-25, which they took. The radio—mostly KFSU, which had enough broadcast power that anybody with more than two fillings in their head could just about pick it up—was full of nothing but *be on the lookout for these dangerous criminals*. It griped McKay's ass to think anybody'd believe that crap. But Sloan said, well, a lot of people'd figure that if the President endorsed it, it had to be so, especially if they hadn't happened to have any personal dealings with the FSE Expeditionary Force as yet. Rogers backed him up. So they gave it such berth as they could.

To McKay's surprise, once they started up the grade into the Sangre de Cristo range toward the Pass, the truck just sailed on as if this were what it'd been waiting for all day. "I'll be damned," McKay said to Chi, who was back behind the wheel. They were the only two up front this time.

Chi nodded. "Yeah. This is it." And he just drove on with a Mona Lisa smile as if this was just what he'd been expecting. McKay suspected he was faking it.

It came down dark quick in the mountains. It was dusk when they started up the pass, and full dark well before they crossed. There'd been a certain amount of debate about mak-ing a run at the mountains this late, rather than waiting for morning. There was a little snow, in dead ground and on north slopes and whatnot, but the sky was clear, and they decided they'd rather make a few more kilometers before calling it a night.

They wound a few klicks past Raton Pass and pulled off onto an unpaved road that serpentined back among slopes clad in Ponderosa pine. By good fortune they found a stream tumbling past a clear spot where they could camp. They set out a perimeter, with the aid of two Claymore mines the Guardians had salvaged from Mobile One, and broke out the chow.

For some reason, during the week just passed, the Guardians and their chance-met comrades hadn't discussed much of what had gone down. Now, here in the thin cold pine-tangy air, a lot of things started pressing to get out.

"That's exactly what we have in mind." Sloan smiled in response to Chi's incredulous query.

Wolfing a bite of canned corned beef and beans, McKay grunted, "You don't have to come along."

Ballou took a last bite from his mess kit, grimaced, threw it down. It clanged on a rock by his boot. "I don't see why we come this far. Don't see it at all."

"You think we should've waited around for more FSE troops to come and hear our story about what happened to all those Russians?" Sandy asked, tossing her braid back over her shoulder. She laughed. "You don't think smart, Ballou."

Ballou glared at her through a lock of hair that had slumped over his water-pale eyes. McKay had a feeling there was something going on here, that Ballou had tried a little too hard to get Sandy to come across at some point. He seemed like the type to push his luck. "We shouldna never done that. We had our orders; just hand these here Guardian fellas over peaceful like. Why the fuck couldn't we done just that?"

"You blind, man?" Chi asked. "Those were *Russians.*"

"So what? You heard the President on the radio. They on our side." He looked wildly around the circle of firelit faces. "Are we crazy? Look at us. We're on the run. We're criminals. We lost three people after not losin' anybody for months. All because we had to go and shoot it out with them Russians. All on accounta these damn Guardians."

He shook his head. "President Lowell's puttin' this country back together, mark my words. And when he's done that, what's gonna be left for us? We're *traitors*, know that? Done burned our bridges right behind us."

Chunky Ski faced him squarely. "You suggestin' we oughta just hand 'em over?"

The night seemed to hold its breath. "Yeah," Ballou said at last. "It's th' only thing to do."

Off to one side, stropping a double-edged Arkansas toothpick on a leather band around one wrist, the man called Runner said, "Listen to the man."

Sidelong, Sloan caught McKay's eye. The Maremont hadn't been fired today, but being a Marine, McKay was cleaning it anyway. He tapped the receiver meaningfully with two blunt fingers. Rogers, sitting over between Mason and Podolski on the other side of the fire, shifted imperceptibly so his right hand was poised for a quick grab at the Galil SAR on the ground beside him. Casey, stretched out on the ground next to Sandy, lying on his left side with his head propped on one hand as if he were watching TV on the den floor, already had easy access to his Dirty Harry horse pistol.

Throughout all this Eklund sat staring fixedly into the fire. The real issue here was her control over her platoon, her fitness to command. Pride wouldn't let her speak in her own defense.

"Bullshit," Chi snorted. He shook his head rapidly as if trying to clear water from his ears. "We ain't turnin' nobody over to no*body*. The Guardians're our buddies, man. They part of the *team*."

"That's all you can expect from a dumb nigger!" Ballou shouted.

Chi grinned at him. "Smile when you say that, mo' fo'."

For a moment Ballou looked ready to go for him. Quietly, McKay closed the M-60's receiver on the first round of his next-to-the-last Aussie ammo box and hoped he would.

"That's enough." It was the voice of Tall Bear, dry and definitive as an ax striking wood. "The sergeant made the decision. She runs this show." Ballou looked at the ground and muttered. "What was that? Why don't you speak up so we all can hear you, Ballou?"

"Said it was a hell of a way to run it."

"That's not what you said when she saved your ass in that shootout over by Lipscomb. And remember the time she covered for you, when you were accused of pilfering from stores, back at Sill? They were shooting people for that sort of thing, Ballou."

He swept his heavy face around the circle, eyes picking out each person like obsidian spearpoints. "Truth is, without the sergeant, a lot of us probably wouldn't be here right now. Or *anywhere*, except maybe rotting by some roadside or in some ruin. She's kept us together all these months. You think you can make it on your own, Ballou, I suggest you go right ahead and try. Walk on out into the darkness and don't look back. But don't go talking against the sergeant."

Ballou said a lot of nothing. McKay let himself breathe again. After a moment, the tension diffused into the surrounding woods. India Three went back to smoking and joking. Ballou went over to sit beside Runner and mutter darkly.

Tom Rogers got up to check Mary Alice, who'd been unusually subdued all day. Sam Sloan moved over next to McKay. "We're going to have to watch those two," he said, inclining his head ever so slightly toward Runner and Ballou.

"Don't I fucking know it."

Next morning they got an early start. It was a bright day, on the warm side, the gauzy clouds starting to unravel overhead. As they rolled out onto the rumpled fringes of the Great Plains past Trinidad their spirits became buoyant. It was as if the mountain barrier they'd crossed was some kind of symbolic barrier as well, that the danger that had haunted them for the past week lay forever behind them. Cruising toward Walsenburg they all started singing "Louie, Louie" for all they were worth. The song was written before any of them were born, and none of them actually remembered the words all the way through, but they had plenty of spirit, and covered the blank spots by yelling, "A-Looway Loo*way, ahhh* ah-ah!" at the tops of their lungs. They may not have been good, but they were loud.

The spirit dampened a bit when Mary Alice started puking up blood just shy of Aguilar. Not five kilometers farther on the engine emitted a very final-sounding thud and expired. Podolski, taking his turn behind the wheel, hauled it off to the side of the road and everybody piled out except for a worried Tom Rogers and his patient.

A flock of crows convened by the side of the road twenty or thirty meters farther along exploded into the sky. Nobody looked too closely at whatever they'd been working over. It was one of those things you learned about life in this Brave New World; you didn't want to *know.* Casey and Chi stood staring into the engine compartment stroking their chins, and this time they shook their heads.

"Like, that's all she wrote, Billy," Casey said.

"That sucker ain't movin' an inch," Chi agreed. "We were gettin' low on fuel, anyway."

McKay sighed. The Sangre de Cristos—the same range they'd just left—loomed blue in the west. Across them lay the San Luis Valley, and across it lay the Freehold, snuggled in among the skirts of the San Juan range. They weren't twenty klicks from the Cuchara Pass that led through the Sangres into the valley, and the valley itself wasn't that broad. Still, it was quite a hike, and a lot of it uphill. His feet ached at the prospect.

Shit, I knew it, he thought. *I'm gettin' soft.*

He shouldered his bulky rucksack. "All right, children. We gotta lot of humping to do."

Chi rolled his eyes lasciviously. "Don't I just wish." From a couple of spare pack frames they rigged a sort of travois for Mary Alice to ride on. She was gray around the edges, clearly in no shape to hike. Tom visibly disliked the idea of moving her at all, but there wasn't a whole lot of choice. They divvied up packs, weapons, supplies, and spare water, and set off toward the cool aloof mountains.

CHAPTER
ELEVEN

"Say, bro'," Rosie said to Casey as they trudged south-west in a long column. "A week ago you look like somethin' try to eat you and spit you out. Now you just walkin' right along. What's goin' on here, anyway?"

Casey shrugged. "No problem, man. I don't have anywhere the load you have to carry." All Tom was permitting him to shag were his sidearm, a couple liters of water, and a rifle they'd brought him from the sporting-goods store, a Remington 700 ADL with a Leupold 4 x 9 power scope. His M-40X sniper's rifle, lost with Mobile One, had been built on a 700 so it wasn't that much different from what he was used to, if you overlooked the fact that this one lacked a stock tailored exactly to his physical dimensions and an electronic scope straight out of *Star Wars*, had a five-round fixed magazine instead of the twenty-round NATO detachable box he was used to, and a few details of that nature. Tom had frowned deeply when Casey wanted to carry that much, his equivalent of a temper tantrum, but Casey insisted. Casey could be as stubborn as a cat when he wanted to, so Tom gave in.

"But you was split wide open," Rosie persisted.

"Yeah," Gillespie said from behind them. "They was pourin' blood into you by the gallon. How do you do it?"

"I've always healed fast. And, like, Tom has us on this special diet. Lots of Vitamin C, growth-hormone stimulants, stuff to promote wound healing."

"It put lead in your pencil?" called Torrance over his shoulder.

"Don't pay him no mind," Chi said. "He got a low mind."

"Must hurt like shit," said Jamake. The huge black hadn't said a word in two days that McKay could recollect.

Casey smiled. "I guess it does. But you've got to just learn to put that aside, man. It's not that big a deal, if you're in harmony with yourself and the universe."

They stared at him with awe. "That's a load of shit," muttered Ballou.

"No, hey, this is serious stuff," Rosie said. "I want to hear more."

"No, you don't," McKay said from the head of the column. It was his turn to walk point; after a heated dispute it had been arranged for him to trade off with Eklund. In America's armed forces, it was a leader's privilege to lead from the front. "He'll have you contemplatin' your navel and sittin' with your legs tied in knots if you ain't careful." And then he heard a sound that raised the hair cropped close to the back of his neck: a many-throated growl of engines.

"Company, Billy," Tom Rogers said over the communicator. Casey unslung his Remington. The other Guardians had their weapons at the patrol position, even though most of India Three carried theirs slung.

Eklund didn't. She was walking right behind McKay holding her M-16 in both hands. "What's goin' on?" she asked. "I could swear I heard engines. Plenty of 'em."

"Get off the road," McKay said.

"Now just a doggone minute—"

"Get off the fucking road!"

Sloan was counting the 40-mm grenades in his chest pouches and looking as if he didn't like the result he was getting—which he already knew by heart anyway. "We could be in for a spell of hot weather here, Sergeant," he said, forcing a cheerful tone.

"What's goin' on?" somebody asked.

"Sound like a buncha cars comin'."

"Off the road, everybody," Eklund snapped. "Odd numbers left, even right. *Move.*"

"Who do you think it is?" Mother Myles asked, setting down his Minimi in the lee of a battered black pickup on the north side of the two-lane highway. He'd been at the rear of the column; now he was nearest the still-unseen vehicles.

Drifting back to this end, McKay told him, "Probably not the Girl Scouts." He went down among high strawlike weeds next to the barbed wire fence that paralleled the south side of the road. They'd been headed down a long easy slope toward a tangle of small ridges and arroyos. He was looking up the incline toward a crestline two hundred meters away. *One hundred rounds,* he was thinking. *This party last's more'n a few dances, I'm in trouble.* At least the lack of a spare barrel, which, like so much else, had been lost with their V-450, was no handicap; he'd burn up his ammo long before he burned out the barrel. A hundred rounds would last maybe a minute in a real firefight.

He glanced back over his shoulder. The stretch of highway appeared deserted. It was like something out of Monty Python: *How Not to Be Seen.* One thing life after the One-Day War had taught the squaddies of India Three was how to stay out of sight.

"I don't see what all this fuss is about," he heard Ballou drawl from somewhere behind him. "It's probably just some kinda convoy."

"If you're a praying man"—to McKay's surprise it was Rogers talking—"then I'd suggest you start prayin' that's the truth."

And then they hit the crest like Howard Hawks Indians.

"*Shit,*" somebody breathed.

"Close enough," Sam Sloan said. "But we usually call them road gypsies."

There were at least a hundred of them strung out along the skyline. Motorcycles, jeeps, pickups, and lots of the barebones dune buggies the road gypsies favored. In the permanent floating depression of the late eighties and early nineties, a lot of disaffected types had turned to popular entertainment, as happened so often in history, for a way to cope with a feeling of powerlessness. This time inspiration came from the Australian *Mad Max* movies, which had done for the gypsies—who had little in common with the ethnic group except the name and a propensity to wander—what *The Wild Ones* and the later Big Bill Smith movies had done for motorcycle hoods. So here they were, big as life—as portrayed on the silver screen—and nine times as ugly in their spikes and leather and outlandish haircuts.

Scanning them, McKay suddenly subvocalized, "Shit. That's a machine gun mounted on that truck, near the left end of the line."

"I make it an old Browning thirty-caliber," Tom said, calm as always.

"Will you look at that?" Rosie said with something like admiration. "Where do they get the gas?"

"Scrounge it, just like everybody else," Sandy said.

"Naw. They gets it from Okie City. They got wells right on the state capitol grounds, refineries all over the place. Whole city smell like a bus station and shit," Chi said.

"I just can't believe the New Dispensation types would give those scum anything."

"Shit, babe, where you been? They thick as thieves."

McKay wondered where she'd been too, though he knew from talking to Eklund's platoon that for some unknowable reason the New Dispensation had kept clear of Sill in their own backyard. But maybe he had a skewed outlook, since he had a certain amount of firsthand experience of the unlikely alliance between the road gypsies and the fundamentalists of Coffin's New Dispensation. Besides, if the gyps could reconcile natural enemies like punks and metalheads into one gang of crazies, and join up with *zombis* who were sworn foes of everything that lived, nothing they did should be a surprise.

"Cut the chatter," Tall Bear rapped. "Hold tight, and maybe they won't see us."

A single rider detached himself from the ominous wall of silhouettes, dark against morning blue. He came curvetting down the slope, zigzagging across the blacktop and kicking up dust to either side as he rode. A hundred meters along he pulled his chopped Harley into a wheelie and pirouetted on the rear tire like a Russian ballerina. *Some ridin'*, McKay acknowledged grudgingly.

The front wheel thumped asphalt on the dotted white line fading into nothingness in the center of the road. "Weary wayfarers, I give you greetings," he shouted in a billow of condensed breath. "Come out and talk to me, dear friends. The Lord Alien addresses you."

"So much for goin' unnoticed," Chi said from his bush.

"He sure doesn't look to have room for all those lungs in that skinny chest of his," Sloan subvocalized wryly. It was easy to see his chest was skinny; it was bare despite the chill, and you could damn near count the ribs from here, they stood out in such stark relief. The Lord Alien wore baggy purple pants like a paratrooper, slashed to reveal orange Danskin tights beneath. He wore a spiked black leather collar around his throat, and bunches of colorful fake feathers, green and orange and pink, at the wrists. The oblong sockets of his eyes were painted black, and he had a white strip painted from one cheek to the other across a hogback ridge of nose like one of Geronimo's Chiricahua out to pay a social call on some white settlers. His hair was caught into an array of waxed green-dyed spines jutting up from a shaved scalp. He looked to be about six six, six seven, even seated in the lowslung saddle of his hog.

"Show yourselves, friends," he called. "You have nothing to fear."

"Fuck this," McKay said. He rose, holding his M-60 in one hand like a tommy gun. "What the hell do you want? The Marine Bill McKay addresses *you*."

"Hearts and minds," laughed Sloan.

"Grab 'em by the balls," growled McKay, "and their hearts and minds'll follow."

"But you display such an awesome weapon," Lord Alien cried. He flung out his pipestem arms, raised them slowly above his head like a great gaunt bird unfurling its wings. "I show myself to you, unarmed and unafraid, filled with good feelings."

McKay let the Maremont drop, caught it by the sling, lowered it gently to the ground. Then he stood at his full height and folded his arms across his chest. "Well?"

"We only wish to entertain you for a while, my friends. Understand that no one travels this path without let and leave of the Children of the Silver Road."

"Silver? She look black as my skinny ass to me, man," Chi said.

"Cut the chatter."

The wind hissed urgent warning about McKay and played dirges on the tailpipes of the derelict pickup. "So, I'll ask nice," he called, pulling a liberated cigar out of a breast pocket and striking up. Miraculously, the match didn't blow out. "Let us go our way. We don't want any trouble."

Painted eyebrows rose. " 'Trouble'? " The gypsy leader looked theatrically around. "I see no source of trouble here. Just the prairie, and the sky, and the clouds, and the silver road our home. And good friends conversing against this lovely setting."

"Great. We're friends. Consider that we've kissed each other hello, and we'll be on our way."

Lord Alien tipped back his unlikely head and laughed like a seal barking. "Such wit! I applaud you, Marine McKay." He turned to his waiting gypsies. They applauded. "But now I really must insist that we all sit down together and entertain one another."

"We got a pressing engagement."

That won another bark. "Your recalcitrance does you small credit, my friend. Don't you owe more consideration to your hosts? This is our road, after all."

"We go where we goddamn please!" McKay said around his cigar.

Lord Alien wagged his head. "Such rudeness! I fear we must teach you a lesson."

"Great," Ballou said.

"You didn't think they was gonna let us *go*, honky?" Rosie asked.

"Ask him if he likes that little dental-hygienist's mirror he's got welded to his handlebars, Billy," Casey said over the commlink.

McKay couldn't *see* the damn thing, but Casey had a telescopic sight, after all, not to mention eyes like the Apache Kid.

"You attached to that little mirror you got welded to your handlebars?"

Lord Alien pushed his head forward uncomprehendingly. "What?"

A shot cracked from behind McKay. Half a heartbeat later the longhorn handlebars jerked violently, and McKay saw a thin splinter of brightness pinwheel up into the sky. He took out his cigar. "That," he said, as Lord Alien wheeled his chopper around and lined out for the hilltop amid hoots and cheers from India Three.

The line of road gypsies vanished as if the earth had swallowed them whole. "That's that," Ski said. His voice quivered with relief. "You told 'em good, McKay."

McKay was examining his cigar as if he thought it might really be a dog turd. "You don't think that's the last we've seen of 'em, do you?"

The next instant they swept over the hill.

McKay was already in motion, hooking the M-60's sling and rolling through the weeds. As he'd anticipated, the truck with the mounted Browning came up spitting .30-caliber death for the spot where he'd stood. That kept it from firing anyplace it might hit somebody. As if on cue Sam Sloan's M-203 hiccupped. Dazzling light flashed from the hilltop as an HEDP grenade blew the cab and gun mount behind into twisted junk.

M-16s started to spit with that deceptively gentle popping noise they made. "Cease fire!" Eklund shouted. The shooting died away as the road gypsies swept down the hill in a long, ragged line.

McKay tried to pick out the attenuated from of Lord Alien, but the road gypsy leader skillfully weaved his bike in among those of his followers so that it was impossible to pick him out. Instead he picked a Nissan sedan with the roof cut away toward the center of the demon cavalcade, and waited.

"They're gonna run right over us!" a despairing voice wailed.

"Steady, dammit!" Tall Bear hollered.

The gypsies were so close McKay could look up the flaring nostrils of the Nissan's driver, see the rings in the ears of the sawed-off shotgunner at his side. "McKay, you're the expert," Eklund called, her voice taut as a garotte. "You give the word."

"Get ready to fire straight ahead," he yelled. The gypsy swarm was fifty meters away. McKay pulled the M-60's butt hard against his shoulder and locked it down with his left hand. He took a deep breath.

"Rock and rolllll!" At his hoarse battle cry he squeezed the trigger like a lover's breast. The Nissan's windshield exploded in a powder of safety glass. The orange and black compact swerved abruptly right, directly in the path of a motorcycling road gypsy in a loincloth waving a submachine gun of some kind. The bike's front wheel hit the car broadside and flipped its rider screaming right over the chopped-down top. An instant later momentum, declivity, and the impact of a half ton of hurtling bike rolled the little sedan right over him.

The starfish of a white phosphorus 40-mm round spread its lethal arms in front of a half dozen bikes. Two ditched in the blast, two others came out screaming, beating at the pellets of burning metal that covered them like killer bees. A fifth was firing a modified Ruger Mini-14 over the handlebars of his hog, ignoring the score of smoke trails whipping back from his hair and leather vest; the last seemed unharmed. In another moment three-round bursts from India Three's M-16s knocked both of them sprawling in the yellow dust.

The improved 5.56 NATO round had better body-armor-piercing capability than the old one, but was still pretty much worthless against even car bodies. And McKay guessed India Three's marksmanship was probably not real scintillating. So he'd had them hold their fire until the gypsies got into eye-white range, and turned a concentrated firestorm on them. Eklund's squaddies maybe couldn't clip the X-ring at half a klick, but they were cool, and that was what was called for.

Mother Myles pumped measured blasts from the Minimi into the onrushing tide of metal and flesh. His buddies and the Guardians turned the ground in front of them into a killzone filled with blood and fire and tortured screams. Their plans for a quick vicious overrun smashed, the road gypsies split into two swarms and swept past on both sides, just as McKay hoped they would.

All except for a pair of bikes and a Jeep CJ with a sheet of metal bolted over the windshield with just a slit for the driver to look through. They flashed past McKay in an instant, the bikes weaving and dodging, the Jeep shedding 5.56 slugs off its makeshift armor plate with a constant tinny rattle. Lips hauled back in a snarl, cigar stub clenched between his teeth, McKay jerked himself upright, trying to swing the Maremont to bear. Sam Sloan popped up out of a low gray-green bush and triggered the M-203 like an old-fashioned wingshooter blitzing a flock of quail. The multiple projectile charge scythed the two gypsies off their machines in a spray of blood, shredded flesh, and white bone fragments. The choppers raced on a few meters like headless chickens, then fell over, spinning their fruitless wheels.

An eyeblink later Mother Myles screamed as the Jeep sideswiped the pickup in a shower of sparks and rolled right over him. The vehicle slowed, wheels spinning in loose gravel. Chi came out of cover in a leopard leap, dropped an apple-shaped grenade in the lap of the startled gypsy firing a lever-action Winchester from the passenger seat, pitched himself backwards and rolled. Eyes bugged, the driver tried to abandon ship. The blast launched him like a rocket assist.

The rest of the pack had blown past like a gust of wind, and were scattering in all directions across the rolling landscape. Several troopies scattered quick bursts after them, till Eklund yelled at them to quit.

Silence burst like a bomb. The only sound was the snarling of engines receding into the tangle of ridges downslope, the moans of the wounded, the crackle of flames, all remote and colorless after the din of battle. "We won, we won, we won!" a high feminine voice chanted.

Sitting, McKay half spun at the sound of gravel under boot-soles. But it was only Tom Rogers racing to Mother Myles. The medic took one look at the machine gunner and shook his head.

"No shit, man," somebody said. "We really whipped their asses." A ragged cheer rose from the prairie like a flock of crows taking wing.

But Eklund shook her close-cropped head. "Don't get y'all's hopes up," she said. "They'll be back. You can bet to that."

CHAPTER
TWELVE ————————————

Perhaps a dozen bodies lay sprawled in McKay's field of vision. Despite the hyperkinetic conversation of India Three speculating how many kills they'd made, McKay reckoned the gypsies hadn't taken much more than a score of casualties. That was fairly heavy, but not heavy enough to discourage road gypsies, if his prior experience with the breed was any indication. The nomads were real hard-core, though he figured it was more a matter of elemental viciousness than courage.

"How many hurt?" he called.

"Podolski got his shoulder laid open, Bone had a finger clipped," Eklund said. Bone was a middle-height black with a weightlifter's build and the knobby face of a prizefighter, who had assigned himself the task of dragging Mary Alice's makeshift travois. He was at least as taciturn as his buddy Jamake. "No biggie."

"That's the good news," Tom Rogers said, "how are we set for ammo?"

That wasn't such good news. With the ammunition scrounged from Amarillo, the 5.56 weapons averaged a little under three thirty-round magazines left per person. Not that shabby, but even with three-round burst regulators, that much could get eaten pretty quickly when it was all on the line.

But the real crunch was on the support weapons. Mother Myles' M-249 was totaled. The RPK-74, like the other captured Soviet weapons and ammo, had been left with the truck as too much dead weight to carry. Unfortunately, that left McKay's M-60 with seventy-two rounds left as the only machine gun—and since the road gypsies would probably be too cunning to try another frontal assault, he probably wouldn't have the option of holding fire till the last minute and then wreaking havoc with a few well-placed rounds again. Even with extra rounds in his pack, Sam Sloan was down to six WP, nine HEDP, and nine multiple projectile grenades for his M-203, along with a few parachute flares. Again, a pitifully low number to use against an enemy that was apt to be very elusive from here on in.

Ballou's twenty-four-pocket vest carried eleven frag grenades, three flares, and two non-incendiary smoke cans for the M-203 he'd taken over after Gutierrez bought it—the same as when the battle started. He started to stammer an explanation. Eklund just told him to swap with Ski, who was carrying a regular M-16 A-2. He looked cold death at her but complied.

Tom and Billy were keeping an eye on the surrounding terrain. "What do we do?" Sloan asked. "It looks as if the gypsies are between us and the best cover."

"Looks that way. I still say we drive on."

"They'll murder us down in those gullies," Tall Bear said.

"Maybe so. But they're not going to be able to take so much advantage of their wheels," Eklund said.

"Right," said McKay. "Let's drive."

They moved off down the middle of the road in an echelon formation, so as to provide the maximum firepower forward as well as to the sides. Eklund put Bone and Mary Alice, who was moaning softly in pain and fear, behind the point between the two files for a modicum of protection. McKay had point again, with little argument from Eklund; his Maremont LWMG could respond to ambush a lot more authoritatively than her rifle.

They were fifty meters from the bottom of the incline when

Gillet shrilled out, "*They're behind us!*"

A group of bikes and stripped-down cars had either circled overland out of sight of the platoon or been waiting in reserve. Now they bore straight down the strip of road toward India Three howling like wolves.

India Three broke and ran. Eklund and Corporal Tall Bear stood in the middle of the road, but as had happened to units caught in the rear from time immemorial they were swept up in unreasoning fear. They streamed past their leaders like water flowing downhill.

McKay fired a burst from the hip, SMG style. A mohawked motorcyclist spilled. Firing from one knee Casey put a round through the driver of a navy blue Ford pickup with flames painted on the sides. Sam Sloan had a high explosive, dual purpose round in his 203. It dropped on the ground and rolled downslope as he popped the breach and tried to fumble a Willy Peter out of his vest.

"Run, Eklund, try to get 'em pulled together and into cover," McKay shouted. She stared at him. The road gypsies were less than a hundred meters away. "*Go*, goddamn it!"

Eklund blinked and took out like a jackrabbit after her fleeing platoon. Tall Bear followed reluctantly. McKay looked at his comrades. "We're seriously fucked. You know that, don't you?"

Sloan fired his white phosphorus grenade straight into the angled blacktop thirty meters away. The sunbright white flash and sudden gush of dense smoke split the charge like a wedge. McKay went to a knee and poured bursts into the gypsies as they veered off the sides of the road, taking the recoil of the heavy weapon by the sheer power of his legs and back. As coolly as if he were sighting in on the range, Casey fired his Remington bolt gun dry, slung it, and hauled out his .44 in time to blast a black-clad *zombi* with a self-mutilated face off his Harley as the man bore down swinging a baseball bat studded with cut nails. Rogers sprayed the road with his SAR. From the hip Sloan fired an HEDP. It socked home between the headlights of a dune buggy and he had to dive to the side to avoid the hurtling fireball.

Bikes and bodies were strewn all over the road. Most of this band of bad guys decided they'd had enough and blew off in all directions like the head puffed from a ripe dandelion. A huge mohawker with a vast paint-daubed beard loomed over McKay, brandishing a samurai sword. McKay grinned, aimed his machine gun for the hairy bare bulge of belly, pulled the trigger. Nothing happened.

Roaring, the bike went by. Down the hill, Bone ran doggedly for cover, drawing a hysterical Mary Alice behind him like a draft horse. The biker ran down on him, hacked him down with the *katana*. Bone went to his knees with a groan, a flash of scarlet diagonal across the back of his battle jacket.

The chopper wheeled, stopped. "No," Mary Alice begged from her pallet. She gagged, and blood spilled down her chin. "No. Please *don't*—"

The sword struck splinters off the sun. Mary Alice's head leapt off her shoulders atop a single orgasmic geyser of blood.

McKay stood. A strange cold fury possessed him. He stepped into the middle of the road. "You're dogmeat, fucker," he called.

The biker turned toward him, grinned gaptoothed. He gunned the engine like nearby thunder. McKay just grinned. The biker twisted the throttle and let in the clutch. The bike streaked for McKay like a crossbow quarrel.

McKay tossed his machine gun into the air. The biker's piglike eyes followed it as it turned over once, lazy in the air. But he came on, raising his saber one-handed for the killing stroke.

The Maremont spun down. McKay grabbed it by the barrel both handed, swung it like a bat, and smashed the steel buttstock through the center of the bearded mocking face as the bike howled by.

Dispassionately he watched as the bike banged over on its side and slid up the road, raising a shower of sparks and a hideous screeching and leaving a red smear on the cold asphalt. Tom and Sam and Casey stared at him.

He examined the machine gun's butt. It was all over blood and matted hair and the plastic stock was chipped, but it didn't seem bent. He popped the receiver, let the empty plastic half-moon box fall, clipped on his last one, less than half-full. "Let's go," he said.

• • •

With late afternoon the sun had worked its way up to being warm on McKay's back, though it couldn't quite compete with the wind that howled through the narrow gullies and up over the ridge on which the Guardians and India Three were hunkered down. Off to one side behind a jut of red sandstone electronics whiz Mason, shot through the throat, was noisily dying, in spite of everything Tom Rogers could do for him.

"They're still out there," gimpy straw-haired Torrance breathed. "Jesus, it's hard. Not seeing them. Knowing they're there, that they'll be back."

Tall Bear lay on his paunch with his M-16 poked through a clump of saltbush. One heavy cheek had been laid open by a tumbling ricochet. "When I was a kid, I always saw these Western movies on the television, where the cavalry was lying in a circle on a hilltop behind all these dead horses, with Indians all around, and they'd go, 'Those red devils are out there watching us. We can't see 'em, but they're there.'" He chuckled, a startling sound. "Always used to piss me off. Us Indians were always the heavies, the cowardly skulking savages. So now the tables've turned; it's the redskin up here on this damn hill, surrounded by lurking white-eyes."

"Glad you can appreciate the irony in the situation," Sandy said.

They were dug in on the end of a ridge like a finger laid against a bend in the road. The Guardians' two Claymores were placed at the back of the rocky fingernail they occupied, slanted inward to sweep the ridge with converging fields of fire without frying any defenders in the backblast. They'd been emplaced after the road gypsies had surprised everyone by trying a rush against their position, booming up over the "knuckle" seventy meters away on a half dozen motorcycles and charging in among them in the time it took to draw a panicked breath. The nomads had left three of their number behind.

Whip-lean Runner, with the black hair and the wild blue eyes, had traded knife thrusts with a bandy-legged biker in cammie pants and a greasy Shriner's fez, the dirk-shaped Arkansas toothpick against a Bowie with a ten-inch blade. They were practically stitched together. When they pried the moaning semiconscious pair apart they found loops of purple-gray intestine tangled like yarn. Half of India Three had puked themselves pale, and so had Sam Sloan, who wasn't quite as seasoned as he thought he was. They smashed the gypsy's skull in with a rock to save ammunition. In answer to Runner's croaked request his buddy Ballou put a bullet in his skull. No one objected. It was the only kind of medicine that would do any good for a man in his condition; that was the world they'd lived in for three quarters of a year.

Mostly the gypsies hung out on the other ridgetops sniping and waiting for night. They'd only managed to nick people, with the exception of the one who'd nailed Mason, and Sloan had paid him off in shrieking white phosphorus death. Still forms on the surrounding high points attested to the defenders' superior marksmanship.

But dark would come down like an avalanche soon. And then . . .

"McKay," Eklund said, crawling up beside him. "Can I have a few words with you?"

He glanced at her. The Maremont stood propped on bipod and buttstock beside him, awaiting an emergency; he himself lay behind a spare M-16 A-2. "Lemme check my appointments calendar." Eklund wrinkled her nose. "What's on your mind?"

"Wanted to apologize for the way we acted back there on the road. Freakin' out and runnin' like that."

He shrugged. "Those are the breaks."

"But if it weren't for you-all, they'd have run us down like a hound takin' a rabbit. We owe you."

"So we're heroes. That's what we get paid for."

She looked away. He wasn't making this any easier on her, he knew. Well, that was too damned bad. "Gonna be night soon," she said.

He nodded. "Listen, I thought maybe we could have Tom exfiltrate after dark, try to make it into the valley for help. They usually have people with radios in the passes. They could send a rescue party."

"No."

"Well, shit. I ain't talkin' about him running out on you people, for Chrissake. It's just we'll never last out the night unless something—"

"Will you kindly please shut the fuck up!" He stopped. She took three heaving breaths. "I'm talkin' about you goin'. All four of you. If Casey can hack it."

He regarded her narrowly. "That'll leave you high and mighty damn dry."

She moistened her lips with the tip of her tongue. Water was another thing in short supply, along with ammo and daylight and time. "We owe y'all one, like I said. Well, this is how we'll pay you back for runnin' out on you. We hold the road gypsies, and you go over the mountains."

"Are you kidding?"

"No. You—you boys're doing something important. I don't know if you can pull off this harebrained scheme to rescue that Jeff MacGregor. But if there's anybody who can do something to help pull this country out of the mess it's in, it's you Guardians. We can maybe buy you the chance." She looked away. "Reckon we owe it to the country, 's well as you."

McKay gazed off to the west. The sun was a fat red balloon getting ready to burst itself on the Sangre de Cristos. India Three were comrades, and you didn't run out on your buddies . . . unless there was no help for it. If McKay believed in anything, if he had religion, had faith, it was in the absolute sanctity of *mission*. The Guardians' mission now was to rescue the President—their President—and excise the cancer of FSE from the flesh of America. And they couldn't very well do that if they left their bones for the crows on some ridgetop in southeast Colorado on account of warm fuzzy feelings for a handful of people they'd just happened to run into.

"We got a while before nightfall," McKay said. Eklund was offering to sacrifice herself and her platoon, the people she had gathered and sheltered and ramrodded and, yes, loved for almost a year for the Guardians and their mission. Her blue eyes burned like suns as she waited to hear him pronounce the death sentence on India Three, and he couldn't bring himself to look into them.

"Got a while till dark," he said. "Let's not decide nothin' just yet."

Eklund rose to her feet and ran bent double back to where Mason's painful gurgles were subsiding. As she went thunder boomed among the ridges. A curious thunder, like the beating of a giant tom-tom.

"Shit, Corporal," Chi yelled. "The natives is restless."

Again the drumbeats, heavy and hard. Like the backspace on a humongous electric typewriter. "Billy," Tom Rogers said, "I could swear that's a machine-gun."

"Only one chopper makes a sound like that. Browning M-2, fifty-caliber."

There was a boom. An orange-red fireball popped up over a hogback, riding a rising black column of smoke. Engines began baying like a pack of hounds. A dune buggy screamed around the curve below on two wheels, straightened, and lined out for the Kansas border. A moment later a whole pack of cars and cycles followed with throttles wide open; gypsies leaned over handlebars with their mohawks flattening in the breeze.

A handful of shots popped from the fingernail. "Hold off," Eklund order. "Let's see what's goin' on."

A lone chopper bombed around the curve. With a skill McKay grudgingly had to admire its rider threw it broadside, rode it through a twenty-meter skid. He sighted the M-16 on the junction of thick neck and denim vest. The rider raised a lever-action carbine single-handed, fired one shot. A fleeing road gypsy bike veered right, ran up the shoulder of the ridge and tumbled back down. An instant later fifteen or twenty more bikes appeared, riders bent low and howling like wolves in pursuit of the fleeing nomads.

"What the fuck?" somebody asked.

"There's your cavalry, Corporal," Sam Sloan said. His voice wasn't altogether steady.

"Yeah," McKay grunted. "But *whose?*"

Creaking and clattering, the boxy shape of an old M-113 armored personnel carrier rolled into view. A man with hair plaited into innumerable long braids lounged atop it, negligently holding the spade grips of the M-2 mounted on its cupola with one hand. He wore an immaculate white jumpsuit and smoked a cigarillo as long and lean as he was, and even blacker.

The APC wheezed to a halt with a banging of loose tread plates. "Hello up there," the dude in the dreadlocks sang out.

"Freehold Fire and Rescue and Choral Society, at your service. We cheerfully accept gratuities."

"Callahan?" Sam said in disbelief. "Dreadlock Callahan?"

"The one and only." He swung long legs over the edge of the vehicle and dropped to the blacktop. "I see my fame precedes me."

"You *know* these people?" Eklund asked.

"One of them, anyway," McKay said.

"Who, may I ask, has the honor of being rescued by my humble self?" Callahan called.

McKay stood up. "Last time I saw you, you were an outlaw biker and a fugitive from justice," he said. "What's with this 'Freehold Fire and Rescue' shit?"

The cigarillo dropped from Callahan's mouth. "McKay? Is that you?"

"The one and only."

"You got Sam and Case with you? And Tom?"

"Yo, Dreadlock," Tom Rogers said. "How's it going?"

"Whoo-*ee*!" Callahan turned and pounded on the steel flank of the M-113. "You in there, break out the Dom Perignon. These're *friends* we done rescued. We're gonna *party!*"

Billy McKay was pissed. In more than one meaning of the word. True to Dreadlock Callahan's words, they had indeed partied, once the unlikely procession of choppers, a couple of carryalls, and the APC had arrived at the Freehold, a scatter of mostly semisubterranean adobe dwellings high up on the west side of the San Luis Valley. Philosophical differences aside, the Guardians and the Freeholders were old buddies, comrades in arms, and reunion was cause for a celebration.

"You see," Callahan told the Guardians as they jounced up Cuchara Pass in the M-113 while Eklund and her people followed in the trucks, "the countryside hereabouts isn't quite so uninhabited as it looks. We got a half dozen radio calls from homesteaders saying the gypsies were hassling some poor sons of bitches. That's why the cavalry happened to ride to your rescue at such an opportune moment."

"You keep saying 'we,' Dreadlock," Sloan said. "But the last we knew of you, you were lighting out from the Freehold without waiting to say good-bye."

Dreadlock gave him a Pepsodent grin. He'd been the leader of a band of bikers pressed—he claimed—into the service of the Church of the New Dispensation in its crusade against the Freehold and the Guardians. Appalled by the excesses of Coffin's stormtroopers, the black-clad Brothers of Mercy, he and his second in command, a woman named Snake, had secretly made their way into a besieged Freehold to talk defection. Under the pretense of having captured them, Callahan and his band marched the Guardians into the presence of the Prophet himself. Coffin's gray eminence—their old friend Trajan—had seen through the ruse. Sacrificing herself, Snake had won the Guardians time to bring their concealed weapons into play. With the timely help of Casey, flying a fighter jerry-rigged from a light private plane and a pair of black-market machine guns, they'd chopped the head off the crusade. Mindful that their status might still come in for a few questions, Callahan and his crew had discreetly vanished during mopping-up operations.

"We came back," Callahan explained. "This nomadic lifestyle ain't all it's cracked up to be. We were never raiders, and we'd kind of lost our stomach for rummaging in the ruins. So we decided to go legit."

"Outlaw bikers join the middle class," McKay said. "No shit."

"Scoff if you will, my friend. We've been in the convoying business, squiring caravans between here and the West Coast." He looked at Casey. "Lady out at Balin's Forge sends her regards. Long redhead, name of Rhoda. Spoke so highly of you it made me jealous." Casey looked at his boondockers and *blushed*. McKay was never gonna understand him.

Callahan took a draw on his cigarillo. "By good fortune we happened to be in port when we got the call. We never pass up a chance to whomp on road gypsies, so out we came."

Now the merriment had died down. Most of the revelers had stumbled back to their own homes, and India Three's survivors had dispersed as guests of various householders. The four Guardians, Eklund, and Dreadlock Callahan sat beneath the massive *vigas* of Angelina Connoly's den, holding a somewhat bleary-eyed council of war by the light of kerosene lamps. It was bleary not just because of the lateness of the hour, the lack of sleep on the part of certain participants, or the nearness of their brush with death. Liquid refreshments had flowed freely during the course of the celebration. McKay couldn't speak for anybody else, but *he* was stewed to the eyeballs. He was also mad as hell.

"These FSE people aren't wasting any time," the stoop-shouldered scholarly type with the glasses and the thinning hair was saying. "Anything not nailed down they're taking. Anything nailed down, they pry up." Roger Kotziades looked like everyone's image of a mousy middle-aged accountant. He was a former lawyer and stockbroker, in fact—as well as a former Navy SEAL with a stainless steel hip joint, courtesy of an alert North Vietnamese militiaman twenty years ago, and military-affairs expert for the Freehold.

"Can't believe Bill Lowell'd let 'em do things like that," said Tom. He'd been drinking beer, which he seldom did. It had the effect of rendering his soft delivery all but inaudible.

"They put him where he is," the compact woman with hair like spun copper who sat next to McKay said. "This is the payoff: anything they can bleed out of America."

"They're getting a lot of cooperation," Angie Connoly said. She was a striking young woman with a wide-cheekboned face and a triangular chin, and black hair that hung straight to her rump when she stood. Right now she and Casey were sitting on a massive sofa covered with a Navajo blanket done in geometric patterns of black and gray and tan. Casey was sipping his inevitable fruit juice and holding Angie's hand. "Forrie Smith's been proclaiming the Millenium till he's hoarse. A lot of local authorities like Dexter White in Kansas City have acknowledged Lowell as legitimate President."

"That son of a bitch," McKay grumbled. He remembered Mayor White too damn well. He thought of a cry for help on the radio in the middle of the night, suddenly cut off, and his fists contracted into huge knots of fury. Ruby Vasquez, the copperhead who sat beside him, patted his forearm soothingly.

"A number of survivors of the armed forces have gone with Lowell too," Kotziades said.

Sloan shook his head. "I don't understand it," he said, his eyes perplexed crescents. "We—Jeff MacGregor, I mean—

never got that kind of support from the military. Hardly got any response out of them at all." A sense of betrayal resonated through his words like harmonics.

"At Fort Sill Major Dugan said we oughta wait an' see," Sergeant Eklund said, plainly embarrassed. She sat off to one side looking uncomfortable; she seemed to have checked her Texas self-assurance at the door. "Said the civilians had made a real ripe mess of things, so he wasn't gonna rush to sign up with this politician or that one."

"The military always favored Lowell," Kotziades pointed out.

"He favored us," Tom Rogers said.

Kotziades shrugged. "Yeah. And this is also a largely military endeavor. Most of this FSE Joint Expeditionary Force consists of American veterans of the fighting in Western Europe. Soldiers over here tend to feel a sense of comradeship with them."

"And expect to join in the spoils, too," Ruby Vasquez said.

McKay glared at her, red-eyed. "That's a shitty goddamn thing to say."

"It's true, and you know it!" she flared at him. "You think everybody turns into a saint when he puts on a goddamn uniform?"

He scowled and sank deeper in his chair. He knew better, but he was damned if he'd admit it. Especially to Vasquez. She was top physician for the Freehold, a woman with no illusions and mean as a ghetto rat when she wanted to be. McKay liked her. They'd never love each other, but they had some pretty good fights. Also she fucked like a crazed ferret.

"Any idea how many of them there are?" Casey asked.

"About ten thousand came over with the first wave," Kotziades said. "It sounds as if that bastard Maximov plans to send more over."

"How d'you know all this stuff?" McKay demanded.

"We've got some of the best computer people to be found anywhere, before the holocaust or after—including our lovely hostess," Kotziades said, pouring himself more Scotch from a bottle on the cable-spool table beside him. "We don't have that much trouble getting into their communications."

"Ten thousand," Ruby said, shaking her head. "That's a lot of the bastards."

"No it ain't," McKay said, pleased to be able to correct her. "Not scattered across a country this size."

"You really intend to try cracking into Heartland?" Angie asked. She sounded worried.

McKay blinked. "Just where do you people stand?"

"Where our feet are," Ruby said firmly. "None of us can speak for anybody else. But I'm in favor of sticking it to these FSE fuckers."

Angie and Roger nodded. "I didn't think you believed in patriotism," Sloan said.

"We don't have to approve of the political setup in this country," Kotziades said, "to disapprove of a gang of foreign thugs invading it. And this is a foreign army, make no mistake, no matter what uniform some of its members wear."

Yeah, McKay thought. That was true. And that was what pissed him off most of all. William Lowell, old Wild Bill the superpatriot. He'd sold America out to a foreign despot. *Sold out.*

"So what's the game plan?" Ruby asked.

"Dunno, exactly," McKay said.

"What can you tell us about the situation in Heartland?" Sloan asked, half apprehensively.

"Nothing directly," Angie said. "I'm not *that* good. I haven't made much headway breaking into the Heartland database." Her voice faltered, scarcely perceptibly; her mother, economist Dr. Marguerite Connolly, was a Blueprint participant who'd been in Heartland when it was taken. The Guardians, however, exchanged a relieved glance. None of them liked the idea of amateurs being able to break into top-secret facilities, even at a remove. On the other hand, somebody had—but they'd had Lowell, and Lowell had all the passwords in his head.

A thought hit McKay like a ball-peen hammer. "What do you hear about New Eden?"

A look of pain rippled across Angie's face. "They took it. There was some shooting."

"Shit."

"What about Dr. Mahalaby?" Casey asked.

"What about Doc Morgenstern?" McKay demanded.

"Dr. Mahalaby· wasn't harmed, we know that. Dr. Morgenstern—" She shrugged. "He vanished."

"Those bastards," Sloan said.

"No, you don't understand. He *vanished*. The FSE didn't get him."

"That's a relief," Casey said.

"So what are you planning to do?" Ruby persisted.

"Try to figure a way to get into Heartland before the Fourth of July," Sam Sloan said. "In the meantime, we thought we'd try to make things hot for the Expeditionary Force elsewhere, draw their attention—and their forces— away from Heartland."

"Won't have much trouble doing that, from what we've learned about the way the FSE's behaving," Kotziades said. "They're acting like a conquering army." He stood up, stretched, grimaced a little at a transient pain in his hip. "Well, we can work out how to save the world in the morning. I'd better hike home." He looked at Eklund. "May I escort you somewhere?"

"Sergeant Eklund's staying here tonight," Angie said, rising herself. "I've got plenty of room." She saw Kotziades to the door, then came back. "If you'll come with me, Ms. Eklund, I'll take you to one of the guest bedrooms."

For some reason Eklund looked at McKay, then quickly away. "Ah—Ah'd be much obliged, Ms. Conn'ly." She looked back at McKay. "You be stayin' here, Lieutenant?"

Ruby Vasquez rested her hand on his arm. "Tom and Sam and Case will. I'll be in comm call range, if anything happens."

"Oh. Well—g'night."

She let Angie lead her off. Tom and Sloan retired to the quarters they were sharing, the ex-Navy man not without a rueful glance at Casey and McKay. With the need to focus on serious talk past, McKay's brain filled promptly with the beer he'd consumed. Suddenly taken by muddled concern he pulled Casey to the side. "Forgot to talk to Callahan," he said. "Shoulda tol' him not to mention nothin' about that Rhoda. Better be careful wh—what you say."

"Oh, thanks, Billy, but that's no problem." Casey smiled. "I already told Angie all about Rhoda."

McKay blinked twice, very slowly. "You *what*?"

"Like, I told her, man. She said she was glad I found somebody nice in California."

McKay looked around, afraid somebody might overhear. "But what if she—I mean, Angie—I mean, if she—"

"Oh, she has. That's cool. She's too young to spend all her nights alone, man. That'd be a waste."

"Sometimes," Billy McKay said, "I think the modern world's too fucking much for me."

PART TWO
NIGHT OF THE PHOENIX

CHAPTER
THIRTEEN ————————

The long winter's passed. But a storm has broken over America. It's no usual storm; its center lies across the Atlantic. Nor is there calm at the eye of this storm. Its center is named Yevgeny Maximov, and in his rage and frustration he seethes with the force of a hurricane.

For he is still denied the one thing he needs, the Holy Grail he obsessively desires. The Blueprint for Renewal lies beyond the grasp of his blunt fingers.

He has, in a manner of speaking, made himself master of America. William Lowell has been reinstalled as President in the impregnable secret fortress of Heartland, and, through Trajan—mad Trajan, whose deterioration has begun to alarm his puppet master—Maximov controls him. But his control is a façade, a hollow shell, a Hollywood storefront. Ten thousand men cannot functionally garrison the over three million square miles of contiguous dis-United States. A certain number of local authorities recognize Lowell—notably Dexter White of Kansas City and the voluble Nathan Bedford Forrest Smith, who owns much of the Midwest Farm Belt in fee simple. And a good many people, loyal Americans of goodwill, find themselves supporting the man most feel to be the legitimate President. They are tired, and afraid, and long for a leader.

But Americans are not Europeans. For many of them, there's little to distinguish these uniformed men with the FSE star-and-map on their shoulders from any other gang of armed thugs—except that they're much better armed. The appetite of an army, even when it's no larger than a pre-war division, is fantastic. And many of these men from across the sea have come with promises of loot, implicit or explicit, ringing in their ears. What they need, they take; what they want, they take. And there's not a lot to go around.

Resistance begins. Spoiled as they are by a generation of prosperity and a tradition of security, there is still a point beyond which Americans cannot be pushed without pushing back. For all their longing to see Wild Bill Lowell as a man on horseback riding to their rescue, more and more are beginning to push back. From the rolling hill country west of the nightmare tangle of rubble and decay that is the Eastern Seaboard, to the California coast, rebellion breaks out like brushfires wherever the FSE Expeditionary Force or its allies are found.

Ten thousand men aren't a lot to hold a continent . . . but they're a lot more force than any potential challenger or rebel can muster. And they do have transport—giant Starlifters, helicopters, state-of-the-art Vertical Takeoff and Landing cargo packet planes; trucks and APCs. Rebellion is met with a crushing, savage response—as the survivors in the rubble of the Chicago metroplex, not four hundred kilometers east of Heartland, are discovering to their regret.

But it's a losing game Maximov is playing. As a master gamesman he knows it. Each punitive operation devours far more resources than its victory can hope to generate in a decade—without the aid of the Blueprint. If the battered survivors don't buckle under soon, sheer attrition of men and matériel will erode the Expeditionary Force to nothing. Maximov doesn't care; if every man of the force leaves his bones to bleach in the hot North American sun, he won't lose a minute's rest; one of his secondary objectives of this scheme was to rid the teetering Federated States of Europe of several thou-

sand mouths to feed. He's made sure the commanders of the expedition ship everything they can pry out of the prostrate superpower back to him in Europe, so the initiative won't be a total loss even if it sinks without a trace.

But if he doesn't get the Blueprint . . . that prospect costs him sleep.

And the Guardians, never to be sufficiently damned— they've been active. Rumors place them all over the continent —here in California's Big Sur, there in the pine woods of Georgia, now in the mountains of Colorado, then whipping on the disastrous revolt in Chicago. Mostly the rumors are just talk; not even men as resourceful as the Guardians could possibly be in all those places, accomplishing that much against the FSE. But it's clear they are sorely hindering the Plan. Maximov has plans cut just for them. Contemplating them is one of his few pleasures these days.

Maximov has been making life very unpleasant for W. Soames Summerill. Every time he gives Trajan a satellite-relayed nudge in the ribs, his puppet sends him something: EMP-resistant computer technology from warehouses in Silicon Valley, an entirely robotic small-arms plant from Gary, Indiana, two hundred beautiful virgins below the age of twenty—the last an Arabian Nights touch that tickles Maximov's vanity even as the sheer ludicrousness of it confirms that Trajan's grip on reality is beginning to go. But nothing helps much—though Maximov's pleased to be able to outfit a new exclusive brothel for his secret police, many of whom have a fascination for American girls.

Time and Maximov's temper run short. But Yevgeny Maximov, that huge yet subtle man, is about to receive good news. News that will be very bad indeed for the people of America.

CHAPTER
FOURTEEN ─────────────

The room lay in pitch blackness relieved only by the fulvous glow of candles in the candelabrum set in the center of the long table. For eyes long accustomed to the total absence of light, then recently flooded with it, it was painful.

"Come on in, Jeffrey," William Lowell said. "It's good to see you."

For a moment Jeffrey MacGregor hesitated in the doorway. He was afraid to risk barking his shins on a chair or on the edge of the table. The way he felt, his bones might shatter like glass. Gradually his eyes became accustomed to the gloom that had been their medium for several lifetimes.

He shuffled forward. His movements were those of an old, old man. His clothing—white shirt, tie, blue two-piece suit, black shoes—felt stiff and scratchy and alien against skin accustomed to nakedness for only Christ knew how long. The filth that had caked his limbs had been scrubbed and blasted off; his skin was raw and pink and seemed to bristle with nerve ends.

Painfully he pulled the elegantly carved wooden chair from the table and eased himself into it. The immaculate Irish linen tablecloth gleamed like a lake of amber. Across it William Lowell's face loomed like a great oblong balloon.

The President had changed little since MacGregor had last seen him, in the office that had once been his. Perhaps the lines were etched a touch deeper, the Mount Rushmore masses of the face more brutally pronounced, the eyes sunk farther and burning brighter. Swept-back gray-brown hair hung lank over the collar of Lowell's suit coat; *that* was something MacGregor had never expected to see. It made Lowell look like a militant Will Geer.

From somewhere a steward appeared. A white-cuffed hand —black, of course—set a plate of tossed salad before MacGregor. The aroma of vinegar and oil dressing was heady as wine in MacGregor's nostrils.

"You make me proud, Jeff," Lowell said as wine was poured. "You've held out this long." The great leonine head shook. "I never thought you had the balls, frankly. Congratulations."

The room seemed to pulse once, slowly, around MacGregor. *Held out? How could I spill something I didn't know?* He fought down giggles that threatened to swamp him like a floodtide. The torture—dear Christ, he'd never imagined anything could be that hideous!—and then the time in the dark, in an unheated cell too small to permit him to stretch full length in any direction, days or months or years . . . he blinked down sudden tears rising hot behind his eyes.

"You look surprisingly good," Lowell said, picking up his wineglass. "Gaunt, a touch of gray to your temples." He sipped. "Makes you look distinguished."

Until recently MacGregor's hair and nails had been growing untrimmed in darkness, until he felt like Howard Hughes of latter days. Right now he was tucking into the salad with a will, trying to pace himself so he wouldn't eat too fast and make his stomach revolt against a too-rapid influx of real food. His diet had been conspicuously lacking in fiber, something that was very important to health-conscious MacGregor. In fact, what food value the sticky gruel that appeared behind the sliding panel of the cubby might have possessed was a mystery, one he'd spent hours poring over: it seemed to lack not just fiber, but protein, hydrocarbons, and any known vitamins. It seemed to consist of curdled polystyrene.

The salad plate, polished to optical flatness, went away. MacGregor stared at Lowell. His gray eyes were huge in the candlelight.

Lowell smiled, the stern but loving father. "You're to be released, Jeff."

It hit him like a sandbag. *Released!* He slumped back in his chair—and instantly stabbed a wary gaze against Lowell's granite visage. "Is this a trick of some sort?" he croaked. If it was, if his being dragged from his cell and barbered and scrubbed and dressed was all a ruse to lower the defenses he'd raised against darkness and fear and discomfort and solitude . . . it had worked. *Dear God, don't let it be! I'd go mad. I can't endure another hour in that box.*

He'd tried, God how he'd tried. At first he'd been semi-comatose from the abuse Summerill's goons had dealt him. Then he straggled back to consciousness, and each second was like a hot iron pressed into his flesh.

He tried to remember the things he'd remembered about prisoners in solitary in Vietnam. He didn't play chess, so he couldn't make up games in his head. He knew some Navy pilot had designed a dream house in his head, then built it, mentally, brick by brick. Jeff MacGregor didn't know anything about construction. But he was a lifelong baseball fan, and so he could use that famed old dodge, assembling a dream league from the great players of all time, mixing and matching, and that ate some time. And he composed poems in his head—dreadful things, just dripping treacle, he knew. He'd never be another Rod McKuen—or, worse, maybe he would. And his fingers—delicately, at first, until the raw wounds where his fingernails had been healed a bit—had explored every square centimeter of the tiny box in which he was imprisoned.

But it was all a stopgap. He was a young man, vigorous, in the prime of life, and here he was folded into a meter-and-a-half cube to rot. The only thing he had to look forward to was the execution of the death sentence that a voice from the speaker grille above his head had announced dispassionately, somewhere in the depths of that timeless eternity. What was happening outside—to the country, to his friends, his people? For a time he'd dreamed the Guardians would come for him, somehow spring him from this, the lowest circle of Hell. At last he'd finally had to let that go for the foolish fantasy it was.

When they'd come for him, he'd smiled. He thought they were taking him, at last, to die.

Now Lowell was saying to him, "No. No trick. You see, we don't need that knowledge you've so resolutely kept locked in that skull of yours anymore."

He stared. He felt his mind reaching, mental fingertips scrabbling millimeters shy of comprehension. "What? What did you say?" His voice tolled in his ears like a great bronze bell.

To Lowell, not three meters away, it was scarcely audible. "Eh? I said we've got it. Our technicians cracked the lock you had put on the Blueprint files. This morning."

I had put on? Well, they hadn't believed his denials before. No reason they should start now. Then it hit him. *The Blueprint files.* The key to America's future.

"Your friends the Guardians have been giving us quite a headache." Lowell's voice was a drone like some vast and distant engine. "You can be proud to have men like that on your team. Too bad they had to turn traitor. But we're going to settle accounts with them soon, never fear."

The steward's disembodied arm floated above his shoulder, laying a huge plate before him, laden with broccoli and mashed potatoes and rare prime rib swimming in its own juices. The smell rolled over him like miasma from a swamp. He lurched back away from the spotless table, turned his head aside. His mouth gushed sour vomit, and he was falling, head over heels, into endless dark.

On the luxurious waterbed in his quarters, W. Soames Summerill lay on his back on burgundy satin pillows and watched the girl suck his cock. She was nude but for a red football jersey with the number 23 on it in white. Her limbs were coltish and slim, breasts muffled by the jersey (but small and perfect, tipped in pale pink; they wouldn't send him anything less than perfect. They wouldn't dare.). Blond hair had been gathered into braids to either side of the oval face. The goosenecked lamp burning over the bed touched it with glints of gold. Her eyes were blue, and slightly puffy; it had taken her a little while to accept the inevitable, with a little help from a cunning electrical appliance borrowed from Trajan's intelligence people.

He watched the taut red circle of her lips go up and down, and he tangled long fingers in one golden braid, and smiled.

It was a celebration, after all. They'd done it at last, pierced the arcane barriers erected to prevent his wringing the secret of the Blueprint from the citadel's fifth generation computer system. It wasn't the whole Blueprint, not yet. But much of it. Enough to buy respite from Maximov's bullying and leaden threats.

And the Guardians, the hated Guardians who'd done him so much damage in the past—and recently. *Their* time was coming to taste his vengeance. If all went well, a matter of days would see them dead, thanks to certain information he'd received. If that didn't work, if once again the incompetence of his minions betrayed him . . . well, Chairman Maximov had a special consignment on the way, due within the week. Trajan was prepared to receive it and utilize it to the best advantage; there would be no escape for the Guardians then.

The tension built within him, that sweet agony, so elusive these days. He grabbed a braid in either hand and pumped.

The intercom buzzed. He froze, pelvis thrust upwards, skinny saggy buttocks clear off the sheets. The girl moaned in terror and rolled her eyes. He poised there, hoping whoever it was would go away, mentally promising retribution for spoiling this of all moments.

The annunciator buzzed again, raucous, insistent. He'd left instructions that he was not to be disturbed for anything less than the most momentous tidings, and his subordinates had received several useful object lessons not only in the costs of disobedience, but of a poor sense of proportion. This was major.

He cuffed the girl away. She crawled into the corner and huddled, whimpering, thin shanks quivering. He rose and walked to the communicator set in the wall, hit the button. "Yes? What is it? What?" The tails of the pink shirt that with a pair of socks was all he wore hung down past his hips. His peter swung limp and damp between gray toneless thighs.

"E-excellency," a voice tremoloed. "We have news."

"Yes? Out with it, or I'll microwave your eyes."

He heard a gulp. "The latest shipment of—" The unfortunate agent up in the operations center almost said *tribute*, but caught himself in time. "—of special materials for Chairman Maximov, that was to leave from the Naval Air Station at Glenview—" He choked. He couldn't go on.

"Yes? What is it, damn you?"

"It was shot down. It crashed in Lake Michigan, off the old Coast Guard station at Wilmette."

"Shot down? *Shot down?* How?"

"S-surface-to-air missiles, Excellency. Stingers. Backpack carried."

"Stingers? What kind of fool do you take me for? Stingers won't bring down a C-141!"

"These were volley-fired, Excellency. At least a half dozen simultaneously. Four strikes were reported by the pilot and have been confirmed by reports of ground observers. The left wing sheared at the inboard engine."

Feebly Trajan broke the connection. *Gone.* Forty metric tons of treasure: fissionable materials, special black-box sensors and targeting devices for fighter aircraft, kilograms of palladium and platinum and other rare strategic metals. A king's ransom to placate the wrath of Europe's ruler. All gone.

His vision misted. *Traitors! Incompetents!* The security officer at Glenview would pay for letting the saboteurs get close enough to bring down the mammoth Starlifter. With interest.

It was the work of the Guardians. He knew it. No one else in this decadent, ravaged land possessed the resourcefulness, the fortitude to pull off such a coup. Almost, he could admire them. Almost. It made his imminent victory over them all the sweeter.

A whimper pierced the swaddling of his self-pity. He glanced sharply at the girl. Pathetic creature. Anger flared in him, and with it a tantalizing prickle in his loins. Perhaps the moment was not irrevocably lost.

He opened a drawer set into the bedroom wall beneath the communicator. He drew forth a short, supple whip. Smiling, he turned toward the half-nude girl.

• • •

"How would you like some of that?" Dreadlock Callahan inquired, eyeing a passing bare haunch with interest.

McKay sipped his beer. It tasted used, but by God it was cold. And *fresh*. "Wouldn't mind," he murmured. "Wouldn't mind at all."

The waitress glanced back over her naked shoulder and smiled. McKay growled deep in his throat. She laughed and slinked away among the tables, smoke, and darkness.

Rosa's Cantina lay off of I-25, the highway that split the continent in two, a few klicks past Douglas, Wyoming, where the great road jogged left to follow the North Platte River skirting the Laramie Mountains on its way to Casper. It was a place where the Great Plains began to rumple up into wind-carved buttes and mesas in preparation for the Rockies; big sky country, drawn in sweeping brush strokes. This was authentic Wild West turf. As late as the 1990s this part of the country still had a very frontier, close-to-the-edge feel to it. Close to the edge it had proven in all fact; the Warren AFB Minuteman complex not so very far away in the southeastern corner of the state had been among the best-nuked real estate in the world during last summer's unpleasantness. From the little town of Wheatland, just a hundred klicks away, the countryside south and east was still not a healthy place to be.

But there was still life in Wyoming, more than in a good many other parts of the country the Guardians had variously visited over the last two months. As hosts to important ICBM complexes, parts of Montana, Nebraska, and the Dakotas had gotten hit hard during the One-Day War, but here the population was sparse, much more widely dispersed than in, say, the East or California. People weren't quite so dependent on the great big network of production and distribution, not up here where the roads were still cut much of the winter. Ranchers were still managing to ranch, miners to mine; a number of truckers had turned trader and were plying routes north, south, west, and east, hauling fresh produce one way and goods salvaged from the ruins of urban centers in the other.

Man's vision of the good life being what it is, it was probably inevitable that an institution such as Rosa's would crop up along the trade arteries of this true-to-life New Frontier.

Douglas, nearby, after having been pretty well depopulated by disease, had grown back, and sported a general store, a dispensary with doctors and—rarer by far—a dentist on hand; stocks of diesel fuel, gasoline, and alcohol for the rolling stock, grain and hay for four-legged prime movers. Sixteen-wheelers loomed over makeshift wagons in the fields west of town, under the watchful eye of well-armed mercenaries. A lot of trade was conducted right there in the transport park. But it was Rosa's, a few klicks west, that was truly the landmark hereabouts.

What Rosa's Cantina was, was a genuine after-the-holocast topless honky-tonk bar. *Inevitable.*

At the moment the piano, squatting beneath a guttering kerosene lantern, lay silent. Soul music blared from unbelievably tinny speakers hung above either end of the bar. An alcohol-fueled generator out back provided current for it, as well as for the bar's refrigerators and the strands of dim Christmas-tree bulbs festooned rather pathetically about the inside of the establishment. Spotlights improvised out of institutional-sized bean cans and tinfoil dribbled light across the sweatsheened limbs of the scantily attired young woman gyrating on the raised stage across the room.

At a table set not far from the stage sat the four Guardians and the dreadlocked biker chieftain, recently reunited. The table was strategically situated diagonally opposite the entrance, which let in past the left end of the bar, so they could keep their eyes on the comings and goings.

"It seems sad," Sam Sloan remarked pointedly, "that a person's whole claim to fame in life should be the ability to make her breasts revolve in opposite directions."

The dancer was a dark-haired young woman with metallic-looking lips and black eyes heavily outlined in mascara, wearing only high-heeled shoes and a spangled bikini bottom. Her breasts were large but firm, not pendulous, the nipples erect, the aureoles broad and black-looking in the particolored light. They were indeed revolving in opposite directions, eliciting appreciative whistles and wolf-calls from the audience.

McKay frowned. *He* was savoring this. He was an old-line habitué of topless joints from his service days. The smells packed into the dark cavern of the cantina brought nostalgia powerfully upon him: secondhand smoke and stale beer, urinal deodorant, Walgreens perfume catalyzed by lady sweat. Rosa's had a filigree of its own aromas laid over the old familiar stinks: the sinus-swelling pong of kerosene combustion, acid remnants of pinewood smoke that had been forced into the burlap on the wall and the wood of floor and bar and the pores of the splitting vinyl upholstery all winter by sheer gas pressure, and was now oozing back out into the air in reverse osmosis. To McKay's mind it gave the place character.

Dreadlock Callahan cocked a thin cynical eyebrow at Sloan. "You're too uptight. Stop and smell the flowers."

Sloan grimaced. "I just find this . . . degrading."

Callahan snorted. "I thank God a lot I wasn't born a honky. Remind me to say a double prayer tonight I ain't a *honky liberal*."

The bar was middling crowded with the usual assortment of truckers, local types in off the ranch in their pointy-toed boots, loggers in checked flannel shirts. Many of them had pistols strapped to their hips. It was the policy of Rosa's Cantina that weapons be checked at the door. Here and now sidearms weren't weapons, but indispensable items of personal apparel.

A half-dozen young women drifted among the tables. They were dressed provocatively, although in this early-summer heat it might also have been termed sensibly. It was hard for the Guardians to remember that not ten weeks before they'd been freezing to death in a culvert in the Texas panhandle. In case one of the waddies or the wranglers got too provoked, a pair of immense bouncers circulated too, keeping bored surveillance.

McKay knocked back more beer that tasted as if somebody'd washed his horse in it. "Got some good-looking girls here. I'm surprised. Usually, your titty bar has a fair number of dogs. And now that things've gone all to shit, I'd think the place'd take what they could get."

"Must grow 'em healthy in Wyoming," Callahan opined.

At a table nearby a gorgeous brunette who answered to the name of Frenchie bent over to talk to a sturdy patron in a John Deere cap, providing McKay an unsettling view of the way she'd pulled her black swimsuit in between the cheeks of her classically molded ass. Suddenly she reared back and gave the guy a good right across the chops. He started out of his chair. A seven-foot bouncer named Lurch, who looked like Lurch from the old "Addams Family" TV show, materialized behind him, literally picked him up by the scruff of the neck, and toted him to the front door.

At the first sign of sudden movement, a lot of guns had appeared at the table. Now the other bouncer loomed over them like a tree about to fall. "Now, gentlemen," he said, laying huge meathooks on Sam and Callahan's shoulders, "I'll have to ask you to take it a bit easier." He was a couple inches shorter than Lurch and looked skinny as a telephone line. Like his comrade he wore the vest and trousers of some kind of light-colored three-piece suit over a white shirt and narrow tie. His hair was slicked back and shiny, very twenties-looking, and his face jutted like the prow of a ship. He was called Rico.

McKay tucked his combat-modified .45 back where it belonged. "What happened, anyway?"

"Gentleman must have made a proposition the lady took exception to."

Despite himself, Sam was curious. He leaned forward. "I would have thought—that is—I mean, don't the women—?"

"He thinks they screw for money," McKay supplied.

Rico's weasel eyes slid fluidly from side to side. "Don't let any of them hear you say that. They ain't prostitutes. What they do on their own time's one thing. But they're no whores." He jerked his head back at the bar. "This is a respectable joint. You say stuff like that, *she'll* get mad."

She was Rosa, proprietor and chief bartender of the cantina, who stood behind the bar polishing glass steins. "Shit," Dreadlock Callahan said. "I don't think I'd like that. She looks like a Russian ladies' field star."

"Got a better mustache than you," Tom Rogers remarked. Dreadlock stroked his Fu Manchu and glowered.

Rico drifted away. "Thought you niggers liked a big-leg woman," McKay said.

Sloan's eyebrows threatened to crawl onto the back of his head. "Obviously, you labor under a misapprehension, sir," Callahan said. "I ain't no nigger. I'm what you call Black Irish."

"And I'm a Jap."

The music cut off abruptly. Rosa lumbered to the end of the bar and spoke into a microphone. "Let's have a big hand for lovely Lydia. Next up—GeNeen." A small, wiry young woman with curly hair and an electric-blue teddy mounted the stage and began to gyrate enthusiastically to the metal strains of AC/DC.

"Would you gentlemen like anything?" A very tall peroxy blonde, leggy and good-looking in a beaky way, stood by the table with a tray in her hand.

McKay glanced around. "We're fine."

Blue eyes surrounded by wide swaths of liner caressed Casey. "How 'bout you, honey? You sure there's nothing I can do for you?" She stroked his cheek lightly with her finger-tips.

"Oh, no. Like, thanks."

"Any time. You need anything, ask for Shiloh." She gave him a last, incendiary look, then sashayed away.

"Shit," McKay said in disgust. "I don't know how he does it. *He's* been getting all kinds of pussy these last few weeks, and look at him."

Casey blushed and looked at the scuffed hardwood floor. Though his California tan had been upgraded by a dose of California sun, he had a yellowish undercast to his complexion. The skin was tightly drawn over his cheekbones, and had a dry, parchment appearance. McKay understood he'd had a strenuous reunion with Rhoda at Balin's Forge north of L.A., though Casey was the last one to brag and give details, worse luck. He had the look of a man who had driven himself too hard and fast since being hauled back from the yawning brink of death two and a half months before.

They'd all gone through too much. Sam Sloan had hit the Southeast, stirring up trouble in the hills and swamps for the FSE. Casey'd gone to California. McKay had been back East—and hardened as he was, he could barely make himself think about it. Was it possible that, on their hell-run from a stricken Washington, D.C., to Heartland, they'd missed the really *bad* parts?

And Tom . . . The ex-Green Beanie just sat there nursing his draft brew, looking as calm and collected as he would sitting in front of the TV set at home, standing in front of a firing squad, or at the bottom of the Marianas Trench, as he always had and always would. He didn't look like a man who had just dealt the ballsiest blow of all to the Expe-fucking-ditionary Force.

"A Starlifter. An entire fucking Starlifter. Right into Lake Michigan." McKay shook his head admiringly.

"The effsees are absolutely berserk about it," Callahan said. He'd come up to the rendezvous from Colorado, slipping out through the siege lines the ever-helpful Northern Rio Grande Valley Federation had thrown around the Freehold at the behest of their new friends Bill Lowell and the FSE. He'd brought word that the Expeditionary Force had sent advisors but no equipment. That reassured the Guardians; until they got some heavy-duty weapons the sad sacks from the NRGVF didn't pose much threat to the Freeholders.

The biker held up his stein. "Here's to tomorrow. You still intending to try and crack the big H?"

The Guardians nodded. For two months they'd traveled around the U.S. by motorcycle and liberated car, lighting fires the FSE would have to bleed off troops to fight. Tomorrow they were to rendezvous with Eklund's platoon and assorted Freehold volunteers in the Medicine Bow National Forest, back among the mountains, to lay their final plans.

"Any idea how you're going to get in?" He wiped his mustache with the back of his hand.

"Nope," Sam said.

"You guys are crazy."

"You're right. But what else are we going to do?"

"What you been doing. Stirring up the people. Hitting the effsees here, there, and everywhere."

"But in a couple of weeks they're going to execute Jeff MacGregor," Casey objected.

"Screw him. He's expendable."

McKay let his attention drift away from the debate. *His* mind was made up. The mission was to spring MacGregor, and that was that. Maybe he was tired of life and just looking for an excuse to get himself offed.

A woman in a black Andalusian riding hat, black vest,

skimpy black panties, and cowboy boots sauntered past. She had skin like chocolate satin, bare breasts like grapefruit in silken sheaths, and the most delectable ass McKay had ever seen. She gave McKay a look with big almond-shaped eyes, and he forgot about being tired of life.

Sounds of a scuffle came from the front door, out of sight past the bar. "Hey!" an angry voice burst out. "You can't—" The boom and flash of a shotgun burst cut him off.

Figures exploded into the room. Light stitched the darkness with a stuttering crash. McKay was already in motion, diving toward the base of the stage. Above him little GeNeen stood with her teddy pulled down around her waist and her pretty pointed little titties aquiver. Her right hip exploded in blood. She screamed and fell across McKay.

BaBOOM! *BOOM!* Still sitting in his chair even as his comrades dived for cover, Casey Wilson had his Dirty Harry .44 Magnum out, firing two-handed. The chattergunner fell back against a table and down. Beside him another dark figure was already raising a pump shotgun to his shoulder, holding down on the pumpkin-sized muzzle flashes, about to catch Casey like a duck on a pond. A bigbellied trucker bounced frantically to his feet just as the shotgun roared. He caught the full charge in the face. McKay had his Colt out by now, fired twice for the center of the shotgun man's body. He went down screaming like a dog run over by a station wagon. Belatedly Casey joined his buddies on the floor.

Men and women screamed in terror, clattering to the floor in all directions. Rico, unarmed, skipped forward, hands cocked in a karate posture. Another submachine gun spoke up, one with the devil's own cyclic rate, like an Ingram or a Mini-Uzi. Red-black dots stitched Rico's immaculate vest from right hip to left shoulder.

The Guardians were prone behind tables and chairs. Sloan's big shiny .357 Magnum Python that McKay hated so much joined McKay's and Rogers's plebeian .45's in axing the man who'd shot Rico. As he went down trailing tendrils of blood like a squid spraying ink another man burst in, crossed the room in a running dive, rolled, and vanished behind the stage from McKay. A man with a sawed-off shotgun vaulted the bar, while a third man fired around the corner from the entryway with something that looked for all the world like an ancient Schmeisser MP-40.

Rosa had vanished. The man behind the bar popped up, loosed two blasts. *Autoloader*, McKay thought. Return fire punched splinters from the bar where'd he'd appeared. The man popped up, fired twice more as the Schmeisser burped again, vanished. Prudently he'd shifted ground after firing the first time.

Hunkered down at this end of the bar, Dreadlock Callahan fired two shots from his Ruger Redhawk, lengthwise behind the bar. A scream and wild thumping and thrashing rewarded him.

"Hold it! Everybody, stay right where they are!" The man who'd thrown himself behind the stage had reappeared. He had Shiloh, the peroxide blonde who'd admired Casey, with her arm twisted up behind her back and the muzzle of a Smith and Wesson M-76 submachine gun cutting into the bare skin over her ribcage. Glimpsed through gunsmoke and darkness he looked to be shorter than she was, with receding hair and eyes that bugged out. Shiloh's eyes rolled like the eyes of a panicked horse.

"Guardians!" the man shouted hoarsely. "We know you're here. Drop your guns and come out or I'll kill her."

Silence. GeNeen was moaning somewhere behind McKay. The man kept ducking and bobbing down behind his hostage, spoiling his enemies' aim. "I mean it! I'll blow her apart, you fuckers, so help me I will!"

Shiloh was making funny strangled little birdy sounds. "If you kill her," Sam's voice called from the darkness, "just think what we'll do to you."

"You're bluffing! I'm counting to ten, and then I shoot. One—" A woman started to scream, the sound rising and falling like an air raid siren. "Two—three—"

Grimly McKay angled for a shot. The unyielding planks pressed hard against knee and elbows, cool on his belly. There was no way he or any of the Guardians were going to sacrifice themselves and their mission for some damn topless dancer. *Helluva waste, though . . .*

"Seven—eight—*nine*—"

An explosion shook the bar. The Schmeisser man flew right over the corner of the bar, the back of his blue work shirt shredded and dancing with tiny blue flames. He landed heavily on his back and stared at the ceiling with undivided interest.

The man holding Shiloh snapped his head around to stare in horrifed amazement at his dead comrade. Chivalrous to the end, Casey got the shot he'd been waiting for, and put two hundred and fifty grains of copper-jacketed lead into the man's right ear. His head came apart like a melon hit with an axe.

Into drifting smoke and sudden silence stepped a figure. A man, small, trimly built, but somehow giving the impression of great power. The first detail visible as he entered a pink spill of light from above the bar was a Close Assault Weapons System super-shotgun, smoke curling from the barrel, looking like nothing so much as a piccolo case with a pistol grip. Above it burned the ember of a cigarette. Another deliberate step and a face became visible in the dispirited glow.

Or half a face. A woman uttered a small yip of terror. The hideous apparition smiled.

"You boys have been hard as hell to track down," Major Crenna said. "But it's good to see you anyway."

CHAPTER
FIFTEEN ————————————

The gunsmoke had mostly settled out of the air, but there was an unpleasant odor of death in the deserted cantina that would take longer to go away. Tom had finished seeing to the several wounded. The dead were laid out in back of the building. They included two patrons, the bouncer Rico, and Silky, the black dancer in the flat Andalusian hat McKay had been admiring when the firing broke out. Also dead were all six of the attackers.

"Woulda liked to ask 'em a few questions," McKay grumbled, as the four Guardians sat down with their commander. They had the place to themselves. Rosa had been found behind the bar, bloody and dazed from a pistol-whipping but not damaged. She'd rapidly recovered enough to begin demanding who was going to pay for the damages, and what about poor GeNeen's leg? "Send the bill to President William Lowell, Heartland Complex, Iowa," Dreadlock Callahan had suggested helpfully. Crenna had a few quiet words with Lurch, the surviving bouncer, who had quickly hustled the owner out to her trailer in back.

"Not necessary," Crenna said, his gravelly voice uncon-

cerned. "You were fingered. That team—native talent, by the
way, not Expeditionary Force imports—followed you here. I
followed them." He lit a cigarette. How he'd followed the
killers—how he'd *known* to follow them—was liable to remain a mystery. Crenna had a habit of playing his cards close
to his chest. For a man like the Major, surrounding himself
with mystery was second nature. It had to be, if he wanted to
survive.

Sloan's square face showed an almost comical look of surprise. "Fingered? By whom?" McKay hid a grin. Sloan was
still an innocent in a lot of ways.

Crenna shrugged and lit a cigarette. "Don't know. Yet. But
the FSE had word you might be making a rendezvous in these
parts in the next few days. Actually, they're chasing your
shadows all over the continent; this is just one of the dogpacks
they've set on you. Since I know your personalities and
methods so well, I was in a much better position to evaluate
the conflicting data on where you'd actually be. So here I
am." He shook out the match, stuck it in the black plastic
Cerveza Cruz Blanca ashtray on the table. "And not a moment too soon."

McKay raised his brows. "Oh so?"

"So. We have to get into Heartland. At once."

"Like, why the rush, Major?" Casey asked. For a while
McKay had been afraid Tom would have to surgically remove
Shiloh from his neck. Dreadlock Callahan had finally been
detailed to escort her the hell somewhere else and calm her
nerves, an assignment he accepted with notable lack of reluctance. McKay's heart refused to bleed for Casey, somehow,
buddy or not. "They're not scheduled to execute Jeff
MacGregor for a month."

"Gentlemen, callous as it may appear, the liberation of
President Jeffrey MacGregor is not our highest priority in in-
filtrating Heartland Complex."

"What is, then?" Casey asked.

"Denying Chairman Maximov and the FSE the Blueprint
for Renewal."

"The sergeant?" giant Jamake said. He nodded down the
forested slope. "She down that trail. Went to the creek."

McKay nodded thanks, started into the trees, carrying his Maremont with a fresh half-moon box affixed, just in case. The deep bass voice stopped him. "Lieutenant." He turned back. "Good to see you."

He grinned and stuck a thumb up. "Yeah. Same."

Overhead Rocky Mountain jays gave each other rafts of shit among the branches of the pines, and a gray squirrel with tufted ears hurled abuse at McKay as he passed. McKay gave him the finger and continued on his way along the trail twisting down the mountainside. Up here it was pleasantly cool. The air had that pinewoods smell, fresh, filtered by millions of needles, and the mountains rose green and sharp and pretty all around. It was almost enough to make him reconsider his addiction to city life.

Almost. But he realized that something was missing. He fished in a breast pocket of his silver-gray coveralls for a cigar, lit up, and drew deep.

Ahead through interwoven branches he saw the green-brazen glimmer of water standing in a pool at the bottom of a little high valley tucked among the peaks. A stream, swollen by runoff from the epic snowpack in higher elevations, curled around a bare shoulder of granite to eddy into an appendix of calm, sort of hanging there to the edge of the current flow. Five meters of short grass separated the trees from the weeds poking up through the still water. Past the weeds he saw a figure sliding between surface and the placid mud of the bottom, a pallid glider, friction free.

The shape rose, broke water with a head of short hair slicked down like drowned plush. It shook, sputtered, opened eyes the color of that startling mountain sky. "Lieutenant," it said with that twangy Texas resonance. "It's so nice to see you."

He nodded. "Likewise, Sergeant."

"You-all just get in? Nice of you to look me up." He shrugged. Wasn't sure why he'd done it himself. Just seemed the thing to do. "But here, Ah'm forgettin' my manners."

The water swirled as she came forward, half wading, half swimming. Then the bottom rose, and she came up with it. Wearing nothing but pure mountain water.

McKay's cigar started to slide off the slope of his lower lip.

He rescued it just in time. "Uh, Miss—Ms.—Sergeant—" For the first time in his life the sight of a naked woman left him with absolutely nothing to say.

Master Sergeant Marla Eklund was quite a sight, all six feet of her, or at least the four feet or so he could see. Her breasts were big and full and set wide, the nipples looking off in different directions like pink eyes. Her belly was a frozen wave of subtly cushioned muscle, her waist narrow, hips flared and round, legs sculpted, smooth, strong-looking. Matted with water her pubic hair looked dark, but it was the same wet-gold shade as the close-cropped hair on her head. Given available evidence, McKay doubted she had feet webbed like a duck or anything. He wasn't even sure he cared at this point.

Thigh-deep and glistening, Eklund put her hands on her hips. "Don't you Yankees know the hostess sets the style for social occasions?"

"Whew," Billy McKay breathed as the aftershocks died gently away. They lay side by side in the short grass next to the pond, sweaty and wet and muddy and happy. Their clothes and weapons were stacked nearby, close to hand.

Marla grinned into his face from three inches away. "Enjoy yourself?"

"Well—" He made a show of looking thoughtful. She grabbed him under the short ribs and tickled him until he managed to pin her wrists together. It wasn't easy. She was slippery as an eel, and a whole lot stronger.

"I tell you what," he said, breathing heavily, once she was incapacitated. "I'm reminded of that old story about the Texan who went to Alaska."

She lay back, stretched, arching her back. Her nipples pointed toward the sun. "Tell me about it. But you make fun of Texas, Ah'll dunk your head."

"Well, this Texan was workin' the pipeline, and he wanted to be accepted as one of the gang. They told him he had to drink a quart of whiskey straight, screw an Eskimo woman, and shoot a Kodiak bear. They serve him the whiskey, see, and he knocks it back, quicker than anybody they ever seen.

"Well, right away they're impressed. This Texan, he swaggers out the door. And don't come back. They wait, and wait, until the sun goes down. Finally they decide he ain't got what it takes after all.

"This great big blizzard comes in. Just after midnight the door bangs open, and in comes the Texan in a big cloud of snow. He looks like shit. Both eyes are black, his face is all over blood, one of his ears is hangin' loose. His clothes are in shreds. He struts up for the bar and drinks another bottle of whiskey, neat. Then he wipes his mouth and says, 'Well now, that's out of the way. Now how 'bout showing me that there Eskimo broad you-all wanted me to shoot.' "

He guffawed. She fisted him in the side. The laughter died in a gasp. "That's *old*," she said. "Why, my momma told me that one while Ah was still teething."

"That may be, lady. But that's still what I feel like."

"You sayin' I got fur all over my body?"

"No, no. Shit, now, don't hit me again, it'll look bad if I come back into camp with more bruises than I got already."

"I cain't help myself. I'm just a warm-blooded country girl."

"That ain't all. How the hell did you get so strong, anyway?"

"Sweetheart, Ah was Texas state women's bodybuilding champion two years runnin'. Only reason I lost the title was I enlisted and couldn't compete no more."

"You're shittin' me."

She pulled herself up on one elbow and grinned down at him. He used to think that damned crewcut looked too boyish. Now he had completely satisfactory evidence that there wasn't anything even remotely boyish about Sergeant Eklund. "Ah am not." She raised her free arm, flexed. Giant biceps seemed to jump right out of her satiny skin.

"Jesus!" McKay exclaimed. "I thought them women bodybuilders all looked like Franco Columbo in drag. Like they had four tits, and that shit."

"No, dummy. Well, maybe in the old days. But now the judges like you to look all rounded and ladylike until you *hit* it. Lot more impressive that way, too."

Slowly McKay nodded, squinting up at the sun. So he hadn't been imagining things. He thought several times while they were going at it that he'd seen surflike surges of muscle he'd never observed in a lady he was putting it to before.

She tangled her fingers in the dense curly built on his gigantic chest. "Penny for your thoughts?"

"Cost you more'n that. Besides, where'd you carry a penny?"

She grabbed his dick, which hung half-deflated between his thighs. "Ah can stroke this here thing nice and gentle like," she said sweetly, "or Ah can give it a big ol' yank. Now, what was you thinkin' there, sweetie?"

"Jesus, where'd you learn to *act* like that?" McKay said, breaking into a sweat.

"My momma taught me."

"Who was your mother, Godzilla? No, shit, *stop* that, you'll pull it off." He looked at her reproachfully. "You acted like you liked it, a little while ago."

"Maybe I liked it so much I decided to keep it as a souvenir. Now, tell."

He sighed. This wasn't going the way he would have planned it, if he'd ever seriously thought he'd get it on with Sergeant Eklund. "I was just wondering why the hell you decided to, uh, come on to me."

"Come *on* to you? You dirty Yankee, I *seduced* you. Don't you got no appreciation for the finer points?"

"No. I just never thought you cared that much for me."

"You were wrong."

"Yeah. Well I thought it was Sam Sloan you went for, if anybody. He was always sweet-talkin' you, and you seemed to sidle up to him."

She laughed. It was enough to set the tree limbs shaking. "Sam's a sweet man. An' he does know how to talk to a lady real nice and pretty, which is more than Ah can say for some individuals. But he ain't my type. Too refined."

"So I'm crude?" he demanded, outraged.

"Bet your ass. Ah like a man with plenty of rough edges." Mongoose quick she got him by the ribs and started tickling again. This time he tickled back. They rolled from side to side, splashing into the verge of the pond, writhing back onto dry land, poking and prodding and laughing. It seemed perfectly natural for McKay to find himself with a double handful of ass cheeks that seemed to be molded of hard rubber over steel, and natural for him to work a couple of fingers down between those powerful thighs, start to probe her furry mound, feeling his prick go hard between their bellies.

Gunfire blatted from the woods. Three little geysers spurted up beside them in the water. With a single spasm of his enormous muscles McKay tossed a hundred and seventy pounds of Marla Eklund off him and into the middle of the pool.

More shots sought him. He jackknifed, slithered like a snake for the cover of a rock a meter around that bellied into the water. Something stung his back, his rump. Splashing mightily he launched himself like a sprinter off the mark, dived behind the rock and tried to make himself very small.

Another three-round burst screamed off the rounded rock. The tumbling slugs moaned disconsolately as they spun off into the woods on the other side of the stream.

"McKay!" It was Ballou's voice. "Might as well come on out. Make it easy on both of us."

"Why don't you come down here," McKay called back.

Harsh laughter. It seemed to be coming from a patch of scrub oak just inside the treeline. "Din't expect to get that bitch-slut Eklund so easy." Alarmed, McKay looked back over his shoulder. There was no sign of the sergeant.

"I'll give you ten seconds to step on out and get what's comin' to you. Otherwise I'll come down and put a bullet in your belly, let you feel that for a while."

"People are gonna hear those shots, cocksucker."

"Take 'em ten minutes to get here, too. You'll be long gone."

The tone was smug, infuriating. Rage built within McKay. He didn't think Eklund had been hit; no doubt she'd hit her head on a rock, filled her lungs with water in reflexive inhalation, and drowned. He was going to make Ballou pay. With interest.

"Listen, asshole," he shouted. "You know as well as me those little .223s got no stopping power. You'll put some into me when I come for you, probably hurt me so I won't survive. But just think what I'm gonna do to *you*, peckerwood."

His answer was an angry fusillade. Despite the white anger within him he grinned. *Goad him into a few more like that, you can take him on the magazine change.* He strained his ears for the telltale click of a magazine release despite the ringing in them from the muzzle blasts of the M-16.

"Got an idea, McKay."

"That's a surprise."

He could hear Ballou draw a ragged breath. "You ain't gonna goad me no more, McKay." *Shit*, McKay thought. "But I got a proposition for you. I'm a sportin' dude, myself. So I'm gonna give you a chance to grab your old M-60 and shoot back at me."

Warily McKay gauged the distance to his Maremont. Five, six meters. "How do I know you won't shoot me as soon as I poke my head out?"

A giggle. *He's around the bend.* "You don't," Ballou said. "But I swear I won't shoot till you lay hand on your piece. Scout's honor."

McKay breathed heavily several times. "All right," he hollered. He had nothing to lose. He hadn't been lying about the stopping power of the little 5.56 rounds. They'd tear shit out of him, he'd probably bleed to death in minutes—but they lacked the shocking power to keep him from getting his hands on the Maremont. Once he'd done that, no power on earth would save Ballou. After that, he didn't much care just now.

A violent thrashing erupted in the bush. *Christ, he's coming for me!* McKay shot from behind his rock as though spring-loaded. He pounced on the Maremont, grabbed it, rolled, came up with it held in both hands just as Ballou lurched out of the scrubby oaks toward him. Teeth bared in a snarl, he pulled back the trigger. *Held* it.

Even as the 7.62 shitstorm tore into him the lanky Southerner was collapsing. Belatedly McKay's brain registered the unnatural way Ballou's head had lolled on his neck when he appeared. He eased off the trigger.

"Jesus Christ you crazy sonuvabitch Yankee bastard what're you trying to do?" Marla Eklund screamed. Naked, wet, and furious, she stepped from the scrub. "I'da known you was gonna shoot my ass off Ah never woulda busted his neck!"

A week later and a thousand kilometers east, Dreadlock Callahan faced Major Crenna and the Guardians across a kitchen table in an abandoned farmhouse in the light and said, "Let me get this straight. The big priority *isn't* springing MacGregor?"

It was nighttime. The early summer heat still squatted on the farmhouse like a prehistoric beast. Outside bullfrogs trilled in the distance. Looking like a nightmare in the glow of a kerosene lamp, Crenna sat back in the straight-backed wooden chair. "When the FSE troops invaded Heartland, some of us managed to lock the computer files containing the data amassed to date concerning the Blueprint for Renewal. Unfortunately, such were the safeguards built into the system to prevent accidental erasure of the data, we weren't able to blank it. Our projections indicate it's likely that the FSE technicians are very near to cracking the protection—if they haven't already." Who *we* were wasn't too clear, even to the Guardians. Presumably Crenna had technical advisors tucked somewhere—or maybe he had a line into Heartland that he didn't want to admit to anyone, not even the Guardians. If Major Crenna had a religion, it was security.

"Our mission, therefore," Crenna went on, "is to break into Heartland and neutralize the computers with explosives. If possible, we will also liberate Jeff MacGregor and the fifteen to twenty Project Blueprint participants we judge are still in the complex."

"Something I don't understand," Callahan said. "How was the FSE able to grab Heartland so damn easily in the first place, if it's so impregnable?"

"The facility was designed as the personal redoubt of President Lowell. They had Lowell—apparently French-Canadian separatists in Quebec rescued him from the wreckage of his aircraft, nursed him, and sold him to Maximov's people. He had all the appropriate codes and recognition signals. They just walked in on us, gentlemen—Sergeant Eklund. We never had a chance."

Three of the Guardians were surprised; never before had any of them heard anything out of Crenna like the bitterness they were hearing now. Only McKay failed to notice. He was glowering at Eklund, who stood with her rump propped on the lip of the long-defunct sink. He hated to see her here so hard he could taste it.

"But why didn't you-all change the codes?" she asked now.

Crenna nodded. "Very perceptive, young lady," he rasped. "We should have. We would—if we'd been able to. But you fail to appreciate the depth of William Lowell's paranoia."

The room filled with attentive silence. "Heartland was to be his ultimate sanctuary in case of ultimate disaster," the scar-faced major said. "Unfortunately—from his standpoint—a facility of the scope of Heartland requires constant maintenance by a substantial staff. And for optimum effectiveness in the event of disaster, it should be kept fully staffed at all times." A writhing smile. "Bill Lowell was deathly afraid of being locked out of his own stronghold. There were conventional access codes those of us with appropriate clearance used to get in and out, and they were changed. Lowell's personal code was hardwired. Built into the system—it couldn't be changed."

"And you don't know what it was." Callahan laughed.

"So how do we break in?" asked the final person in the room, who stood behind Callahan. He was above average height, and wasn't carrying any excess weight. He wore an olive drab T-shirt, camouflage pants, a red scarf tied around his forehead. He had curly black hair, a mustache, and a Bren 10 millimeter pistol strapped to his hip.

"Excuse me, Major," McKay said. "You know I ain't used to questioning orders—"

"Bullshit," Crenna said softly.

McKay laughed. "Okay. But still, I got to ask—just what the hell are all these people *doing* here?"

"They're going with us, with the exception of Dreadlock Callahan. He's in charge of the outside diversionary force."

"All of them?" McKay swept narrowed eyes around the room. They kept coming back to Marla Eklund. He wasn't happy about the dude in the headband, who was one of Callahan's people who answered to the name of Pirate. He claimed Special Forces training; if ex-SF Major Crenna, who'd talked to him personally, accepted that, McKay would too. But Marla—

"That's right."

"You can't be serious, Major. Sergeant Eklund's hardly suited for this kind of operation."

He heard an angry intake of breath from Marla, ignored it. "On the contrary. Her record proves that she's tough, smart, and survival-prone. We've got a lot on our plate on this job; as it is we're going to have to take another of Sergeant Eklund's people in with us, I'm afraid."

"But, Major, I didn't think we worked on the 'warm bodies' principle," Casey said, concerned. "These people—they don't have the training we do."

"That's true. But in this case, we *do* need warm bodies. I'm primarily concerned with shepherding the prisoners to safety once we do liberate them; you'll remember from your counter-terrorist training how difficult newly freed hostages can be to handle. You—and I—will do the primary work in disabling security devices, gaining access to the facility, and dealing with hostile forces. We may not have the breathing space to act as nursemaids too."

"Speaking of security devices," Sam Sloan remarked dryly, "just how *are* we planning to get in?" As the electronics expert on the team, he would bear the brunt of finding and incapacitating sensors. There were certain to be many of them —hard to find, hard to get at, hard to take out.

Crenna grinned a death's-head grin. "Lowell had the place built," he said, "but I had a hand in building it."

"Know an easy way in?" Callahan asked.

A chuckle. "There are none. What I do know is a *possible* way in." He spread a piece of butcher paper on the tabletop and took a felt-tip pen from his pocket. "I'll show you."

CHAPTER
SIXTEEN ─────────────

Heartland Complex was secret only in a manner of speaking. You don't keep secret scooping a junior-grade mountain of rock and yellow soil out of the Iowa countryside, or filling it back up with tons of cement and sophisticated equipment and sodding it all over again. Not in an age of sophisticated spy satellites that could just about read the nametag at the back of a site foreman's collar—or in an open society such as America, in which the neighbors watched the proceedings and discussed them with interest. The Russians knew it was going in. So did anyone else who was even mildly interested.

The only thing to do was to fabricate a plausible cover story. With no little subtlety—"Wild Bill" Lowell was nowhere near the bumptious buffoon his opponents painted him, nor the lead-pencil-simple country boy portrayed by his own publicists —the President and his advisors cooked up several different explanations. A couple of layers down lay the tale that it was intended as an internment center for dissidents in case of war or some other national emergency. This lined up fairly well with the view Lowell's opponents held of his draconian outlook, and was universally accepted by those cynical enough to probe beneath innocent surface explanations. You don't keep digging after you hit a treasure chest.

Ostensibly, Heartland was intended as an agricultural research station. Why an agricultural lab needed to be underground, to say nothing of being surrounded by a ten-meter-thick layer of especially dense oil sealed between layers of stressed concrete, was something of a mystery. Of course, for a secret presidential redoubt it made perfect sense; the oil was present to dampen shocks from nearby nuclear blasts and had extremely fine fillings suspended in it to form in effect a giant Faraday cage to shield against the disruptive effects of electromagnetic pulse.

Official access to Heartland was through a discreet cluster of official-looking red brick buildings near the crest of the artificial hill beneath which it was buried, or through a pair of titanic concrete doors set into the hillside, overlooking a combination parking lot/helipad. There were several *sub rosa* entrances concealed in structures scattered at seeming random throughout the area. Major Crenna and his seven-person infiltration team would of course avoid all of these. They were constantly, heavily, and scrupulously guarded—and in the event of entry being forced into any of them, the adit connecting it to the underground complex could instantly be sealed by the simple expedient of a hundred-ton cement plug dropping from the ceiling.

Since sewage departed the premises via pipes too narrow for humans to negotiate, the only available *unofficial* access was through the ventilation system. The four great vertical shafts —two intake and two exhaust—and the myriad horizontal ducts that radiated from the ducts that pierced the hollow hill like round atria were an inevitable and obvious weakness in Heartland's armor: highways opening into the heart of the citadel. They were of course engineered, therefore, to be virtually impenetrable, and a number of sensors and other clever contrivances installed to ensure that any intruder was a) quickly detected and b) unpleasantly surprised. Combined with regular foot and vehicle patrols of the grounds, the ventilation system's static defenses seemed no more penetrable than the entrances.

Nor were they. The Guardians' dream of breaking in to liberate Jeff MacGregor had been just that: a dream. Cunning as they were, skillful as they were, courageous as they were, the four of them would have required a miracle to get inside.

The miracle was called Major Crenna. Byzantine subtlety came as naturally to the Major as breathing. He had been among the men who conceived the onion-layer cover story concept for the secret facility, as well as one of Heartland's designers. Just as William Lowell had anticipated the possibility his loyal servitors might try to lock him out of his bolthole, Crenna had conceived the eventuality *he* might someday want to break in.

In the early-morning darkness a few hours after the conference in the derelict farmhouse, the Guardians found themselves staring at what appeared to be a World War Two vintage pillbox, or perhaps a silo ten meters across that had sunk into the earth until only three meters of wall and a kind of cement witch's hat protruded above the earth, ghostly pale in the starlight. The constant white-noise hum of a huge fan was loud in the still night air. Even with the extra personnel —Eklund, Pirate, and stocky Podolski from India Three—the intruders had no trouble slipping in past the patrols.

They'd been equipped for this expedition by visits to several special caches scattered in the vicinity—or so they surmised; Crenna simply turned up with the stuff at the farmhouse. They were dressed like latter-day *ninja*, all in black, and their hands and hair and faces were smeared with black nonreflective paint, as if they were a pack of hopefuls auditioning for the Al Jolson role in a nostalgic remake of *The Jazz Singer*. Under the shirts each wore a lightweight Kevlar vest. At their belts rode gasmasks. Pushed up on their foreheads were infrared goggles, each with a tiny built-in IR flashlight like a third eye.

Most of the team carried the handy-dandy MP-5 SDX submachine guns in .45 ACP along with several magazines of special Teflon-coated ammunition designed to defeat personal body armor. This was the stuff that was banned all over the country almost as soon as it was invented, lest criminals foresightful enough to spring for the hundred and twenty bucks or so for a Kevlar undershirt be inconvenienced by fear of citizens' *still* being able to get at them as they plied their trade. The story was put around that the ban was meant to protect cops from criminals armed with the things—the very class of person best connected to buy them on the black market. It worked as well as most prohibitions.

Crenna, Sam Sloan, and Marla Eklund carried CAWS 12-gauges for social work once quiet was no longer an issue, after their inevitable discovery. Aside from their capacity to put a lot of fast-moving metal particles in the air on short notice, the super-shotguns could fire fat depleted-uranium slugs that did great things at punching through obstacles. Additionally, each person carried a sidearm, several flash-bang grenades, and a rucksack full of the sundry explosive and electronic gadgetry necessary to penetrate the fortress. That was another reason for the extra bodies: *somebody* had to hump all this stuff.

Pirate eyed the meter-and-a-half gap between the walls and the "hat," screened with grating invisible in the dark. "We gonna cut that?"

Crenna shook his head. "Wired in tight. Cut it, lights go on on a console a hundred meters below us, and we're out of luck." Like the biker he pitched his voice to a low murmur that carried less than a whisper.

"Bypass?" Sloan asked, sizing it up. "Could be done." He grinned as he spoke; *never thought this mother's son would be discussing breaking and entering as a skilled professional.*

"Tougher than you think. Also unnecessary."

"So how the hell do we get in?" McKay demanded.

"We cheat."

Crenna moved to the side of the foreshortened silo and began to dig with his hands. McKay shrugged and helped him. In a few moments they'd unearthed the ummistakable outline of an access panel.

"Oh, come *on*," Casey whispered, scandalized. "The designers had to know how easy it'd be to find something like that."

"This wasn't exactly in the blueprints, son. Not supposed to be any way to get in or out."

"How'd they clear out the birds' nests and such?" Eklund asked.

"Climb up the inside." Crenna slipped a small plastic card into a slit beside the hatch. A small panel popped open, revealing a keypad. He punched a combination, and the hatch in turn opened. "Not exactly easy to break in, even if somebody stumbled onto it."

He hit the transmit button on his pocket communicator, breaking squelch three times to let Dreadlock Callahan, lurking off in the darkness with the diversionary forces, know they were going in. The voice-activated mikes were turned off, and the miniature radios were tuned to the same wavelength the patrols used. They were sitting on a mountain of some of the fanciest communications and detection gear on the planet, so it didn't pay to take chances.

Once they were inside, the signal to Callahan to strike up the band would ride Heartland's own broadcast system, thanks to Sloan's wizardry. With the complex's metal skeleton and dense iron-filled amniosis surrounding them, it was the only way to radio out. There was no way at all for Callahan to reach them, so they just had to pray nothing went haywire on the outside.

"Everybody, rope up," Crenna said, "it's all downhill from here."

"Christ," McKay said, "I hope you're as lousy a prophet as you are a stand-up comedian. Sir."

The first obstacle was the huge-bladed fan that sucked stale air from the guts of Heartland and forced it up and out. Its armature contained an access hatch, this one perfectly legit; even the fittings in ultrasophisticated secret installations need maintenance. Since Heartland's occupants knew about this entrance, the codes had no doubt been changed since the take-over. That was why Sam Sloan was low man on the string. He lowered himself to the platform in which the fan was set and went to work.

Clinging to the metal rungs a few meters above him was Tom Rogers. Above him was Podolski; since he was judged most likely to fall, they put him as near the bottom as they dared. Next Crenna, then Eklund, then Pirate, and finally, waiting to clear up at the top, McKay. As the strongest member of the team, he had the comforting task of anchor—

supporting them all if *everybody* peeled. Everybody caught a breath and hung on to it. Even though the really nasty stuff didn't begin until after this first barrier.

Gingerly, Sam laid aside his little computerized safecracker. He subvocalized a brief prayer remembered from childhood, an embarrassed agnostic, and lifted the hatch cover.

Silence thundered in his ears.

He descended through the mantle of oil and down into the earth.

"They don't have motion sensors," Major Crenna had explained, back in the farmhouse. "Birds and bats can get in the damnedest places, and they can't always be sealing the complex for false alarms. They do have two kinds of sensors, though. Each rung of the maintenance ladder has a piezoelectric unit in it. Anybody putting weight on one will trigger off the alarms. This one isn't hard to cope with. The system's modularized. Every thirty meters we stop, lower Sam on a rope, and he shuts off the next circuit."

"Piece of cake," Sloan had said dryly.

"The other system's a bit trickier. Infrared beams crisscross the shaft at random intervals, shining on miniature photocells. Your goggles will permit you to see them. You must avoid them at all costs."

"What happens if you don't?" Pirate had asked.

"A microchip-controlled laser mounted on a swivel on the wall shoots you."

McKay had rubbed his chin. "Saw a movie like that, when I was a kid."

"The Andromeda Strain," Casey the science-fiction fan had supplied.

"This isn't quite like that," Crenna had said. "Laser technology's come a long way in the last twenty years. These lasers don't buzz. They crack like a gunshot—they ionize the air in their path."

"What happens if one hits you?" Eklund asked. McKay had winced. Dammit, this was why he didn't want her along— he didn't want the worry. He remembered the last time a lover had accompanied him against his better judgment into action. It had been not so very far from here, not quite a year ago. . . .

He had forced the unbidden pictures of Tanya Jenkins dying on the scuffed linoleum of the Luxor, Iowa schoolhouse away from behind his eyes.

"That's the other difference, Sergeant, in case you saw the movie too. They don't just burn a little neat hole in your cheek like a hot needle. They flash-boil the water in your tissues when they hit, causing a steam explosion. It's like getting hit with an explosive bullet. Also, tripping a beam will set off the alarms. So *don't do it.*"

"It looks like the inside of some kind of cathedral." The echoes of Sam Sloan's reverential whisper chased each other down the great shaft during a respite from the gruelling descent.

Resting on a handhold to which he'd gratefully secured the safety line, Billy McKay grunted. Cathedrals for him summoned up sensations of boredom and discomfort of the starched choirboy variety. For him the network of fine lines, white-glowing in the IR goggles, that filled the airshaft put him in mind of a web woven by a really big goddamn spider.

It had been woven pretty damn tightly, too. Too tight in some places for a human to pass by any conceivable contortion performed climbing down the ladder or dangling from the exotic high-test rope. They never would have made it this far, a hundred meters below the surface, if Sam hadn't had the inspiration of shining the miniature infrared flashlight set into his goggles like a miner's carbide lamp onto a photocell, keeping the circuit opened while his comrades scuttled through the beam. It was tedious work, unbelievably grinding. Everybody's blackout suit was drenched in sweat, and they weren't comforted by the blast of hot stale air driven up at them from the great driver fans far below. It felt as if they'd been at it for years.

"Looks like a wasp's nest, to me," Eklund commented. "All these little holes." The holes led into meter-and-a-half-high secondary exhaust ducts. These, unlike the central shaft, weren't boobytrapped. They had to be entered too often for maintenance. But their floors were thickly and randomly sown with pressure sensors.

"Where are we, anyway?" McKay asked.

Sloan swung the beam of his mask-lamp to a doorway set into the curving wall. "Iota, looks like. Mostly technical stuff, this level." Like the other Guardians he'd spent a lot of downtime exploring the fortress in between missions. A number of areas were marked off-limits, even to them. Instead of feeling offended, each man had regarded it as a personal challenge to defeat security measures and snoop and poop as he pleased. That kind of thing was second nature to them all; it was one reason they were Guardians.

Crenna, dangling from a rung like a small spider invading his larger cousin's den, flipped up the Velcro cover of his digital LED watch. "Better get going. Callahan's a pretty stable type, but some of the people he has to work with aren't." In the event of the Guardians' intrusion being discovered they'd radio word to their friends outside. Callahan and his mixed bag of bikers, India Three, and what SFers termed "indiges"—rhymed with "ridges," meaning locals— were to raise enough of a commotion outside to force the defenders to divide their attention. Rogers and Pirate nodded subconscience assent. Old cadremen themselves, they understood just how volatile indiges could be. They blew hot and cold—as a rule when the chips were down they either boogied or ran suddenly amok. Billy McKay was mostly grinning in haggard amusement at anyone characterizing Dreadlock Callahan as "stable," but he got the point.

He studied his teammates as they unclipped carabiners from rungs and got ready to move. The Guardians and Crenna of course were unfazed. Pirate was acting as if he'd done this every day of his life, which was natural if in fact he'd been Special Forces. Though her face was drawn, Marla Eklund was holding up as well as any of them, much as it chafed McKay to admit it; that he admired her as a woman made it somehow difficult to regard her as a soldier.

The weakest link, though, was Podolski, male chauvinism aside. McKay would have preferred Tall Bear, but somebody had to boss the rest of India Three while the sergeant was gone. Eklund had picked Ski as the steadiest alternate. Remembering the way he'd been afraid to stand up to Ballou over Polack jokes, McKay had his doubts. But the stocky little squaddie had a grim, almost pathetic, determination to make it. The way his lips were pressed together so tightly they disappeared and his mouth pooched out around and his eyes stood out from his round face, he looked like a dark-haired Mickey Rooney in the midst of a particularly trying bowel movement. But he hung in there.

"How much farther?" Eklund asked as Sloan probed cautiously down to disable the next level of piezoelectric sensors.

"Detention cells are mostly on Phi—twenty," Crenna answered. Back at the farmhouse he'd sketched the rough layout of Heartland for those unfamiliar with it, but if they had to split up—likely—at least one man who'd been inside would pair up with each who hadn't. "They may be keeping the scientists under guard on one of the dorm levels though."

"Computers?" Pirate asked.

"Sigma. They're buried that deep for protection against shock. We'll be splitting up there, going our separate ways."

"Got it," Sam Sloan called softly from below.

McKay looked to Podolski. "Ski? How's it goin'?"

Podolski gave him a manic grin and shaky thumbs-up. "Piece of cake."

McKay grimaced. The eerie descent began again.

In order to keep Heartland's appearance nice and innocuous, its various proprietors had never done anything so brazenly menacing as clearing fields of fire around the fence perimeter. In a stand of trees not twenty meters from the wire, a tense group of indiges clustered around an ancient 90-mm recoilless rifle, under the skeptical eye of Dreadlock Callahan.

To his judgment, which if not that of a military professional was at least that of a seasoned player in the post-holocaust Western Athletic Conference of hassling, they were a pretty sorry-looking lot: a dozen men and women armed with an assortment of long arms. The only uniform thing about them was the wildness of their eyes. That strange dude with the mask for the left side of his face had told him they all had some kind of score to settle with the FSE. Given what he'd seen of the way President Lowell's supporters behaved, that wasn't hard to believe. Callahan just wasn't sure it followed they'd be much use.

Oh well, what the hell, he thought. They weren't supposed to fight a pitched battle. They were just there to die noisily and draw some heat off the infiltration team. Callahan's bike was parked behind a wooded bluff behind him. When it hit the fan, he'd fade back there to lead his people riding around hollering and firing off guns and in general making a nuisance of themselves without, preferably, getting killed. What happened to this gang of looney-tunes wasn't of much concern.

From somewhere off in the leaden night came the creaking rolling clamor of an armored vehicle, rising above the sawing of field crickets. The group tensed around the recoilless. "They're coming!" hissed a woman with a shock of dark hair Callahan might have found foxy if weird emotions hadn't warped her face into such harpy lines.

Taking out a cigarillo, he patted the air with his free hand. "Take it easy. It's just the track on patrol."

"Track?" asked the gaunt-faced youth crouched like a troll beside the gun. He looked to be about college age.

Shit, don't these people know anything? "Armored personnel carrier, man. Just makin' the rounds."

A colorless tongue flickered over thin lips. "Animals," the young man hissed. "They're all animals."

"Shit," Callahan said. He scratched a match alight with a thumbnail and lit the cigarillo.

There were three recoilless guns, scrounged from God knew where, sited under cover in a roughly equilateral triangle about the complex's perimeter. Random patrol sweeps outside the wire would've spotted them in half a second, but it seemed the effsees couldn't be bothered; something Crenna had termed *fortress mentality*. The feeling that nobody could hurt them in their high-tech castle.

The other two guns were in the charge of that six-foot fox Eklund's troopies, who at least were liable to know how to shoot them. Not that there was much to it; this one was sitting pretty on its cute little tripod with a high explosive round wired into it. All these would-be liberation fighters had to do was close the contact and keep clear of the backblast and they'd make a pretty flash and nice loud noise. Aiming through the optical sight so they might actually *hit* something was optional. Of course, it hadn't escaped Callahan's notice that firing the beast would spotlight its location clear to Low Earth Orbit. If that happened he didn't intend to stick around. Survivor type, Crenna called him; he got *that* right.

Rattling like a drawerful of hardware being shaken vigorously, the APC rounded the shoulder of the artificial hill. An M-113, just like the one Callahan had ridden to the rescue in Colorado, with a bored-looking dude in a beret sitting up in the cupola, holding on to the M-2—more to keep the long barrel from swinging around and hitting him in the face, it looked to Callahan, than with any expectation he might ever use it. Foregoing his usual ostentation for the occasion, Callahan was decked out in dark like the others, black pants and army pullover. He cupped a palm over the ember of his cigar and just stood there watching, enjoying a little thrill of not-too-great danger.

When it had closed to two hundred meters, Young Joe College let out a bloodcurdling shriek: *"Die you fascist cocksucking swine!"*, grabbed the recoilless's pistol grip, jerked it toward the M-113, and fired. Flame bellowed from both ends of the tube.

Callahan took his cigarillo from his mouth. "So much for surprise," he remarked.

"I hit it! I hit it!" gibbered the kid, doing a sort of Indian war dance. Thin shrieks like a sheet flapping in a high wind came from the cottonwoods. Someone had disregarded dire warnings about standing behind the 90-mm, and gotten fricasseed in the backblast. Callahan watched with interest as flaming figures exploded out of the APC. It was really true; God *did* look out for fools. He had His work cut out for Him. Callahan did a quick fade back and around.

His crew waited with engines idling at a low growl. One of them jerked his chin at the yellow light glaring from the other side of the bluff. "What the fuck happened?"

"Some kid decided to play Sergeant Fury and his Howling Commandos with live ammo." He mounted his own bike. "Let's ride, Desperados."

"Ain't you gonna let the Guardians know the balloon's gone up?"

"Can't," Callahan said. There came the heavy-metal stutter of a .50-caliber. He smiled.

"Reckon they'll find out soon enough."

CHAPTER
SEVENTEEN ─────────────

From hundreds of ventilation ducts in all directions burst a strangled, labored whooping, like a gigantic baby trying to spit up. "Alarm," McKay said unnecessarily.

"Son of a bitch," said Major Crenna, who seldom swore.

"Some indige couldn't keep it in his pants," Pirate said sagely.

"Drive on," Crenna said. "They don't know we're inside yet."

They continued, the sirens burping hollowly at them. It wasn't loud, but something about it seemed to go right into their bones and vibrate. Podolski's eyes rolled like the eyes of a frightened horse. His hands shook on the steel rungs.

"Take it easy, Ski," Eklund said reassuringly from above him.

"We're almost there," Tom Rogers said.

They climbed down, past Nu to Xi. The toe of Podolski's boot slipped on a slick handhold. He kicked frantically to regain his purchase. Instead his sweaty fingers slipped.

"Catch me!" he screamed. "I'm going!"

Braced above him, Crenna said, "I have you, son." Below,

Tom and Sam tensed to take the shock of him hitting the end of his slack. He dropped level with Rogers, flailing wildly. Rogers took the jolt with his legs like a pro.

"You're okay," he said. "Relax."

Ski turned a camouflaged face toward him, an eerie black balloon, and reached out a spasmodically clutching hand. The motion changed the direction of his pendulum swing.

White light burst dazzling in the shaft. Thunder roared, almost drowning Podolski's scream. The back of his blackout suit exploded in a sheet of flame. His legs kicked so hard he turned momentarily upside down. Then he fell back again. And hung.

The others had their faces pressed against the cool concrete walls as if trying to melt into them. A penetrating stink of burned meat hovered in the air. "Ski?" Eklund choked.

"He's had it," Tom said. He was already scrambling back up to Nu, seemingly unaware of the literally dead weight he was hauling up with him. As he was slapping finger charges over the lockplate of the access hatch—no need for silence, now, and all the need in the world for raw speed—Sam was unstrapping a satchel charge slung to the bottom of his ruck.

"Fire in the hole," Tom called. He dropped beneath the hatch while Crenna held his place above it, his CAWS unslung and ready in one hand.

For a frozen moment Eklund stared at that pathetic spinning, smouldering body, her eyes wide with horror.

Knew it, McKay thought. *She can't hack it. She's freaked.*

At the last instant she hugged the smooth unyielding wall. The finger charges blew with a deafening crack. Crenna slid down and kicked in the hatch, covering with his shotgun. Apparently no one was on the other side. He slipped inside and Tom scrambled in beside him.

Eklung gave McKay a quick look. Then she too disappeared into the hatch.

While the other four covered the corridor in both directions McKay and Sloan hauled Podolski's body up to the lip of the hatchway. McKay anchored the corpse while Sloan hit the quick-release button on Podolski's chest. The cloth around the fist-sized hole blown in the dead man's back still smouldered, trailing an evil brown-blue smoke that smelled of burned meat. Sloan was obviously having trouble holding in the beans he'd forced down hours ago. He disentangled the ruck from limp arms, dropped it behind him, then cut the rope with an almost vicious pass of his combat knife.

Podolski went cartwheeling down. Lasers went off like machine gun fire as he tripped the IR beams. He was beyond reacting to the probing fingers of coherent light, but tissue exploding from hits made his corpse jerk in a hideously lifelike way as he fell. Gagging, Sam twisted the fuse-dial on his satchel charge to ten seconds, tripped the initiator, and chucked it in after him. The blocks of Composition C-4 would blow hell out of the giant fan at the bottom of the shaft, but the real intent was to spread confusion as to the location and intent of the intruders.

He turned. They were in a corridor that almost shouted normality, the soft subliminal flicker of fluorescents shining from panels in a dropped ceiling, doors lining either side, directions to the Nu Level Lounge embossed on a plastic sign a few meters from the gaping hatch. As the others had, he jerked down his goggles to hang from their elastic strap around his neck. Behind him the boom of the satchel charge going off floated up like a huge burp.

"Company," Tom Rogers said. "Mask up."

To the right a man in a tan uniform and red beret trotted around the corner of an intersection twenty meters away, carrying a Steyr AUG. Kneeling by the wall, Crenna shot him with his CAWS. The triple-ought Teflon-coated buckshot spun him clear around before it let him drop. If he had buddies, the shotgun's boom, terrifying in these confines, served the desired purpose: It kept their heads down until Tom could pitch a tear gas grenade into the intersection. It popped. White smoke blossomed. Choked curses and coughing broke out.

"Time to split up," Crenna said, voice muffled behind his gas mask. "Good luck. Watch for TV cameras, keep your communicators open, and don't stop for anything." He raced into the swirling CS cloud, followed by Sam, Tom, and Pirate. They were bound for the computer room on Sigma Level.

McKay led Casey and Eklund—Podolski had been his fourth—in the other direction. Their objective was the detention blocks where, with luck, MacGregor and the captive

Blueprint personnel were being housed. The awful crack of a flashbang going off around the corner to stun any bad guys who weren't busy enough weeping made them wince, and then they heard the booming of Crenna's and Sloan's shotguns on full-auto, and the hard rapping sound made by the two silenced SMGs.

McKay halted at the next intersection, looked both ways. Nothing. As he recalled, there were stairs to the right, not far away. On the theory that the nearest stairwell was the most likely to be jampacked with security forces, he led his team straight ahead, toward where the next nearest ought to be.

Most of Heartland's interior was laid out on a sensible grid plan, oblong blocks of offices, apartments, labs, and whatnot divided by spacious, well-lit corridors. That meant intruders could find their way around with a minimum of hassle, especially if they could read the signs conveniently posted at every intersection, pointing the direction of stairwells and non-sensitive locations like johns, gyms, and commissaries. On the other hand, the grid made it very easy to vector security teams onto any invaders. More to the point, people had to live and work here, so the layout couldn't be too confusing.

The first objective of the two teams was to put as much space as possible between themselves and the blown access hatch, the location of which was flashing red on monitors in every security squadroom in the complex. There were television cameras mounted at intervals in the neutral-painted corridors, but it was still going to take a live human being doing a visual check on the right camera at the right time to spot them—and since the area was very shortly going to be filled with armed men, there was a small but definite possibility that even if they were spotted they wouldn't be identified.

Unfortunately, their destinations were two of the most obvious targets for infiltrators. They were not going to be easy to reach.

After the brief massacre of half a dozen FSE troops Crenna's team made the stairwell without more encounters. Callahan's diversion was no doubt paying off; the men controlling the defense forces were so distracted watching the show outside their iron mountain they'd been slow to react when things began happening within.

But they didn't drive straight on down to Sigma. Instead they hurtled down three levels, Tom leading the way, suppressed H&K at the ready, and stopped. Rogers opened the steel door a hairsbreadth, peered out. An unarmed soldier in American uniform with FSE shoulderpatch stood talking to somebody who looked as if he ought to be guarding Darth Vader's private crapper in the Death Star: a man in navy blue uniform, battlejacket bulky over full Kevlar body armor, with a coalscuttle helmet equipped with polarized visor to prevent him being dazzled by clever little flash grenades of the very type the intruders were carrying—open at the moment. In gloved hands he held a short version of the Enfield Individual Weapon, the British bullpup battle rifle.

The stun grenade would have had the desired effect of stunning the pair, but it made too much noise. The men stood broadside to Rogers, so he had no shot at the security man's unarmored face. Onehanded, Tom aimed his SMG for the center of the blue-uniformed torso and fired a short burst. The Teflon slugs performed as advertised; the man went down. Rogers stepped into the open. The unarmed man faced him, mouth hanging like a door with a sprung closing mechanism. Rogers shot him through the forehead. There was no time for chivalry.

"It's clear," he said. The others followed him out, down a corridor to the left to a deserted lounge equipped with wall-sized TV/VCR, a few soft drink machines, and furniture that looked as if it had been salvaged from a dentist's waiting room. Sam tossed in what looked very much like a string of firecrackers, and they were off again for another set of stairs.

They *were* firecrackers. Loud ones. Thirty seconds after Crenna's team departed, what sounded like a very spirited firefight, complete with a couple of light-fixture rattling grenade booms, broke out on that level. Gleefully, armored security teams converged on the spot.

Skulking in a dark office, McKay, Marla, and Casey listened to booted feet pound heavily by outside. This made three times they'd heard bad guys coming and successfully ducked out of sight. On the way they'd scattered a couple of firelight-simulators themselves. Now they were just three levels above their destination, and things were starting to get hairy.

Cautiously McKay checked the passageway. Nothing. "Let's go." He shouldered out the door and turned in the same direction the boots had gone.

Following him out, Marla Eklund screamed. *"Look out!"*

He dropped and rolled. Another Death Star type had materialized in the corridor behind him and was holding down on him with an Enfield IW. Eklund fired first.

The round in her CAWS's chamber was a depleted uranium armor-piercer; they were loaded every third shell in the ten-shot magazines. It caught him under the wishbone. The metal inserts of his armor weren't enough to spark much of a ther-mochemical reaction in the three-quarters-inch-wide heavy metal slug. But then again a few kilos of carbon and calcium were pretty puny compared to the thick armor plating the DU projectile was meant to defeat. The guard's upper chest and shoulders just seemed to vanish in a spray of flame. The lower torso went one way, the head, still faceless in its helmet, the other.

Two more guards had boiled out at the back of the first. Casey and McKay opened fire simultaneously. One of them went down, the other popped back the way he'd come. McKay reached for his belt.

Marla Eklund still had her assault shotgun poised by one hip, but she was staring at the corpse of the man she'd shot. "Ah'll be damned," she breathed. "Ah never did nothin' like *that* before."

"Get back," McKay gritted. Eklund snapped out of her fascination, blasted two buckshot charges down the corridor to keep noses back, and ducked into the office. Casey followed as McKay lobbed a grenade.

It bounced off the far wall of the intersecting corridor and went ricocheting up among the unseen guards. McKay scrambled back into the office. Its walls shook an instant later to the report of a grenade.

"That wasn't a stun bomb," Casey said, eyes wide.

"Nope. Willy Peter." Screams rang. "You don't think I put all my faith in them cherry bombs, do you?"

Sigma level swarmed with armored guards. Attack on the computer room was sheer suicide. So Crenna's team didn't attack—on Sigma.

On Rho Level one of Heartland's many data-processing centers occupied the block directly above the computer room. It wasn't precisely a pushover. Sentries stood at all four intersections surrounding the processing center, with two more at both of the entrances. Security control for this level wasn't taking any chances. It thought.

A short block away the four men in black gathered behind the intersection. Tom Rogers hunkered with his MP-5, Pirate stood next to him. At Crenna's count they both swung around and fired a single shot, Tom for the far guard, Callahan's man for the near. Even as both dropped, shot neatly through the head, Sloan was running for the intersection with a primed stun bomb in hand. He threw the flashbang down the long side, waited for it to go off, pivoted around the corner firing. The two guards at the entrance halfway down never had a chance. It was coldblooded murder, but somehow Sam felt no more than a microsecond's twinge of guilt.

. The intersection guard at the far end of the data-processing block hadn't been watching the grenade when it went off. He fired a long burst in Sam's direction from his M-16. Sloan ducked back with plaster dust stinging his cheeks.

He fired a return burst to no effect. Crenna arrived and threw another stun grenade. This time the guard was caught flatfooted. Sloan shot him and they all ran for the door.

Inside perhaps a dozen male and female technicians huddled behind smooth-contoured consoles of dove-colored nonglare plastic. Crenna chased them toward the far exit while Sam and Pirate crouched behind consoles and covered him. Tom had his rucksack off and was rooting purposefully through it.

The two remaining door guards were trying to breast the brief tide of panicked techs streaming out of the center. One of them finally poked his head around, collected a bullet in the left eye. His buddy ducked back. The door closed. Crenna flowed across the floor and locked it.

Entrances secured for the moment, Crenna, Sloan, and Pirate took up watchful positions around the perimeter of the room. Since Heartland had been built as a bomb shelter among other things, the floors tended to be of very solid construction. You couldn't hope to bust through them with any regular demo charge that wasn't big enough to flatten nonload bearing walls for a hundred meters in every horizontal direction.

The thing Tom Rogers set with loving care in the center of the carpeted floor was no ordinary demo charge. It looked like nothing so much as a giant inverted black flower pot of maybe four kilos capacity set on a tripod that telescoped to a meter's height: a shaped charge, designed to focus its destructive force on a single point.

For security reasons the doors to the data center were steel, very sturdy. Muffled voices shouted at one another outside, and something metal and heavy pounded against the one they'd entered through, but it would take a while before they could be broken down. Sam took a turn of line around a work station and tied it off with an aplomb only a formal naval cadet could muster as Tom finished wiring an electric handdetonator to his infernal device. They all hid behind things.

Tom flipped up the detonator's protective cover. "Get ready. Five—four—three—two—one—"

A volcano erupted right there in the middle of the data processing center.

McKay, Casey, and Eklund ran into a six-man squad in American uniforms coming up the stairs two floors above Phi, where the cells lay. They bowled four of them over; the other two ducked out the door of the landing below. Moving gingerly to avoid turning his ankle on one of the steel twelve-gauge casings littering the landing, Casey went to the railing and peeked down.

Fast as he was he barely had time to yank his head back before a shot cracked straight up. "Guys in armor down where we want to go, man," he explained.

"Shall we rush 'em?" Eklund asked eagerly.

"Jesus, lady, hold your horses," McKay whispered. He reached into his pack. "They're waiting for us. This is gonna take *science*."

His was a simple strategy, planned for in advance and predicated on the extreme sturdiness of Heartland's construction. Casey Wilson chucked a stun grenade out the door of the landing they were on, looked out to see asses and elbows departing toward both ends of the corridor. Then Billy McKay yanked the cord on two fused blocks of C-4 held together with black electrician's tape, made a long arm, and dropped them into the upturned faces of the security men waiting on the Phi landing. Then he and his companions stepped out the door, closed it, and waited for the very loud noise.

For a long moment it didn't come. "I am going to look like a prick if that thing's a dud," McKay announced.

Eklund snickered. "Naw. You'd have to shave your head all the way before—"

The floor lurched beneath their feet. A huge fist buckled the steel door, slightly but unmistakably. "Science," McKay said with satisfaction.

Sure enough, the stairwell down on Phi was intact. But the security squad that had been clumped on the landing wasn't. The door to the corridor was blown out. They went through it at the run. Two more guards in black were staggering around the hall, stunned despite their fancy helmets with the armored visors. Casey and McKay killed them both.

A short way away a locked security booth with firing port and armor-glass front kept watch over the sliding steel grate that sealed the detention corridor. Casey slapped a sticky-fingers charge onto the door and blew it. McKay tossed in a flashbang, and they went in to take custody of two very stunned guards.

McKay pushed them against the wall. "Open up the cell block," he told the little skinny one with blood streaming from one prominent ear.

"Fuck you," the guard said. McKay shot him.

He turned to the tall middle-aged one whose belly had begun to lop over his belt buckle. "Open the cell block."

"Yes, *sir*."

Leaving Casey to keep an eye on things, McKay and Eklund went in past the opened grating.

And a baldheaded officer type in shirtsleeves stepped out of a squadroom to one side and shot Marla in the belly with his sidearm.

CHAPTER
EIGHTEEN ─────────────

Flashback: *Tanya Jenkins screaming, thrashing, mindless with the pain of pulped guts.* "*You son of a bitch!*" McKay roared, turning to the officer to crush him with his massive hands.

Leaning against the wall, Eklund raised her CAWS and shot the officer. At this range the buckshot charge didn't disperse at all to speak of. It just punched a huge hole right through to the middle of the man.

McKay was at her side. "Marla—"

She grinned at him. It was a puny grin, but a grin nonetheless. "Din't . . . penetrate," she gasped. "Who-ee. Feel like I been kicked by a mule."

Briefly he squeezed her arm. "Let's get to work."

Jeffrey MacGregor sat on his fold-down bed reading an article on cormorants in a two-year-old *National Geographic*. A few minutes before, he'd felt the floor shake, heard a distant rumble like midsummer thunder. Since he'd long since given up any such adolescent daydreams of hoping to be rescued, he just shrugged and gone back to reading.

He was dressed in a green and black soccer shirt, blue jeans, and Adidas. His captors had had to dig up new clothes for him; his time in the box had melted kilos from a frame that hadn't been carrying much excess to begin with. He'd got some weight back since he'd been returned to this apartment-like cell—if indeed it was the same one. He honestly didn't know.

It didn't matter. Hardly anything mattered any more. He got up whenever, went through a vigorous session of calisthenics because it was harder not to, ate whatever materialized in the dumbwaiter, which was usually decent if unimaginative, and settled in to wait until he was drowsy enough for sleep. His esteemed hosts had even taken to supplying him with reading material, though it wasn't much more distinguished than the cuisine. But he didn't care. Not really.

His death sentence wasn't the cause of the dull haze of apathy that lay like fog on his brain. It was his complete and total powerlessness. Somehow his liberation from the crawling discomfort of the box had only pointed up how helpless he was, how totally at the disposal of others. He had failed; his country was being raped by plunderers from across the sea, and there wasn't a thing he could do.

The door opened. Incuriously he looked up. What he saw was unusual enough to blow some of the mist away: what appeared to be a young woman made up for a minstrel show, taller than he was and dressed all in black. Carrying a large, peculiar-looking gun.

For a moment she stared at him, seemingly as astonished as he was. "Mr. President," she said in a Texas accent that couldn't possibly be real, "Ah've come to take you out of here."

A figure materialized in the doorway behind her, huge enough to make her seem normal-sized. A figure MacGregor had never expected to see again.

"For Christ's sake, Jeff, will you get off your ass?" Billy McKay said. "We got to get going."

"Major, we've got them," McKay said into his communicator. "I say again, we have the goods." He stood keeping watch at one end of the cellblock. Amazingly, the navy blue boys weren't swarming down the stairs—yet. Looked as if no one on duty down here had had time or presence of mind to call for help, so hard and fast were they hit. Of course, McKay had no doubt that would change real quick if anyone happened to be eavesdropping with some good unscrambler software to hand, which was unfortunately quite likely. This was Heartland, after all.

Casey and Eklund were popping people from their cells, herding them like sheepdogs, calmly but insistently. Eklund caught his eye and grinned; he grinned back. She was a hell of a good troop. Moon-faced Marguerite Connoly, Angie's Neo-Keynesian economist mom, was helping an old man teeter out. It looked as if he'd been beaten up in the not-too-distant past. Dr. Connoly handled him with the brisk maternal efficiency of a head nurse. Down at the other end of the block, pulling guard with an AUG, was Jeff MacGregor, looking like an apprentice to the Four Horsemen. He seemed to really want to *use* the funny-looking rifle.

"Your objective secured?" McKay asked.

"Negative."

One word, so simple that it took heartbeats to sink in. When it did, he wouldn't accept it. "Say again?"

"Negative. We didn't get through. Charge didn't penetrate." He sounded a million years old.

McKay wasn't given a whole lot to Existential ruminations, but right now it seemed as if the entire universe was turning inside out. Crenna, Tom, and Sam—*failed?* "Need assistance?" he asked. It was going to be hell for the holidays getting out of here with any of these people alive, but canceling the FSE's deathgrip on the Blueprint held absolute priority.

"Negative to that, McKay. They'd got it sewn up tight. We'd never get in alive." Not *out;* that wasn't an issue. But Crenna said that not even he and his elite team could make it in to blow up the computers, and that meant no one could.

Failure settled in on McKay's shoulders like a uranium raincoat. The very idea that the Major could fall short of an objective twisted his mind out of shape. He knew that was silly. Crenna was human too. But Crenna was such a total master, total professional, totally in control of every situation McKay had ever seen him in. Somehow McKay always figured failure was something the Major had outgrown, like masturbation.

Gunfire popped from the other end of the corridor. Someone screamed. McKay hardly noticed. "I'm sending Tom,
Sam, and Pirate down to help you break out. I'm going to
complete the mission."

"Say again? Thought the computer room was a no-go."

"Affirmative. This is an alternate objective." A pause that
somehow spoke of weariness and self-disgust. "I should have
done this earlier. But I thought there was another way. I was
wrong."

"Get the President out, McKay. Get as many people out as
you can—especially yourselves. America needs you now,
worse than ever. The going should get easier for you in a few
minutes. Crenna out."

"But Major, wait! I'll come with you—"

"Negative, McKay. That's an order. It's a personal request
too—I know how you handle orders. This is up to me, son.
Got that?"

"Yes," he said sullenly.

"Good. Good luck, McKay. Give my regards to the rest.
Crenna *out*."

McKay stood staring at the little pocket communicator
resting in the palm of his hand. He felt as if God had just
called him to say He was retiring and the shop could mind
itself from here on in.

Several minutes later Casey's communicator spoke up.
"Case, this is Sam. We're coming down Stairway Nineteen.
Don't shoot." The three came down behind a squad of guards
trading shots down a corridor with Eklund and a middle-aged
man the two Guardians remembered collecting in western Ten-
nessee. A quick vicious crossfire settled the issue. "Where's
Billy?" Tom asked as they joined up.

"Said he was going ahead to help clear the way," Casey
said. One of their possible escape plans was to have somebody
infiltrate through whatever security forces were closing in on
the detention level and do what he could to divert and weaken
them so the escapees could win through to the garages behind
the big doors. Risky, with little chance of success—like everything they'd done so far.

"I hope he'll be all right," Jeff MacGregor said.

"Of course he will," Eklund said serenely.

For McKay, who'd grown up playing hide-and-seek in the streets of Pittsburgh, it was child's play. There were all these offices and storerooms to hide in, and a lot of security forces tromping around with their big feet, advertising their approach. McKay didn't screw around with heroics. He hid if he could, shot if he had to. Twice he bumped into groups, one the armored security, one a bunch of squaddies in American OD. In both cases he simply dropped a CS grenade and ran like a motherfucker. Six-to-one firefights weren't going to get his mission accomplished.

He did what he could to draw heat off his buddies—and Crenna, wherever he was and whatever he was doing. He zigzagged along the corridors and up the stairwells, sowing the noisemakers, occasionally letting himself be seen. The bozos in Security Central hadn't thought to freeze the elevators; he sent a satchel charge riding up to Delta Level, timed to explode shortly after arrival, as near he could judge from his own myriad trips in these elevators. Anything to keep the fuckers guessing.

But his primary purpose wasn't diversionary. He had a mission of his own now. Something that had been growing in him since the first awful millisecond of the ambush in Texas, since the first gut-twisting certainty of betrayal. A drive compounded of rage and outrage and sense of duty, stronger than hunger, stronger than sex, stronger than the imperative for self-preservation: a *mission*.

He popped up on Theta, where their old quarters were, and found his own. No one seemed to be living here; plenty of room in Heartland. He barely spared the little apartment a quick glance around. It had no more hold on him than a cheap hotel room, and since the cases of Coors beer the Freeholders had given him after the Coffin thing were history he had no personal effects. Instead he quickly turned on the computer, accessed the complex's database, keyed in a request to write all files pertaining to Project Blueprint to this terminal, with hard copy. When he hit return the cursor didn't bounce to the next line as it should; it just sat at line's end blinking at him like an eye with a tic. He grinned. No matter what else was going down, someone would notice what he'd just done; the system was programmed to make sure people noted unauthorized data-access requests, and he bet the effsees had set all kinds of flags on keyword *Blueprint*.

He made a quick stop two doors down and left Theta Level without looking back.

Hanging out in a convenient utility closet, McKay held the door open a hairline and watched a squad of armored security grunts thunder past. Wonderful things, utility closets. For the aspiring infiltrator, in fact, there was no greater boon than the need for sanitation and maintenance. Somebody had to sweep the floors and change the light fixtures, and you couldn't run the janitor through an entire strip search every time he wanted to check out a mop. In Heartland they didn't even lock the doors to the closets, a common oversight. Who the hell was going to steal Lysol from a top-drawer classified base?

His second and last Willy Peter grenade pitched into an unoccupied bedroom a good many corridors away was drawing a satisfactory amount of attention away from the place McKay was headed, acting on a wild-hair intuition. When the squad was gone he waited a few seconds to make sure there were no stragglers, slipped out, and went back the way they'd come.

This was one of those restricted zones where he'd played an adult version of hide-and-seek with Heartland security in the good old days. He knew how to get where he was going, though he shouldn't have. He moved quickly but quietly on rubber soles, every nerve end cranked up to maximum receptivity. He wasn't naive enough to think he'd sucked away all security from his destination.

Right and behind him a door popped open. He spun, MP-5 ready. Anyone with reflexes less superb would have simply fired as he turned. McKay trusted his abilities enought to wait to make sure of his target.

And so avoided blowing away this teenaged blond girl dressed in a filthy once-white men's shirt, skinny and shit-scared. She recoiled away from the sight of his brutal, black-painted face. He grabbed her wrist before she could jump back into the room. "Who the hell are you?"

"You're not one of them." It was a statement, delivered in a voice balanced like a tightrope walker crossing a pit of boiling lava on a strand of dental floss. She quit trying to pull away.

"Hell, no." He didn't know who "they" were, but he had a shrewd guess.

Tears bubbled from puffy discolored eyesockets. She didn't sob. McKay realized the girl had been knocked around pretty badly. Her lids were so swollen he couldn't tell if her eyes were green or blue, and where the unbuttoned shirt hung negligently open he saw what looked grimly reminiscent of a cigarette burn on the modest swell of one breast. She didn't sob. "So I'm not in trouble," she said in that voice of awful calm.

"Trouble?" This was too weird. "What're you talking about?"

He'd released her arm. Now she caught his wrist and tugged. Something told him to follow. "I couldn't stand it," she explained, reasonably. "I couldn't take him hurting me anymore."

They were walking up the short foyer of what seemed to be a pretty opulent suite. The living room was tastefully appointed in Frankish Modern or Louis XXV or whatever it was rooms were tastefully appointed in; not even Guardians training covered interior decorating. McKay looked around cautiously, MP-5 held out before him like a bug's feeler. "They called on the intercom. He started yelling, it was terrible. Something real bad was happening."

She guided him toward a door to the left, half-open. He put a palm on its immaculately white-painted surface, gently pushed. "He always hurt me when he got bad news, like. And I couldn't take it. And there was this chair over past the night stand, and I got up real quiet, and I picked it up, and I hit him. I hit him." Disbelieving: "I *hit* him, you know? *You know?*"

Billy McKay gazed down on W. Soames Summerill, dba Trajan, post-war head of the Central Intelligence Agency by right of treachery and force, ace operative for Yevgeny Maximov and the FSE, lying there on his side by the wall, buck naked. Every detail of that aquiline countenance had been forever burned into his brain during the nightmare hours of torture by the Brothers of Mercy in the Denver Federal Center: every sculpted contour, every discreet aristocratic pore. It was a good thing. Summerill's head looked as if it had been trampled by an elephant. Repeatedly.

"You won't hurt me will you? You won't punish me?" The voice was now like that of a four-year-old, contrite, confessional.

"*Punish* you? Shit. Wha'd you say your name was?"

"Sally."

"Great. I'll get you a fucking medal, Sally—but first we gotta get out of here alive."

It was another suite, even lusher than the first. Somehow he wouldn't have expected that. But his quarry had already surprised him in more fundamental ways.

Sally was stashed in another handy utility closet, ordered neither to stir nor make noise under pain of pain. McKay stole silently down the abbreviated hallway, coat closet to his right.

A thin young man with thinning hair and an American lieutenant's uniform came around the corner. "Just a moment, sir, I'll get your—" He stopped and stared at McKay. His mouth gaped. His eyes were stretched wide in bovine fear. McKay shot him.

As the body slumped McKay went past in a tiger bound. The living room's only occupant straightened from where he was messing with the suitcase on the couch and turned with majestic deliberation. "Lieutenant McKay," President William Lowell said. "I was expecting you."

McKay's throat was dry. "Goin' somewhere, sir?"

The massive shoulders shrugged. "Making preparations. I always believe in being prepared for the worst." A smile, rugged, masculine, but somehow roguish—polished by the caress of half a billion TV cameras. "As the existence of this facility amply proves."

He stood regarding McKay as calmly as if he were some junior White House staffer he'd called on the carpet. Under the pressure of that gray-hazel gaze McKay quailed. This man was *authority*. Embodiment, at one time, of the nation McKay loved more than his life. A man whose life he had once sworn to protect at any cost.

"You don't seem to've experienced much difficulty getting past my guards."

McKay's turn to shrug. "I been trained, sir."

A nod of an old lion's head. "Yes. You've been trained. Well trained. America needs people like you, Lieutenant."

McKay said nothing. His eyes kept hitting Lowell's gaze and bouncing off. Lowell held out a hand, eroded, age-spotted, but in the bones and sinews that stood out in stark relief there seemed to be strength to powder rock. "Join us, Lieutenant. It's not too late. We'll rebuild America. You and I and our allies from across the sea."

Something snapped. McKay raised his head. His eyes were like bluewhite pits. "Allies? They're invaders. I don't sell my country to foreigners, Mr. President."

The hand faltered. "Don't take that tone with me, Lieutenant. I did what was necessary to recover my rightful position. Don't you see, son? MacGregor was letting things fall to pieces. I did what I had to do to get a strong hand back at the helm."

"Yeah," McKay said in a voice like armor plate. "Maximov's hand. You sold out, sir. You're a traitor."

Lowell blanched. The heavy face was blotched with age and anger, and something else. McKay thought maybe it was corruption. "You idiot. You can't win. I know you and that renegade Major tried to blow up our computers. You failed. You will fail. Give it up, Lieutenant. Give up before it's too late." He started on a whining note, but toward the end the voice tolled with its old accustomed thunder.

"Sorry, sir," Billy McKay said. "It's already too late."

With a single fluid motion he brought the submachine gun to his shoulder and fired once. Amazed eyes stared at him from beneath the blue-black hole in the center of the great cliff of forehead. McKay had seen in countless movies and comic books where the bad guy, struck down, had turned out to be some kind of ancient evil sorcerer who immediately decayed to dust. What happend now was like that. Bill Lowell, that huge powerful presence, seemed to dwindle, collapse in on himself, till what remained sprawled on the floor seemed no more than a dwarf.

McKay was just dragging Sally out of the closet where she'd been huddled and letting the sobs she'd held back earlier loose with a vengeance when a new set of sirens kicked in. This was a sort of rising-falling wail that cut through the klaxons that McKay no longer even heard like a *samurai* sword. "*Now* what the fuck?" he asked the air.

It answered in a voice borrowed from God for the occasion: "ATTENTION ALL PERSONNEL. TERMINATION SEQUENCE COMMENCED. THIS COMPLEX WILL BE DEMOLISHED IN TEN MINUTES."

CHAPTER
NINETEEN ────────────────

"Major!" McKay bellowed over his communicator. "What the hell's going on? Major?"

"I'm here, McKay," the voice said in his ear. "No need to yell."

"What's the matter? Your voice sounds funny."

"I've been hit. Nothing serious."

"Bullshit. Give me your location. I'm coming for you."

"Negative. I've locked myself in. It's a special, secret little room even Lowell didn't know about." A chuckle like a handful of gravel dropped on a tin roof. "They know about it now. Must be an entire company of security trying to batter down the door. Not that it matters if they succeed."

"Tom, Sam, do you read? See if you can triangulate the signal."

"Never mind, McKay. You'd never reach me in time. You've got to get clear. You and the others. The future . . . you're the future." He was fading.

"Major, Major, you've got to get out!"

"No. Not even I'm about to get out of this one. The mantle's passing to your shoulders, McKay. Thank God they're broader than mine."

"*Major—*"

"Shut up and soldier, soldier. Casey, Tom, Sam?"

"Yeah."

"Major."

"Yo."

"It's been a pleasure serving with you men. You've made me proud. Crenna out."

McKay hit the squelch button savagely twice, but there was no response. "EIGHT MINUTES!" boomed the public address system.

Hesitantly Sally reached up and touched his cheek. Her fingertips came away moist, beaded with droplets in which swam flecks of black face paint. "You—you're crying!"

"Bullshit," McKay husked. "Come on. Or I'll leave you here."

A bullet from up the stairs had just caught Pirate in the side when the ten-minute warning started rattling the walls. The boys in the helmets and the armored battle dress just evaporated off the landing above. Tom moved to Pirate's side.

"I'm okay." The biker paused in pounding at the cocking handle of his H&K, which had suffered a stoppage, and waved him off. "Let's just go."

They'd gone. Now they were all clustered near a door that opened onto the great echoing cavern of the Mu Level garage. "I don't believe it," Sam Sloan breathed. "I wish things always worked out this well."

Trucks and jeeps and FAVs were parked in neat ranks. The personnel of Heartland Complex were swarming over them like soldier ants, and the immense clamshell doors were groaning open onto starry darkness and the intermittent flashes of shooting off among the hills. But that wasn't what Sloan couldn't believe.

What he couldn't believe was the Cadillac Gage V-450 Super Commando, twin to the late lamented Mobile One, parked off to one side in its own little yellow spill of quartz-halogen light as if it were waiting just for them. They'd known, or guessed, there were other similar vehicles stored in Heartland in case something happened to their car. But this one was obviously prepped, freshly checked-out and ready to roll, like a new car parked out in front of the showroom window with keys inside.

"The good Lord's providin'," Eklund said.

Sloan gave her a skeptical eye, and not just because he was an agnostic. He had a bad feeling about this. It was saving their bacon now, but the presence of that car tickled his brain with ominous implications he couldn't quite delineate.

"TWO MINUTES TO TERMINATION."

"Maybe we should skip the metaphysics," Dr. Connoly suggested, "and just take advantage of Providence."

They moved out, Guardians and Eklund fanning out into a sort of flying wedge. Instantly they began taking fire. A noted systems-analysis expert gave a cry and stumbled, blood starting to seep into the front of his white shirt. Jeff MacGregor grabbed him around the shoulders and helped him along, firing his Steyr one-handed as he ran.

A machine gun chattered at them from between two trucks to the right. Pirate hurled a concussion grenade, sprayed fire from the M-16 he'd liberated to replace his jammed MP-5. The MG stopped. Limping a little, Pirate ran on.

They were halfway to the V-450, strung out in the open, when a helmetless security officer sprinted from between two trucks to the armored car, which stood angled off to their left. Shots flurried like sleet, but the man was already behind the angular snout hauling open the side hatch. "Oh, holy shit," Sam Sloan said. Once the man got behind the awesome M-2/M-19 combo in the turret, they were dead. He put on a burst of speed as the man vanished inside the car, knowing it was hopeless.

The blue-clad man reappeared, seeming to melt back out of the hatch and slump to the cement. Billy McKay appeared from between the two trucks, his MP-5 in one hand and a little blond girl's wrist in the other. "Jesus, Sloan, you're the runner. Can't you do better than that?"

Sloan reached the car and put a hand on its sloped bow to support himself. "I'm a marathon man, not a sprinter," he puffed. "God, it's good to see you."

"Yeah." A bullet spanged off the 450's hull. "But let's save the glad reunion for later. Casey, Tom—get MacGregor in the car and go. Sam, Sergeant, help me get these people in the trucks."

Sally hung back, staring around wildly. "You go off on a mission and look what you come back with!" Casey shouted in McKay's face. "You can't yell at me anymore."

For the first time since McKay'd known him the kid sounded outraged, genuinely aggrieved. Stress hits people in funny ways. "Jesus," McKay said. "Quit lookin' at me like that, Eklund. I rescued the goddamn girl—she rescued herself —shit, I didn't go *lookin'* for her."

"ONE MINUTE."

The one-man turret suddenly traversed left and fired a shuddering burst of .50-caliber toward a knot of men firing at them from the cover of a bunch of trucks parked seventy meters away. Tom Rogers was back on the job. Casey started to climb in after him as people started piling into two trucks.

"Case," McKay said. The former fighter jock looked back. McKay took something out of his blackout shirt and tossed it to him. Puzzled, Casey unfolded the crumpled object. A look like Christmas morning spread across his face.

"My cap! My *Born to Run* Bruce Springsteen cap." He sounded as if he were about to cry.

"It was in your fucking room. All the time."

Casey jammed the cap on his head and bounced into the car. A minute later its diesels growled awake—a well-remembered sound. The sound of . . . home.

Jeff MacGregor helped Sally into the car and shut the hatch. McKay was already in one of the trucks. "They left the keys. Considerate of the pukes."

The far door opened and Eklund slid in beside him. She leaned over, kissed him quickly on the cheek. "You shittin' me about that girl," she said sweetly, "and Ah'll break your arm, Yankee."

"It's nice to have friends."

"THIRTY SECONDS TO DETONATION."

Sam boosted Dr. Connoly over the tailgate with an apologetic hand on the rump and raced around to jump in the driver's seat. Pirate rode shotgun, M-16 poked out the window. Sloan keyed his communicator to OPEN mode. "Casey, Billy, we're ready to go."

The Super Commando roared ahead. An FAV spurted in front of them, men in Belgian uniforms firing the two machine guns frantically. The V-450 slammed into the car and sent it rolling away like a toy into a pair of parked HMMVs.

"FIFTEEN SECONDS AND COUNTING. THIRTEEN. TWELVE."

An M-113 bulked suddenly in the door like a dumpy dinosaur. Tom slammed a burst of HEDP into its front plate. It burned. The 450 swerved around, scattering fleeing vehicles like frightened chickens, and was gone.

"SEVEN—SIX—" Sloan's vehicle slalomed around two pickups and a deuce and a half and spurted into the night.

"FIVE."

Panicked, the driver of the bigger truck veered and collided with one of the pickups, locking the two vehicles together blocking McKay's path.

"FOUR—THREE—"

"Cover your face," McKay said. He put the pedal to the metal and aimed for the juncture of the wrecks.

"TWO—"

The truck hit in a shower of glass and sparks and screeching noise.

"ONE—"

A hanging endless moment. *Christ, we're caught!* McKay thought. Then the pickup was scraping down the left side of the cab and they were through. McKay cranked the wheel hard left and the truck shot out at an angle to the yawning entranceway.

"ZERO," the voice announced. For the first time McKay realized it was a recording of Major Crenna's voice, distorted beyond reason by amplification. "SEE YOU IN HELL."

And with Crenna's last macabre joke still hanging in the heavy Iowa air, a tidal wave of orange flame gushed out of the cavernous entry.

Sam was trying to drive and watch the other truck in the rearview at the same time. All he saw was fire. "Billy? *Billy?*"

"We're fine," McKay's voice came. "Just licked our tailgate."

Sam put back his head and let loose a Rebel yell. Startled remonstrations cracked back from the other Guardians. Not very abashed, he turned to Pirate and grabbed his shoulder. "We made it, Pirate. *We made it.*"

The biker's head flopped over on Sloan's hand. The cheek was already cool.

The V-450 hit the wire and never slowed. The two trucks followed through the gap it made. It boomed cross country, Tom Rogers throwing heavy artillery at anyone who even looked interested in them. They passed the wreck of an M-113 and a burning patch of woods with the broken outline of a little 90-mm recoilless rifle silhouetted pathetically against the flames. As they rounded the flank of the wooded bluff Dreadlock Callahan's bikers joined the procession bent low and howling like the Wild Hunt in triumph and exhilaration.

The cavalcade tumbled like an avalanche for the nearest road. Behind them Heartland was burning. McKay kept watching it in his rearview with hypnotic fascination. A gigantic funeral pyre, lit for the just and the unjust: a lot of men just doing their duty, which happened to be dying to keep the Guardians out; some innocents, perhaps; two genuinely evil men for sure.

And Crenna, one real-live goddamn American hero. Who hadn't died in vain.

Richard Austin
Trial by Fire £3.50

The second adventure in the blistering new series

World War III is over . . . and the ultimate battle for
control has begun.

From the blasted ruins of World War III came the Guardians . . .

Armed with awesome combat skills; equipped with the most
devastating weaponry ever devised; trained to hair trigger tautness;
the Guardians have been entrusted with freedom's last hope . . .

. . . the top secret Blueprint for renewal!

The Guardians' first task has been accomplished – the President is
safe in the fortress known as Heartland. Their next step: to hunt
down the hi-tech experts – for only they can put the Blueprint into
operation!

With time running out, is this Mission Impossible for the fighting
elite?

The future lies in their hands!

All Pan books are available at your local bookshop or newsagent, or can be ordered direct from the publisher. Indicate the number of copies required and fill in the form below.

Send to: **CS Department, Pan Books Ltd., P.O. Box 40, Basingstoke, Hants. RG21 2YT.**

or phone: 0256 469551 (Ansaphone), quoting title, author and Credit Card number.

Please enclose a remittance* to the value of the cover price plus: 60p for the first book plus 30p per copy for each additional book ordered to a maximum charge of £2.40 to cover postage and packing.

*Payment may be made in sterling by UK personal cheque, postal order, sterling draft or international money order, made payable to Pan Books Ltd.

Alternatively by Barclaycard/Access:

Card No. | | | | | | | | | | | | | | | | | | | |

———————————————————————————————

Signature:

Applicable only in the UK and Republic of Ireland.

While every effort is made to keep prices low, it is sometimes necessary to increase prices at short notice. Pan Books reserve the right to show on covers and charge new retail prices which may differ from those advertised in the text or elsewhere.

NAME AND ADDRESS IN BLOCK LETTERS PLEASE:

....

Name ——————————————————————————————

Address ——————————————————————————

——————————————————————————————————

——————————————————————————————————

——————————————————————————————————

3/87